Murder
At
Fort Revere

Frank J. Infusino Jr.

Bob,

Friends from youth
to "older" times,
always appreciate your
support and friendship.
Best wishes
always,

Frank

Murder at Fort Revere
Copyright ©2018 Frank J. Infusino Jr.

ISBN 978-1506-905-96-9 PRINT
ISBN 978-1506-905-97-6 EBOOK

LCCN 2018937281

April 2018

Published and Distributed by
First Edition Design Publishing, Inc.
P.O. Box 20217, Sarasota, FL 34276-3217
www.firsteditiondesignpublishing.com

"In a small town where everyone knows everyone it is almost impossible to believe that one of your acquaintances could murder anyone. For that reason, if the signs are not pretty strong in a particular direction, it must be some dark stranger, some wanderer from the outside world, where such things happen."

John Steinbeck
East of Eden

Prologue

The priest and the assassin began their careers on the same day in cities over two thousand miles apart, in two different countries. The priest was twenty-six years old, the assassin fifteen, a *Sicaritos*, teenage killer for hire. The priest was chosen because of his piety and devotion to Christ, the assassin because he was desperate and expendable. One entered his profession with pomp and circumstance, the other hidden in shadows.

The priest, John Francis O'Shea, was ordained in the Cathedral of the Holy Cross in South Boston, the mother church of the Archdiocese, in a Mass resplendent with pageantry and steeped in centuries of tradition. The congregation embraced O'Shea and his fellow "ordinands" — candidates for the priesthood— and sought heavenly protection and guidance for them. Their voices echoed through the cavernous church as they chanted the Litany of the Saints: *Holy Mary, pray for us, Saint Peter, pray for us, Saint Paul, pray for us, Christ, hear us, All you holy men and women, saints of God, intercede for us...*

Light streamed through the ornate stained glass windows of the Cathedral, reflected off the massive gothic arches and settled on the four white robed young men lying prone before the altar, a sign, perhaps, sanctifying the chosen ones.

In Ciudad Juarez, Mexico no such divine signal anointed the assassin and his cohorts. The former heroin addict and street urchin waited in an alley with two other young hit men to ambush a local police commander who had rebuffed a cartel's effort to add him to their payroll. Rats the size of cats scurried across the feet of the terrified boys and flies buzzed and pummeled their faces. One boy gagged as the stench of rancid meat and rotting fruit assailed his nostrils.

In the pristine Holy Cross Cathedral an aroma more inviting to churchgoers hung in the air—a mixture of lingering incense, burning candles, flowers, furniture wax and perfume. The ceremony progressed as each ritual brought the candidates closer to ordination. They knelt before Cardinal Bernard Law, Archbishop of Boston, who laid hands on the head of each young man in turn, a gesture signifying the transfer of the power of the priesthood from the Cardinal to the "ordinands." John Francis O'Shea beamed with pride at the Cardinal's touch. At peace, with no reservations, he was committed, through the vow of celibacy, to lead a chaste life devoted to the service of Christ.

In Ciudad Juarez, Mexico, only the passing of time moved the assassin nearer to his goal. Rudolpho Gonzales, the oldest of the three *Sicoritos*, rested his hands on the shoulders of his two co-conspirators. No allocation of power; a simple act to calm them. Gonzales, though more experienced than the others had, to this point, never killed anyone. Trained in the jungles bordering Guatemala, he had participated in gun battles with rival gangs and even the Mexican Army, ordeals that hardened him to the dangers ahead. His brown, deep-set eyes were vacant, not so much unafraid as uncaring.

His companions shivered, though it was not cold, and shifted their weight from one leg to the other, excited but fearful. A puddle of yellow liquid formed at the foot of one boy whose eyes darted from Rudolpho to the end of the alley as if seeking comfort or a route of escape.

"You'll be okay," Rudolpho whispered and encircled the boy's shoulders with his arm. He took a deep breath and puffed out his chest in a display of bravado. "Soon you will be famous, respected. Get all the chicas you want. Follow me. Shoot and keep shooting till you can shoot no more."

In the Cathedral of the Holy Cross, the ordination rite reached the point where the "ordinands" were officially priests. Cardinal Law draped the men with the vestments required to celebrate Mass—the stole and colorful poncho-like chasuble. As he did so, he intoned in a stentorian voice: "Take these vestments of the priesthood which signify charity; for God will anoint you with charity and perfection."

The *Sicoritos* needed no official uniform to confirm their status as killers. They wore the only clothes they owned; hoodies pulled low over their eyes, dark greasy pants and black Nike running shoes with the white *Swoosh* on the sides. Their clothes hung on the boys as if made for someone older; each was malnourished, their growth stunted, their faces gaunt. They struggled to hold the Uzi submachine guns they carried although each weapon weighed just a little over seven pounds.

In the Cathedral of the Holy Cross, Cardinal Law, wearing a Mitre on his head and holding a crozier in his left hand, bent down to plant a Kiss of Peace on each kneeling newly ordained priest; this act was replicated by visiting priests attending the ceremony as they filed in front of the men, a sign of unity with their brethren in the Ministry of Christ.

In Ciudad Juarez, the police commander and his bodyguards, fueled by many margaritas during lunch at a nearby restaurant, stumbled down the road laughing and singing oblivious to danger as they approached the alley where the trio of assassins waited.

With a dip of the head signal, Rudolpho Gonzales and the two other *Sicoritos* charged onto the street firing their guns wildly though their intense fire struck the targets again and again. Each boy emptied his Uzi of all thirty-two rounds. One boy vomited upon seeing the blood, bone and human flesh from his victims blown into the air. Unaffected, Rudolpho and the other boy stripped the bodies of wallets, watches and other valuables.

In the Cathedral of the Holy Cross, the Mass concluded, new priest, Johnny O'Shea, walked out of the church with his arms around his parents surrounded by friends and well-wishers. He ignored, or did not see, one former classmate who stood apart tears streaming down her face, grieving for what might have been. Susan Wilson, O'Shea's high school sweetheart, resented the church for stealing her Johnny away. The knuckles of her hands turned white as she gripped the back of the pew stifling the anger seething inside, not a woman to be snubbed or betrayed.

In Ciudad Juarez, the *Sicoritos* bolted down the alley away from the carnage they had wrought, stumbling over mounds of garbage and sending rodents scurrying in all directions. They dropped their weapons as they ran and emerged on an avenue where they slowed to a walk and mingled with a group of shoppers. The two younger boys lengthened their steps, shocked by what they had done, impatient to get away. But Rudolpho Gonzales took slow, measured strides, emotionally drained but exhilarated by the chaos, the noise, the smell of gunpowder and the shouts and screams of his victims. He was eager to do it again.

The priest and the assassin, Johnny O'Shea and Rudolpho Gonzales, would never meet, but their lives would later intersect with deadly consequences.

Part One

Secrets and Lies

We dance round a ring and suppose, but the secret sits
in the middle and knows.

Robert Frost
The Secret Sits

Chapter 1

Hull, Massachusetts
(Twelve years later)

The nightmares stopped years ago. The ache remained, of innocence lost, a childhood wrecked, a faith cast aside, men once admired, now despised; an escape from alcoholism no cure for the demons lurking in his subconscious.

It began with a stolen sip of wine. As an altar boy he filled the cruets used during mass to celebrate the Eucharist. He and his fellow servers tapped the bottle sometimes; just a little, to show off in front of each other, to keep a secret from their parents, from the priests.

One day, alone in the church sacristy, a small room adjacent to the altar where the celebrants dressed and prepared for mass, a priest caught him with a glass of wine in his hand. The young priest, red haired, green eyed, tall and lean, milk white complexion, soft hands, defined handsome. His intricate sermons baffled many parishioners yet he was well liked, an object of lust for adolescent girls, a role model for devout Catholic boys.

Instead of being angry when he discovered the young acolyte sneaking wine, the priest smiled, got his own glass and refilled the boy's. He urged the youngster to sit next to him on one of the straight-backed wooden chairs used for visitors. Later that day, the boy's memory of the encounter was hazy, but he was uncomfortable with the way the priest gestured as he spoke, sometimes touching him intimately.

He remembered subsequent incidents in the Church and at the rectory where the three priests who served the parish lived. They plied him with wine, forced him to undress and stroked and fondled him.

Later, the red-haired priest, more aggressive, hurt him. Racked with guilt, the boy blurted the details to his mother, a strict Catholic, who disbelieved him until the day he came home crying and bleeding. The skeptical police took a report but embraced the pastor's claim, which dismissed the child's tale as pure fantasy. No action was taken.

Traumatized, the youngster never set foot in church again. Anger consumed him. Sleepless nights drained his energy. He drank to excess, experimented with drugs. Only after years of therapy did he understand the blame rested with his abusers, not him. He had done nothing to encourage the priest's advances. He blocked the memories most of the time yet often became anxious, restless. At those times he found solace at the old fort, less than a mile from his home. At night, he would sit on the picnic benches and stare at the lights on a nearby island in Hull Bay or watch the beacon on Boston Light flash its signal to ships offshore. The solitude and view calmed him.

The nightmares did not resurface, but sleep came in fits and starts. His wife, a fervent Catholic, dismissed his protests and attended church faithfully. He hadn't divulged his secret to her.

Worse, his daughter belonged to the Catholic Youth Organization (CYO) and often had contact with the new local priest who gave her rides home from night meetings. She once claimed he touched her inappropriately but later backed off saying she misunderstood his actions.

The man knew better. That's how it started, with misunderstandings. The police took a report; it went nowhere as it had with him. He vowed not to let his child become a victim. The priest had to be stopped.

He went to Fort Revere often to think and plan.

Chapter 2

Tucker Richardson was pissed.

Like the brooding former altar boy, he had a beef with the pretty boy local priest.

He sat at a table in Jo's Nautical Bar, an Irish pub located in the basement of a home a short distance from the high school at the tip of the Hull peninsula. His third shot of whisky in front of him.

Tucker was prone to violent outbursts and had been eighty-sixed from Jo's at least three times; the last when, in a drunken rage, he pounded on the false door purportedly leading to tunnels under Boston Harbor and demanded access. This was his first time back since that episode; allowed to return with the caveat that a repeat flare-up would earn him a permanent ban.

Tucker was a hulk, sweaty, the buttons on his white shirt strained to contain his massive chest. His fleshy bull neck overlapped his unbuttoned collar while his two-day stubble gave his face a maniacal look. A scar above his right eye, a souvenir from one of his many fights, completed the picture of a dangerous man.

He sat opposite a smaller companion, a co-worker and friend, one who nevertheless Tucker intimidated, not uncommon among those close to the big man.

"You've heard the rumors, right?" Tucker asked as he downed his whisky and signaled for another. "My wife and that black robed bastard."

The man nodded, sipped his beer and remained silent. Not about to say the wrong thing like the poor slob Tucker pummeled in the bar's parking lot for making a crude remark about Elaine, the wife.

"I know the bitch spreads her legs for other guys," Tucker said. "But a priest! I'll kill the fucker."

Richardson's friend couldn't verify the rumors but he was among the legions of men who sniffed around Elaine. He had sneaked a peek more than once down her low cut blouses or up her tight short skirts when she sat on a bar stool and gave everyone a spectacular view of her sometimes panty-less crotch. Hell, he'd rubbed up against her a time or two and let his hand stray to her bare thighs when Tucker was in one of his drunken stupors.

"Calm down," the man said. "It's gossip. You know Elaine."

"Yeah, I do," Tucker responded. "She flashes her assets all the time and I've caught pecker-heads feeling her up when they thought I wasn't looking."

The man's face reddened as he slugged his beer, afraid Tucker might be referring to him.

Tucker gulped another whisky brought over by the female bartender and renewed his rant.

"I got no complaints. Elaine's great in the sack. I wish she'd dress up all-sexy like just for me and not every swinging dick in places like this."

He slumped back in his chair and gestured toward the bar for another drink. His companion thought he was about to doze off when Tucker shot up straight, danger reflected in his narrowed eyes and furrowed brow.

"The talk about Elaine and the goddam priest better not be true. You can't report those sons-a-bitches to the church. They'll stonewall, cover it up or transfer him like they always do. If he's diddling Elaine, I want him to pay. And I'm just the guy to collect."

Richardson's buddy swallowed the remainder of his drink and felt a trickle of sweat at the base of his spine.

No telling what Tucker might do.

Chapter 3

Homicide detective Vince Magliore arrived at Logan Airport in Boston at 5:30 a.m. on a Jet Blue "Red Eye" from Long Beach, California. Sleep eluded him on the flight as he tossed and turned grappling with both physical pain and emotional anguish. He had been wounded in a celebrated shootout with a renegade ex-LA cop who thought killing other cops and their families' proper payback for having been fired.

Magliore managed his physical agony with prescription painkillers; his mental torment proved more difficult to combat because in taking down the rogue cop he committed an act contrary to his oath of honor—never to betray the badge, his integrity or the public trust.

On medical leave, he hoped by returning to his boyhood home, he could restore his body and get his mind straight. His destination was Hull, a narrow peninsula community about thirty miles south of Boston where he planned to spend a few weeks in quiet contemplation of his future. He might never return to police work.

He picked up a Ford Escape at the central rental car outlet and exited Logan via Route 93 and the Ted Williams tunnel. Sixty minutes, and one wrong turn later he crossed the Weir River Bridge into Hull traveling north on George Washington Boulevard, one of the two main roads into town. Despite the paucity of traffic, he was forced to stop at the second stoplight he encountered to allow a car entering from a side street to cross in front of him.

As he sat drumming his fingers on the steering wheel, he glanced around. The Nantasket Pier was on his left and a restored children's carousel on his right. The two landmarks were vestiges of a more prosperous time for the town. The pier once handled daily steamboats that dislodged hundreds of vacationers from Boston during the summer and the carousel served as the centerpiece for Paragon Park, a major tourist attraction. The dollars spent by the many beachgoers and fun seekers filled the town's coffers and helped pay for public services. That income dried up with the Park's closure and the demise of the various businesses supporting it. The town has struggled to replace those funds and attempts to reinvent itself as an attractive tourist destination and supportive business environment have failed.

The town's economic plight did not interest Magliore who had no desire to become embroiled in local issues. He was focused on his own immediate needs, to escape crowds and the craziness of southern California. And so far his brief look around convinced him his decision to come home was a wise one.

At this early morning hour, the pier was deserted and the carousel closed—no pedestrians on the sidewalks and no other cars on the roadway. Magliore lowered his driver's side window. The only sound was a squawk from a seagull circling over the nearby bay in search of food. He grinned. The stillness and lack of activity reinforced his hopes for a peaceful recuperation.

He should have known better.

***

Vince Magliore was single, thirty-eight years old, never married, several relationships having ended badly. In addition to the more lofty goals of dealing with his physical and emotional angst while in Hull, he had one less grandiose objective—to bed one Maria Martinelli a high school crush who had spurned his many advances and damaged his adolescent psyche during their school years.

Maria Martinelli, she of the dazzling smile and movie star profile, had performed in a few forgettable movies and lived in Beverly Hills among the glitterati, divorced for the third, fourth or fifth time, he'd lost count. He expected to dazzle her with his sparkling personality at their high school reunion four days hence, his first appearance since graduation. The grapevine tom-toms heralded Maria's anticipated attendance.

Maria was unaware of his plans, of course, which increased the challenge. *They were both Italian, unattached, and once classmates, how could she resist*, Magliore reasoned.

After breakfast and a self-guided tour through town to acclimate himself to the sites he hadn't seen in twenty years, Magliore checked in early at the Nantasket Beach Resort Hotel, formerly a Clarion. He reserved a room with an ocean view, a romantic setting if he succeeded in luring Maria up to his room. Few people knew of his homecoming, so the blinking red message light on the phone surprised him when he opened the door to his room. Unless the hotel concierge was calling to offer him a free bottle of champagne for being an honored guest, he suspected he would not be happy with the call. Cops are suspicious beings; a trait developed while working with the dregs of humanity. They mistrust most people and, when off-duty, shun telephones, text messages, twitter and emails. Without fail, any communication will entangle them in something they will not enjoy.

Adhering to that philosophy, Magliore ignored the phone and walked into the bathroom. After flying three thousand miles across the country in a cramped seat, waiting in line for his luggage and rental car and driving sixty minutes to town, a shower and nap beckoned.

It would turn out to be the best part of his day.

Chapter 4

Refreshed after his shower and brief snooze, Magliore listened to the phone message he ignored earlier. The caller was the Hull Police Chief and former high school classmate, Randy Hundley who didn't offer a reason for his call. "Hey Mags," he announced, "call me at the station."

Everyone in Hull refers to police headquarters as the "station" which also doubles as the Town Hall and houses a fire truck or two. It's a small town.

Magliore dialed the number and got a polite female voice, an actual person, who inquired how she might direct his call.

Magliore, also polite, requested to speak to the chief and after a short interrogation to determine, he suspected, if he might be a nut case on a crusade about broken street lights, noisy neighbors or some other crucial issue, he was put through.

"Mags," the chief answered, "welcome home." His cheerful response did not disguise an anxious quality in his voice as if suppressing a less upbeat feeling than what he conveyed.

Wary, Magliore challenged him: "How did you know I was here?"

Nonplussed, Hundley responded: "I am the police chief."

Hundley deflected more of Magliore's questions and asked to meet at the Dunkin' Donuts shop at the corner of Nantasket Avenue and Washington Boulevard, a site that had once been a cafe. Magliore agreed to be there in thirty minutes though the walk from the hotel would take less than ten.

When Magliore entered the donut shop, Hundley sat at a window table with two large coffees in front of him. He appeared lean and fit. Black hair cut short, well-defined laugh lines around the eyes and mouth, blue eyes clear and sharp. He wore a short sleeve blue and white striped polo shirt and jeans, no uniform.

Seeing Magliore, he grabbed the coffee and motioned with a dip of his head to go outside. Magliore attempted a smart about face but the maneuver degenerated into an awkward, jerky motion, the result of his injured left leg.

On the sidewalk, Hundley handed a cup of coffee to Magliore and shook his hand, grip firm, his huge paw a reminder of why he dropped so few passes as a receiver on the football team.

They crossed Nantasket Avenue and sat on separate wooden benches near a memorial to Louis, "Papa Lou" Anastas, a town legend. The old man once owned the convenience store across from the donut shop; a jovial, gregarious guy who dispensed home grown wisdom with the sodas, candy and other goodies sold each day. The store is now "The Corner Café," and no longer belongs to Papa Lou, gone to his reward somewhere in the universe.

"Good to see you, buddy," Hundley said when they were seated, "but what's with the limp? Fall off a bar stool?"

"Occupational hazard," Magliore said without further explanation then asked: "Not to sound suspicious but to what do I owe this one man welcoming committee?"

Hundley smiled. "Can't fool a big city detective, huh!"

Magliore returned the smile, took another sip of coffee and waited

Hundley scanned the area to ensure privacy and stunned his friend with his next comment: "I'm being blackmailed."

Chapter 5

Who blackmails a police chief?

Anyone that dumb, Magliore thought, either had huge stones or a death wish but he asked the obvious. "Any idea who it might be?"

"Not a clue," Hundley responded, putting his coffee on the concrete slab in front of him. He inhaled deeply and leaned back on the bench. "Not a clue."

"What do they want?"

"Not a clue," he repeated prompting Magliore to consider punching him.

He resisted the temptation and ran the possibilities through his mind. Blackmailers often want to make a quick buck either by promising to withhold information embarrassing to a public figure, like explicit emails or photos, or by agreeing to return something of value in their possession, like a snatched kid or some incriminating document. Students, involved sexually with a teacher, try to extort them for grades. Drugs are often sought as a reward for keeping quiet.

"You must have some idea?" Magliore demanded after a brief pause. "And don't say 'not a clue' or I walk."

"Money probably. They haven't spelled it out yet."

"Money. Did you hit the lottery? What's so incriminating they believe you'll pay to keep it quiet?"

Hundley shrugged but his eyes betrayed him.

"What did they say?"

"They claimed to know my secret and would contact me again soon with instructions."

"What secret?"

Hundley shifted his position on the bench, crossed his right leg over his left, ankle resting on his knee, and stared out at the ocean. He maintained that pose for a minute or two before making eye contact with his friend. "I'm having an affair," he said, dropping his gaze to the ground.

In high school, Hundley, a handsome star athlete, deflowered more girls than could be counted on two hands. Magliore thought those days ended when he married Karen Phillips, one of the few girls in their class who did not succumb to his charms or line of bullshit. Their marriage was one of the longest of their group with two great kids, a boy and a girl, both college graduates with great jobs. He'd reached the top of his profession, leading the good life.

"An affair," Magliore said, incredulous, and leaned back on his bench. He reached into his pocket, dumped two pills out of a plastic container, popped them into his mouth and washed them down with another swig of coffee.

Hundley raised his eyebrows when Magliore took the pills but did not comment. Neither man spoke for several minutes. Magliore was digesting the blackmail bombshell and it wasn't going down well, like a piece of meat caught in his throat. His stomach churned. His leg throbbed.

Hundley, content to remain silent, let his friend recover from the shock.

Magliore stared into the ocean, unfocused and shivered as if struck by a winter gale off the Atlantic. He'd seen too much as a cop to be shocked yet this staggered him.

He turned back toward Hundley, a boyhood pal, a respected police chief, now in deep trouble.

"An affair," he repeated, shaking his head to rid the thought from his mind.

Why did he answer the damn phone?

Chapter 6

Magliore wanted no part of this drama. He came back to Hull to get away from his own demons. He even contemplated a new career or retirement in the sun somewhere. Certainly not soiling his hands or mind with some two-bit blackmailer. His high school buddy was about to suck him into a morass from which neither of them might emerge untainted.

"What do you want from me, Randy?" he asked.

"You're a detective, man. I need you to detect."

They both laughed but found no humor in the situation. "I'm out of my element here, man," Magliore said. "I'm a cop in California with no authority in Massachusetts."

"I don't want you acting in an official capacity," Hundley assured him. "Do your thing under the radar. You grew up here, know the town, still have friends here. You can make inquiries without raising a lot of attention. And you don't have to follow all the rules."

Magliore sipped his coffee, now bitter, reflecting his mood. He had other plans, like lying on the beach, getting a suntan, and chasing Maria Martinelli around his hotel room.

Hundley detected his indecision. "Come on man, I need your help. I've got no one else."

Magliore's stomach ached and his head pounded as if someone on the inside was clawing to escape. He leaned forward, placed his elbows on his knees and rested his chin on his hands, a bad imitation of "The Thinker."

After a few moments, he sat up, pushed his back against the hard bench and asked the question he knew would embroil him in his friend's mess.

"When did this all start?"

Hundley grinned and Magliore's heart flipped. About to be trapped.

"I got a call about two weeks ago. The guy didn't sound familiar. When he told me what he knew, I almost lost it. My job, my family, everything I've worked for could go up in smoke. Shook me up, I can tell you. Still can't sleep."

"What proof did he offer?"

"He says he's got pictures. Dates and times at hotels."

"You haven't seen any of it?"

"No!"

"So he could be bluffing?"

"Doubt it. He identified my lover and I thought no one knew."

Now Magliore smiled though not amused. Every guy who ever stepped out on his wife thinks he's being careful. But someone always finds out, and many times it's the wife herself; a cell phone or email message, a forgotten note left in a pants pocket, even the clichéd "lipstick on the collar," serve as clues to give the poor slob away. Randy, of all people, should know this. His little soldier was leading him around, always a bad thing.

Magliore was pissed his friend would stumble into this quagmire and now draw him into it as well. "So! Where do I start, Chief?" he said, using Hundley's title to jack him up.

Magliore, an experienced interrogator, read the expression on Hundley's face. He was about to bullshit him so he cut him off. "Look Randy. I came here for some rest and relaxation. I'd much rather be doing anything else than get involved in this crap. So level with me now, give me something to go on or I walk."

Hundley took a deep breath and again gazed out at the ocean, his eyes moist. Then, once again, caught Magliore off-guard.

"You owe me Mags," he said.

Magliore threw his head back as if he'd been shot. "I owe you. I owe you," he stammered, sounding like a bird making some kind of mating call. "I owe you."

"Yeah!" Hundley deadpanned. "If it hadn't been for me you would never have gotten a football scholarship to a school in sunny California."

Chapter 7

He was right.

The two boys slashed across the New England high school football landscape like the Four Horseman of the Apocalypse, minus two. A slight exaggeration although they did set state passing and receiving records, Magliore the QB, Hundley the sure handed wide receiver. A reporter for the Quincy Patriot Ledger compared Hundley to a former NFL Star, Bucky Pope, nicknamed the "Catawba Claw" for his skill in catching thrown footballs. Alas, the "Hull Claw," "Pemberton Claw," or "Pirate Claw," never caught on and they never won a league championship. Their best chance was thwarted in their senior year when they couldn't recover from an opponent's punt that traveled over ninety-yards blown along by the gale force winds that raged through the Hull "Gut," a narrow waterway bordering the football field.

Nevertheless, both boys received scholarship offers from schools large and small. And after a brief stay in a Catholic seminary, Magliore accepted one from San Diego State to get as far away from snow and ice as possible. Hundley chose to go to a local community college and remain close to his sweetheart.

Taking different paths, they both wound up in law enforcement. Magliore, despite a decent college career, attracted little attention from the big boys in the NFL. He graduated with a degree in Criminal Justice, attended a police academy in Orange County, California and joined the Anaheim PD where he now served as a homicide lieutenant. Hundley went to a Massachusetts academy, snagged a spot on the Hull force and worked his way to the top.

It was a stretch, but Randy could take credit for helping Magliore attain a scholarship and flee to warmer climes. He played on their friendship now and that undeniable fact.

"OK! Forget the bullshit, Randy. I'm going to help you."

Hundley exhaled and the tension drained from his body. "Thanks. And you're going to stay with Karen and me," he said.

"No way, I can't face her knowing this."

"You've got to man. If these guys decide to play rough they might go after my family. I don't know what they're capable of. The kids are no longer here but Karen's home. She's vulnerable. They'll think twice if they see you there."

"I'm booked at the hotel until after the reunion," Magliore said.

Hundley didn't hesitate. "OK. After the reunion."

15

Magliore sensed his vacation slipping away along with his much-needed solitude and his designs on Maria Martinelli. Not the homecoming he pictured.

"OK!" He said. "After the reunion."

Hundley smiled and Magliore shuddered sensing bad things to come.

Chapter 8

Police Chief Randy Hundley left Magliore sitting on the bench and strolled across Nantasket Avenue to retrieve his car in the Dunkin' Donuts parking lot, gliding across the street on his toes, lighter now after sharing his burden with his unhappy pal.

Magliore dropped his no longer drinkable coffee in a nearby trashcan, cut across a small patch of grass and limped back toward the Nantasket Resort on the concrete walkway paralleling the beach. Waves, propelled by the high tide, lapped against the sand and in some places the seawall. The cool breeze brought some relief from the unseasonably warm temperature.

It was a weekday morning, school in session, most adults working so there were few sun-worshippers around. A couple of toddlers digging in the sand with colorful pails and shovels under the watchful eyes of their mother populated this stretch of beach. Magliore, invigorated by the offshore breeze and the smell of the ocean, bypassed the hotel and continued to the rest station at the end of Hull Shore Drive.

The station contained restrooms, showers to rinse the sand off your feet when leaving and an overhang with a picnic table underneath. Two young girls in skimpy bikinis lay face down on towels on the rocky sand nearby ensuring, Magliore thought, a battle with skin cancer later in life.

Jesus. Had he turned into an old fogy?

He leaned against the iron railing separating the rest station from the beach reminded of the past when he jogged along the water's edge to get in shape for football, when he patrolled as a lifeguard a few hundred yards north and when he partied at the base of Allerton Hill until the cops came, confiscated their booze and sent everyone scurrying home with warnings not to return. No arrests; small town, different times.

The partygoers included Randy Hundley, his now wife, Karen Phillips, Johnny O'Shea and his latest squeeze, other athletes and cheerleaders; a fun group without a care in the world, except for the usual teen angst. They could not have predicted the events that would bring some of them together again in tragedy and recrimination.

Magliore was about to turn and walk away when one of the girls pushed up from her towel. She had unfastened the straps to her bikini top and as she rose up exposed her breasts. She smiled at Magliore, waved, then covered up.

He shook his head. *I am an old fogy.*

Chapter 9

Entering the hotel lobby after his beach sojourn, Magliore noticed a rack with three different newspapers, the Boston Globe, the Quincy Patriot Ledger and the Hull Times. The headline in the Times caught his eye: **Redevelopment Plan Approved.**

He grabbed the paper, paid the gal at the registration counter and sat down in one of the overstuffed chairs to read. For years, a 13acre rectangular parcel of land sandwiched between Nantasket Avenue, the town's main thoroughfare, and Shore Drive, a more scenic route, lay vacant despite numerous efforts at development. Previous plans failed for a multitude of reasons, taxpayer opposition, state and national recessions, environmental concerns, disagreements among town politicians. Now, after more than fifty-years, the redevelopment was moving forward.

The proposal called for a mix of retail stores, condominiums, two parks, townhouses and another hotel straddling Nantasket Avenue with many of the structures having a view of the Atlantic Ocean, the Hull Bay or both.

Selectman Carter Fitzgerald was effusive in his praise of the elaborate venture. "This will put Hull back on the map and draw visitors other than in the summer months and allow us to compete with Plymouth and the Cape as an attraction."

Fitzgerald recalled the history of the town when its beaches and grand hotels attracted celebrities and political leaders from around the country. He was obsessed with the idea this one project could revive a bygone era when such luminaries as Presidents Cleveland, McKinley and Coolidge summered here and heavyweight champion John L. Sullivan prowled the bars quaffing free drinks while displaying his championship belt. "This is the most beautiful property on the East Coast," he proclaimed. "It can't miss and is long over-do."

A Boston design firm created the project plan and the Quincy development company, Finch & Sons, was chosen to initiate and complete construction. "The Finch Company," Fitzgerald bragged, "has extensive experience in building and managing residential housing as well as commercial and industrial space throughout the South Shore. They will be great partners with us as we move forward."

Roger Finch, President and CEO of Finch & Sons, touted his firm's expertise: "We can take a site from conception and permitting to completion. Our experience and know-how is unmatched."

A few townspeople worried the ambitious plan would fail like so many in the past while others lauded the effort and hoped it would generate necessary tax revenue. The town's roads and other infrastructure needed repair and sources of income were scarce.

Skeptical yet hopeful, having spent his formative years in Hull, with friends here, Magliore wanted it to succeed though the town's location on a narrow peninsula away from the flow of traffic from Boston to Cape Cod and its inaccessibility during snowy, winter months, was problematic.

And Magliore didn't know, as others didn't, that Selectman Carter Fitzgerald had a connection to the Finch Company he championed, one that could sabotage the entire scheme.

Or worse.

Chapter 10

Chief Randy Hundley did not return to his office after leaving Magliore at the "Papa Lou" memorial site. Instead, he turned left on Nantasket Avenue and pulled into the beach parking lot near a now closed restaurant and diagonally across from a building that had once been a bathhouse, a failed motel and a charter school.

He exited his car, walked down a slight incline and climbed onto the rocks forming the coastline at the bottom of Green Hill, a favorite party spot for he and his pals while in high school. He now came here often to think. He sat high up to avoid the spray from crashing waves. The sky was clear, Boston Light visible in the distance.

Head in his hands, he cursed and thought about his predicament. For years he fought urges. Never acted upon them. Married his long time sweetheart, had two wonderful kids, a fulfilling job and was respected in the community. The proverbial local boy makes good story.

Now everything was unraveling. He gave into those long suppressed feelings and paid the price, a victim of blackmail, his relationship with Karen beyond repair.

He'd misled Magliore. The blackmailers didn't want money, never demanded any. The threatening calls "suggested" he stick to fighting street crime in Hull and back off his investigation into the town's redevelopment plans.

The threat shocked him because he had informed no one of his concerns or his unofficial inquiry. He heard rumors and did some research confidentially, he believed. If the rumors proved valid, some bad men would go to jail and some good men would suffer along with the entire community; another blow to Hull's effort to reinvent itself. Magliore offered some hope. If he could identity the blackmailers, Hundley might be able to survive, keep his job and reputation though probably not his marriage. He sat on the rocks for a long time, his fate and that of the town beyond his control.

Chapter 11

Selectman Carter Fitzgerald put down the copy of the Hull Times. The report on the redevelopment project should have pleased him. He'd led the fight for years. The new plan had great potential, would revitalize the town. Might even lead to a statewide office for him as some friends suggested and encouraged. Yet, something he'd discovered a few days earlier threatened everything.

A long time Hullonian, Fitzgerald attended Hull public schools and graduated from the University of Massachusetts, Amherst, in business administration with a minor in finance. A free-lance CPA, he worked with some of the largest companies in Boston and on the South Shore, lived in his boyhood home and served on the Board of Selectmen. A staunch Catholic, he was also a member of the Knights of Columbus, the right arm of the Church.

Carter never claimed to be a descendant of one of Hull's most famous residents, John Francis "Honey Fitz" Fitzgerald, former mayor of Boston, father to Rose Kennedy and grandfather of John Fitzgerald Kennedy; he never denied it either. He would just offer a knowing smile when asked about the connection. The many pictures dotting the walls of his home featuring "Honey Fitz," Joseph P. Kennedy Senior and JFK, who as a fledgling congressman helped dedicate the Hull Memorial School, cemented in the minds of many Carter's relationship to the famous clan. It hadn't hurt his budding local political career and might aid a future one if the redevelopment plan succeeded.

In his capacity as a CPA, Carter met Roger Finch, who with his brother Adrian, owned and operated Finch and Sons Construction. The company built high profile buildings in Boston, subcontracted work on the Big Dig and constructed residential housing and shopping malls in Quincy and Braintree. Their political contributions helped gain support for their building efforts, a fact not lost on Carter.

But despite his political ambitions, he was an honest man, and his faith in Finch Construction took a hit during a payroll audit. The company supervised three jobs in Quincy and one in Chelsea going on simultaneously. Not unusual and good for business. Yet something did not compute. On two jobs in Quincy and the one in Chelsea the names of workers were the same, their specialties different. Three men on a Quincy job working for an electrical subcontractor had the same names and social security numbers as those on a job in Chelsea where they worked as plumbers. Three other men in Quincy toiled as dry-wallers while in Chelsea the same three men were listed as roofers. In addition, the quantity of materials purchased for these jobs appeared excessive. Fitzgerald worried customers were being scammed.

He should have turned the records over to state authorities. But as a town selectman, he championed the Finch Company to handle the work on the Hull redevelopment projects. A hint of fraud endangered the venture as well as Fitzgerald's reputation. He would look the fool, or worse, be suspected as a party to malfeasance. If he covered up his findings, the truth might be discovered later and he could go to jail.

Conflicted, he sought out his parish priest, Father John O'Shea, for advice. He first blurted his misgivings in confession reasoning fraud was akin to stealing. He also met with the priest privately to discuss options. O'Shea recommended he go to the authorities.

Fitzgerald also expressed his concerns to Kathleen Maxwell, an administrative assistant with the Finch Company whom he trusted. They had developed a personal relationship and, truth be told, he craved a more intimate connection. She was shocked when he repeated his discussions with Father O'Shea and urged caution before he acted. She suggested there must be a reasonable explanation for his findings, a misunderstanding or inaccurate documentation. She promised to reexamine the records and get back to him.

Fitzgerald, torn between the advice of his priest to go to the police and the urging of caution by a woman he cared for, hesitated.

His indecision proved catastrophic.

Chapter 12

The Finch brothers inherited the construction company from their father, Atticus, named after the principal protagonist in the book, "To Kill A Mockingbird." Daddy Finch hadn't the scruples of the fictional Atticus and neither did his sons. They cut corners whenever possible using substandard materials, padding payrolls, bribing city and county officials and forging connections with unsavory characters, both local and foreign. Savvy American businessmen!

At 8:10 this morning, the brothers sat opposite each other at the rectangular table in a conference room separating their opulent offices. Executive assistant, Kathleen Maxwell, a thirty-eight year old graduate of Boston University and their right hand lady, sat at the end of the table between them. All three had steaming cups of coffee in front of them. Adrian Finch munched on a cheese Danish.

"We have a problem," Maxwell said, looking from one brother to the other. She was aware of some of the nefarious dealings of the Finch Company, of course, but unaware of the true level of corruption.

"What kind of problem?" Adrian responded his words muffled as he chewed his Danish.

"Our CPA, Carter Fitzgerald, found some irregularities when he examined the personnel records on a couple of our jobs. Guys working at different sites on the same day in different specialties."

"Why is he inspecting the personnel records anyway?" Roger Finch demanded.

"He's trying to reconcile the books so he examines payroll and material costs, overhead, etc."

"How big a problem is it?" Roger asked. "Would a little extra cash in his pocket take care of it?"

"Don't think so," said Maxwell. "He's very Catholic, very principled. I've put him off for now. His parish priest suggested he report his concerns to the police. We need to straighten this out. I'm sure the logs got mixed up somehow. I'll go over them with him."

The brothers thanked Maxwell for the heads up, dismissed her and ogled her backside as she left. They both knew first-hand the pleasure that backside offered.

"This issue is small potatoes," Adrian said, "but an investigation could hurt us and if Kate probes deeper, all hell could break loose."

Roger agreed. "We've got to deal with Fitzgerald."

"We're getting in deep, bro. I didn't bargain for this," Adrian complained.

"Too late now, pal."

They sat for several minutes before Roger spoke again. "We've got to stop Fitzgerald from reporting his findings to the cops. I'll let our friends know. They'll handle it."

Adrian sipped some coffee. His hand trembled as he held the cup to his lips. He dipped his head in agreement and took the last bite of his pastry. Their friends scared him.

Chapter 13

Adrian Finch had reason to fear their friends.

The 2008 recession blew through the construction industry with the force of a gale. Jobs dried up. Residential housing projects, corporate office building and shopping mall developments stalled across the country. Skeletal buildings stood decaying in the sun and wind; abandoned roads and home pads resembled ghost towns.

Roger and Adrian Finch, desperate to save the company their father built and never sticklers for following the rules or averse to cutting corners, were rescued by a colleague whose company also faced catastrophe. He offered to put them in contact with an investor.

"An investor?" Roger asked, sitting opposite his friend in a restaurant booth. "Someone willing to put up money now, in this environment?" He glanced at his brother next to him.

The man smiled and two days later introduced the brothers to Rudolpho Gonzales, who was accompanied by two intimidating other men with shaved heads and thick necks.

Rudolpho had come a long way from the scared *Sicoritos* in the alley in Ciudad Juarez to his present position as the point man for a Mexican cartel seeking to expand its influence in delivering drugs to the American Northeast. Nicknamed "Little Hammer" for his use of that instrument in killing and torturing his competitors, he had moved up the cartel's chain of command to be a member of the inner circle of a new group challenging the dominance of the Sinaloa's under the now imprisoned Joaquin "El Chapo" Guzman.

Gonzales stood apart from his two companions. Clean-shaven save for a small moustache, he wore a brown tailored suit, white shirt, blue striped tie. A bit paunchy, he had gained weight and muscle since his days on the streets. He plunked his briefcase down on the seat across from Roger and Adrian and offered his hand to both.

"I understand you are seeking investors," he began in a muted voice.

"We are open to suggestions, sir," Roger responded.

Gonzales smiled and outlined his simple investment strategy. "My company is seeking to buy construction equipment. We will purchase tractors, back-hoes, skip loaders, anything you can spare; and pay a premium price."

"How are you able to do this?" Roger inquired, glancing sideways at his brother. "There aren't many jobs out there right now."

Gonzales stared at Roger and spoke in a chilling voice. "That is no concern of yours, señor. Do you wish to do business or not?"

They disregarded their concerns and within minutes agreed. Gonzales presented no contract, no documents of any kind. He shook hands and told them they would be contacted in three days.

The Gonzales plan was a money-laundering scheme by CJNG, a Mexican drug cartel. The cartel, using a straw buyer, purchased all equipment Finch offered. They paid in "Narco dollars." The straw buyer then sold the tractors and other heavy items at auctions in Texas and to brokers throughout the southwest. The cartel often took a loss in these transactions but the money used to purchase the equipment was now clean, part of a legitimate business deal. It could be wired to Mexico or elsewhere through the banking system.

The cartel helped facilitate other schemes in addition to the equipment scam. Adrian and Roger created over ten shell companies, without actual employees or assets, which they identified as subcontractors. They cut checks to these companies to pay their employees, who didn't exist, and used an entity called "Quick Cash," to cash the checks themselves. This money was then used to pay undocumented workers provided by CJNG at various work sites.

The plot allowed Finch & Sons to hide its actual numbers of employees, which reduced the company's insurance premiums and payroll. This also enabled them to submit lower bids for work. The company thrived even in the recession when many competitors folded or cut back on workers.

The arrangement, while profitable in the short term, portended trouble but the money blinded the brothers to the danger ahead.

Chapter 14

After the meeting with his brother and Kathleen Maxwell, Adrian Finch secluded himself in his office, completed some paperwork, returned phone calls, skipped lunch and began his afternoon ritual around 3:00 p.m. He had a well-stocked liquor cabinet behind his desk and took a drink in the afternoon to calm his nerves. Since the pact with CJNG, this habit started earlier in the day; one drink became two, then three. Not as strong physically or emotionally as Roger, he found it difficult to concentrate. He feared they no longer controlled their own company. Audits like Carter Fitzgerald's might destroy them, send them to jail, or result in an even worse fate at the hands of their new "partners."

As Adrian sipped his third whisky, he peered through the open door to an adjacent workroom. At 5:00 p.m., the office was deserted except for the cleaning staff. He got up from his chair with his drink and tottered to the open doorway. The cleaning woman, a young girl, had her back to him as she scrubbed a countertop. He stepped into the room unnoticed, moved in behind her and crushed his body against hers covering her mouth with his left hand. She struggled but his bulk pinned her; he weighed over two hundred pounds. He whispered something in her ear and she stopped resisting.

Encouraged, he dropped his hand to her breast as her shoulders shook and tears ran down her cheeks and fell on the counter. Adrian fondled her with one hand, put down his drink, reached under her skirt and lifted it to her waist. She wore bikini panties, white. He caressed her buttocks and thighs, slipped his hand between her legs and pulled her underwear down to her knees. Hard, he rubbed himself against her soft skin, exploded in seconds and fell against her with all his weight. He recovered in moments, wiped his ejaculate from her body with her skirt and cleaned himself.

Ignoring the sobbing girl, he returned to his office to finish his drink. Goddam her he thought. She, and those like her, had been the solution to their problem, now they might be the instruments of their demise.

He knew she would not report his behavior to anyone.

Chapter 15

The cleaning woman, seventeen-year old Angelina Suazo, dared not report Adrian Finch's assault to the police or anyone else. Angelina, like all of the cleaners at Finch and many of the construction workers was an illegal immigrant supplied to the company by the CJNG Cartel and Rudolpho Gonzales.

Angelina fled El Salvador, dubbed the Murder Capital of the World, caught between two warring gangs, the Mara Salvatrucha (MS-13) and the Barrio 18. Civilians like Angelina had no place to hide in her chaotic and lawless South American country. The gangs preyed on anyone and everyone. She, her family and friends could expect to be extorted, robbed outright, carjacked or kidnapped on any given day. A friend her age, who had the audacity to sell tortillas in one gang area while living in another, was gunned down on a sunny afternoon while crossing a street. No one would be held accountable. The police and government were impotent and corrupt.

Angelina also sold tortillas from a stand by the side of the road in her village outside San Salvador, the capital. Her meager income helped her impoverished family survive. One day, an older friend, told Angelina she could get a high paying job in the United States and send money back to her parents.

Eager to escape the constant fear she experienced, Angelina and her relatives scraped together the $500 to pay a "coyote" to help her navigate the 3,600 miles from her village to El Paso, Texas. She survived the dangerous journey with a dozen other immigrants and faced another hurdle at the border. The "coyote," who worked for the CJNG, JaliscoNueva Generacion Cartel, a growing organization and rival of the feared Zetas, demanded an additional $5000 before he would help her cross into Texas. Unable to pay, of course, she agreed to work off the debt once she got a job in the United States. She was driven from the border to Houston by one of the many people willing to transport immigrants for a fee and later delivered in a cramped truck to Boston. She and three other girls wound up at Finch & Sons, as had some male counterparts. Their promised salvation and good life in America a lie.

Chapter 16

Kathleen Maxwell sat at her desk and reflected on the morning meeting with the brothers Finch. No doubt both undressed her as she left the conference room, her fault. Early in her career at the company she suffered their groping without protest, minor caresses but degrading nonetheless.

A graduate of the Boston University School of Business, she didn't need to use her body to climb the corporate ladder but convinced herself it was a small price to pay for future advancement. Yet she was drinking more lately and avoiding the bathroom mirror.

She chastised herself for turning a blind eye to the company's excesses, excused them as part of the construction game. Many companies cut corners. Her father, an executive in a building company himself, described how it worked: substitute low cost materials and bill the premium price, pad timecards, pay minimum wage to non-union workers whenever possible.

Maxwell did not comprehend the depth to which the Finch brothers had stooped to save the firm, avoiding bankruptcy when other companies succumbed during the recession. She expected to be promoted to Executive Vice President soon, a pledge made to her often. With more influence she could exert pressure to change company practices. They didn't have to play this game. There was now enough legitimate work to increase profits and operate ethically. She would have gone to the police without hesitation had she been aware of the cartel. But she didn't know, so she conveyed Carter Fitzgerald's concerns to Adrian and Roger. She regretted throwing Fitzgerald under the bus but couldn't afford trouble now on the verge of a promotion. Fitzgerald might be fired but he'd be fine. CPA's always found work.

She would later regret her naiveté.

Chapter 17

Roger Finch sat in a back booth in Darcy's Village Pub in Quincy. At 11:00 a.m. the lunch crowd had not yet arrived. Finch, not a regular, chose the place to lessen the likelihood he would be seen with the man across from him, Rudolpho "Little Hammer" Gonzales. Finch was unaware of Rudolpho's nickname and would have been appalled and frightened had he known. He knew, of course, he and Gonzales engaged in illegal activity but was convinced anyone in his position would do the same.

"So my friend," said Rudolpho, opening the conversation. "What can I do for you? Is there a problem with our little arrangement?"

"No no," Finch assured him. "We have a situation I thought you might be able to help with."

Rudolpho smiled revealing a gold tooth on the right side of his mouth. He had a round face topped by long, unkempt hair, an attempt to conceal the scar on his left temple extending an inch or two below his ear. His smile did not hide the malevolence behind his dark eyes. "So how can I help you," he asked.

Finch peered around to ensure privacy. Two brown skinned, broad-shouldered men sitting at the end of the bar watched them, bodyguards for Gonzales, whose menacing appearance kept others away.

Finch sipped his tap beer to remain calm. His request might lead to terrible consequences; not acting could bring down the company.

"In a recent audit," he said, "our CPA found some irregularities which could expose our relationship."

"Did he go to the *placa*?"

"What?"

"Police."

"Oh. Don't think so. He did report it to our administrative assistant, a loyal employee who notified us of his concerns."

Finch sipped his beer and wiped his forehead with a napkin before continuing. "The man is a devout Catholic and our assistant believes he might seek counsel from his priest."

Gonzales knew about priests and counseling. He attended mass every Sunday with his wife but avoided the confessional. His eyes bore into Finch. "So what would you have me do, my friend?"

Roger hesitated before blurting out what he came to do. "We, my brother and I, hoped you would talk with him, persuade him to perhaps alter his audit findings."

Gonzales' eyes narrowed and he leaned back in the booth. " I need the man's name and address and his priest's too."

"His priest?"

"A precaution, my friend. In our business it pays to be cautious—you understand."

"I, uh, don't know his name but he's the lone parish priest in the town of Hull."

"Good. Be assured we will handle this situation," Gonzales said.

Finch felt a trickle of sweat creep down his back; his hands trembled but he couldn't turn back now. He reached into the briefcase beside him, removed a piece of paper and wrote down the contact information for Carter Fitzgerald.

Their business complete, Finch and Gonzales ordered lunch. Roger left most of the meal on his plate.

Chapter 18

The Hull High School reunion dinner did not begin well for Vince Magliore. He stood near a portable bar sipping a glass of Merlot when the ballroom door swung open and Maria Martinelli swept in like a Nor'easter draped on the arm of a tall thin man with movie star looks and a California tan. Maria was ravishing; blond locks cascading to her shoulders, short black dress clinging to every curve and a plunging neckline revealing all but the nipples on her silicon-enhanced boobs. Magliore's stomach flipped then sank. His intentions toward Maria would not be consummated that night. Her escort presented an insurmountable roadblock. He gulped down the remainder of his wine and switched to a vodka tonic, determined the night would be finished in an alcoholic stupor.

No sooner had he made that decision than the door opened again, and Randy and his wife Karen walked in with much less attention than Maria and her arm candy had drawn; Randy handsome, Karen stunning. A click shorter than her husband, Karen dressed in a form fitting blue print dress with a slit up to the clouds, black hair cut short with bangs covering her forehead. Her hazel eyes swept the room, settled on Magliore and she glided to his side in a few long strides.

"Great to see you, Mags." she said, giving him a firm hug and a peck on the cheek. "Randy said you'd be here."

"Randy knows all," Magliore responded looking into her eyes. "He is the police chief, you know."

She laughed as Randy stepped beside her, joined in and offered a forced chuckle. Karen eyed her husband and in a too sweet voice said, "Randy dear, please go save us three seats together. I want to find out what this guy's been up to all these years."

Randy blinked, gave Magliore a furtive glance, and marched off to a nearby table where he placed white napkins on the back of three chairs. The tables were set for ten people ensuring classmates would sit shoulder to shoulder.

As Magliore watched Randy perform his husbandly duties, Karen squeezed his arm, said she would catch up to him later and headed off to a group of former cheerleaders. Magliore appraised her curvaceous figure as she sashayed away and again wondered why Randy cheated on her.

Now alone, Magliore scanned the room and spied two men and three women standing together a few feet away. Even without nametags, he recognized the guys, two football teammates, Johnny O'Shea, a former running back and Rob McCaffrey, a mountainous ex-tackle. O'Shea, now a

Roman Catholic priest, eschewed his Roman Collar for an open necked white shirt.

Magliore also remembered one of the women, Susan Wilson, selected as class flirt in the Senior Superlatives Section of the yearbook. Dressed in a low cut, thigh high red dress, she displayed as many curves as the California Coast Highway, and just as scenic. Her plunging neckline exposed half-moon breasts while a heart shaped tattoo on her left calf completed the picture of a sensuous woman. Glassy eyed, she held a bottle of beer in one hand while draping an arm over O'Shea's shoulders.

The other two women dressed far more conservatively, one in a white blouse and black slacks, the other in a sleeveless blue outfit with red, white and blue neck scarf. Their nametags disclosed white blouse and black slacks was McCaffrey's wife, not a classmate, and the other, Nora Roberts, a Hull graduate in the class behind this one. With a school as small as HHS, multiple class reunions were not uncommon.

Magliore sidled up to the group, shared fist bumps with the guys, hugged Susan Wilson and shook hands with the other women. The men reminisced about the good old days while the women acted enthralled. Susan draped herself over O'Shea running her free hand over his chest; the priest not fazed or embarrassed by her attention.

The group's banter droned on until the entrance into the room of Hull selectman and former class president Carter Fitzgerald distracted them. Fitzgerald escorted an attractive lady on his arm. Spying Magliore's group, he waved and walked over, shaking hands, slapping backs, and wrapping everyone in politician like bear hugs.

"People," he shouted as if calling a meeting to order, "please meet a colleague and friend, Kathleen Maxwell."

Maxwell smiled, turned her attention to Magliore and grasped his hand. Maria Martinelli might be Hollywood glamorous, but Maxwell glowed, red hair, green eyes, alabaster complexion, warm smile.

Maria who?

Magliore stood dumbfounded trying not to drool, ignoring his classmates and their ladies. He caught O'Shea eyeballing Maxwell but the priest turned back to the group laughing, fighting off the advances of a giggling Wilson who planted a kiss on his priestly lips.

"Nice to meet you Kathleen," Magliore stammered like a dumbstruck teenager.

"Call me Kate please," she said, her eyes never leaving him. "May we sit at your table?"

"Of course," he said, and made sure she was seated between he and Fitzgerald.

The night might not be a bust after all.

Chapter 19

The night was not a bust.

Kathleen Maxwell and Karen Hundley, sandwiching Magliore between them, pressed their warm bodies against him. While Karen was a tall woman with a firm, muscular build, Kate was petite with a narrow waist, tiny arms, small, delicate hands, her skin clear and smile bright and wide. *Perky*, thought Magliore.

As the table conversation about jobs, health problems, children and planned vacations rambled on, Kate found Magliore's hand under the table and squeezed it. That coupled with the pressure of Karen's thigh against his, though not deliberate, put a smile on Magliore's face. And gave rise to happy thoughts and other things. Those looking at him must have assumed the discussion captivated him.

Carter Fitzgerald prattled on about the town's growth potential, its history and the Redevelopment Plan he proclaimed would usher in a new era for Hull, one equal to its former glory as a playground for the rich and famous.

"Movie stars, athletes, actors and even presidents used to come here," he asserted, "and could again if we're bold and forward thinking."

He took a breath before continuing. "They came for our beaches and Paragon Park, once the Disneyland of its time. The Park's gone," he conceded, "and we need to repair the beach, but the new shops, condos and hotels will provide the money to do that."

He raised his voice and arms like a preacher imploring God to bless the scheme. He didn't mention during the Golden Age he heralded, booze flowed, gambling thrived and prostitutes plied their trade without fear as cops looked the other way, paid off by the flamboyant "Boss Smith" who ran the place.

Most present were ignorant of the town's history, good and bad, and greeted Carter's enthusiasm with polite nods; a clear sign they doubted the proposal would ever come to fruition.

Magliore half tuned in as Kate's nimble fingers danced up and down his open palm. She smiled the whole time and he blushed as if he had too many vodka tonics, which he had.

Karen Hundley leaned in to him and whispered, "Is Fitzgerald full of shit or what?"

Her warm breath on Magliore's neck and the scent of her perfume had a predictable effect on his male physiology though Kate presumed her fingers were responsible. While he enjoyed the dual sensations of Karen's proximity and Kate's manipulations, Fitzgerald's diatribe diverted his attention.

Fitzgerald was a big man, balding, with a round pudgy face and a stentorian voice reverberating over the cacophony of multiple table conversations and the rattle of silverware and plates as the servers moved about the room. "This town is headed for a resurgence, I know it," Fitzgerald barked. "Heck. Many former summer cottages along the beach have been refurbished and are selling for millions."

Two others offered contrary opinions. They'd heard it all before, seen plans crumble to dust or revert to the weeds that covered much of the empty field Fitzgerald pronounced a future wonderland.

Undaunted, Fitzgerald persisted, seeking support across the table. "What do you think Chief?" he asked Randy Hundley supposing the Chief embraced the same rosy outlook as him.

But Hundley had no desire to get drawn into the debate. He raised his glass. "We all need to lighten up and enjoy the festivities. A toast. To all our classmates, those here and those not."

Everyone echoed Hundley's words and the rest of the night proceeded as reunions do. There were a couple of speeches from class officers, a video of some of their high school moments taken primarily from the yearbook and spoof awards for the least amount of hair, traveling the farthest, having the most children.

After the prizes were awarded, the D.J. coaxed the group on to the dance floor, playing such past hits as: Un Break My Heart, Truly Madly Deeply, I will Always Love You and Nothing Compares to You.

Magliore danced with Karen Hundley and Kate Maxwell despite still limping from the wounds he sustained in the California shootout. His movements defied the concept of dancing as he shuffled his feet from side to side. The benefit of such awkwardness though allowed him to cling to Kate, their thighs pressed together.

Kate also danced with Carter Fitzgerald, her escort and Randy Hundley but kept them at arm's length. Susan Wilson gyrated with Johnny O'Shea and even the married McCafrey, rubbing herself up and down their bodies and exposing a boob when she spun around a little too enthusiastically.

By midnight the hall emptied with only the echo of laughter remaining. There would be little to laugh about in the days ahead.

Chapter 20

Susan Wilson and Johnny O'Shea left the reunion and drove separately to Fort Revere. Both were intoxicated and shouldn't have driven anywhere but they had made arrangements before the reunion to do this and neither wanted to renege. Wilson was horny and Johnny never turned down a woman in heat especially one as hot and sexually adroit as Wilson.

They parked their cars close together, O'Shea slipping into the back seat of Wilsons much larger four-door Toyota Avalon. Wilson's short red dress had risen to her waist, exposing her matching red panties. O'Shea slid a hand up her inner thigh, planted kisses on her face and neck and with his free hand unzipped her dress.

After O'Shea helped her wiggle out of her tight dress, she unbuckled his pants and pulled them to the floor. He caressed her breasts while she stroked him. Their fevered contortions rocked the car, the closed wndows muffling Wilson's ecstatic squeals. Their fevered, sweaty coupling ended with Wilson lying atop O'Shea holding him in a viselike grip.

They got dressed and left the car to stand by the low monuments to the French servicemen who had died on this hill during the American Revolution. She wrapped her arms around him from behind.

"I love this view," O'Shea said gazing at the lights of the town

"Me too, wish we could come here more often, be more public."

"You know that's impossible, Sue. I'm not going to stop being a priest."

"Yeah," she said. "And I know I'm not the only one you're doing this with."

She later discovered the awful truth of that statement.

Chapter 21

Johnny O'Shea lingered on the hill after Susan Wilson had driven away. Though still flushed from their fervent coupling, he felt empty, alone. He wasn't often given to introspection and with good reason. He broke the promises made to God on the day of his ordination many times. If he examined his behavior, he would have to admit he had failed the Church, himself, his family and his parishioners.

Somehow, the psychological and spiritual training he received in the seminary did not suppress his sexual urges. His vow of celibacy weakened over time and he succumbed to his desires. At first, he took solace in the knowledge his encounters were with consenting adults, women who chose to be with him, like Susan.

But guilt tormented him. He prayed for help often and even confessed his sins to a priest in a distant city where he wasn't known. Nothing helped. He continued his dangerous behavior to the point of a dalliance with a married woman.

Yet, he denied he was a predator like his colleagues caught up in the Church sex abuse scandals. He never had sex with the young girls who also flirted with him, at least not in the biblical sense. The caresses he shared with them were innocent expressions of the love he had for all of his congregants.

As he stood on Telegraph Hill, among the ruins of Fort Revere, tears streamed down his cheeks. He longed to be the young man infused with piety when he donned the vestments of the priesthood over a decade ago. He wished he could live up to the pledge he had made to serve "worthily and wisely" and to celebrate the mysteries of Christ "faithfully and reverently." The tears he shed were for that lost young man and for the bright future wasted.

He did not see the man sitting at the picnic table under the tree a few yards away. A man who hated the priest's very existence and whose hatred was further inflamed by what he had just witnessed.

Chapter 22

Vince Magliore, arm-in-arm with Karen and Randy Hundley, left the reunion about fifteen minutes after Susan Wilson and Father John O'Shea. As they exited, a couple of Lotharios at the bar put the moves on two female classmates they had ignored in high school. A few other classmates posed for pictures they would file away as soon as they returned home, promises to keep in touch, notwithstanding.

The Hundley's walked Magliore back through the hotel to the elevators. Their awkward goodbyes included a shoulder hug/handshake with Randy and a prolonged embrace with Karen. They parted as the elevator doors opened, Karen sneaking in an over the shoulder smile as they walked away. Magliore waved, a booze induced grin on his face.

His room was on the third floor at the end of a long corridor. He stumbled out of the elevator and put one foot in front of the other taking care not to ricochet off a wall, the wine and vodka working its magic; his pronounced limp not aiding his progress.

He opened the door to his room using the key card, flipped on a light, shed his jacket and tie and went into the bathroom to splash water on his face.

As he tended to his ablutions, a knock on the door startled him. His first instinct was to ignore it, but he staggered to the door and opened it a crack. Kate Maxwell stood there, shoes in one hand and a bottle of wine in the other.

"Hey," she said. "May I come in?"

Magliore, dumbfounded, stepped aside as she bee lined to the one chair in the room and plopped down, her short dress riding high on her magnificent thighs. She held the bottle up. "We'll need a couple of glasses."

Magliore's face contorted into a lopsided grin, one eye closed, a cheek raised. He snatched the wine and went back into the bathroom to unseal the bottle with an opener he always carried on trips. He extracted the cork, filled the two glasses the hotel provided and returned to the room. Kate was passed out on the chair.

His smile faded and he stood immobile, his brain addled by booze, unsure of what to do next. He could let Kate sleep it off on the chair, wrinkling her little black dress, or he could wake her and let her sleep on the bed.

He tried the second option, couldn't rouse her no matter how hard he shook or how loud he shouted.

He needed a Plan B.

He pulled the covers back on the bed, lifted Kate as gently as possible and turned to place her on the bed. He lost his balance and fell forward with Kate in his arms both landing with a thud, his face buried in her chest. She didn't stir.

Now he needed a Plan C. If he left her as she was, her little black dress would be trashed by morning and no one would need much of an imagination to figure out she had slept in it.

So, as chivalrous as he could, he rolled her on her side, unzipped the dress, and slipped it off her shoulders, over her thighs, and off.

He hung the dress in the small closet and sat down in the chair ogling Kate lying there in black bra and panties fighting back all the urges common to a horny middle-aged man.

His inner altar boy beat back the Devil's thoughts. He covered Kate, lie down on the very edge of the king-size bed beside her and fell asleep, visions of sugarplums dancing in his head.

More like visions of Kate flitting around the room naked.

Chapter 23

Magliore awoke to the smell of brewed coffee. Rubbing the sleep from his eyes, he rolled over on his side noting the depression once occupied by Kate Maxwell. She now sat in the lone stuffed chair in the room, knees pulled up to her chest, draped in one of his white dress shirts. She raised her cup in the air in a toast. "Grab some Mags. It's very good. Not the usual bland hotel room brew."

He got up, padded into the bathroom, closed the door to take care of business, and rejoined Kate, a cup of coffee in hand.

"Sorry about last night," she said. "Too much vino."

She paused and her eyes sparkled. "You at least got a look at me in my underwear."

"I did," he said and smirked.

"And you hung up my dress."

"My mother taught me manners although she never covered last night's scenario in her briefings on etiquette."

"Bet she didn't," Kate responded.

"You hungry?" he asked.

"Famished."

"Great. I know a place nearby that serves a wonderful breakfast. Let me shower first."

He gulped his coffee, returned to the bathroom, stepped into the tub and turned on the shower. As he closed the curtain, the door opened and Kate slipped in wearing only a smile. "Interested in a shower buddy?"

His smirk provided the answer.

***

They left the hotel refreshed and stimulated. Magliore drove the short distance to the Saltwater Diner in Kenberma and found a metered spot on Nantasket Avenue not far away.

They seated themselves at a window booth and both ordered coffee. Magliore examined Kate in the daylight and even without make-up she was stunning; her skin pink, her red hair pulled back in a ponytail, her round green eyes alive with mischief.

"What?" she asked as he stared at her like an idiot.

"Checking to see if you're real," he said; a line he thought both original and romantic.

She laughed but offered neither a putdown nor encouragement.

"The least you could do after spending the night in my bed and sharing a shower is tell me about yourself," he said. "How did you wind up as Carter Fitzgerald's date at our reunion?"

"It wasn't a date. Carter is a free-lance CPA who does the books at the company I work for, Finch & Sons Construction. He invited me to accompany him and I thought it might be fun. Haven't been to Hull since high school. We went to Paragon Park each summer. I loved the saltwater taffy at Lahage's."

"Where have I heard the name, Finch Construction?" Magliore asked, ignoring her nostalgic reminiscences.

"We've been awarded the redevelopment contract here in town, thanks to the efforts of Carter. Another reason I thought it prudent to come to the reunion. Doesn't hurt to schmooze people who can help the company's bottom line."

Magliore couldn't disagree.

When the waitress, an older gal in a multi-colored apron came to their table, he ordered eggs, bacon and wheat toast while Kate chose a grapefruit and English muffin.

No wonder she was petite.

"Not to be rude," she said breaking the silence. "Why the limp? You struggled while we danced but the contact was nice. What happened?"

"Occupational hazard," he said, his stock answer that avoided lengthy explanations.

"No way. You don't get off that easy," she said. "If we're going to get to know each other better, you need to come clean. Unless you don't want to."

He took a sip of coffee and considered the options. He could stick with his response and undermine a relationship not yet one day old or tell the truth.

"OK. I'll give you the Reader's Digest version."

Pleased. She reached out and touched his hand.

"You may have read about the incident in the newspaper or watched it on TV. An LAPD cop who thought he had been unfairly terminated opted to kill other officers and their families and threatened to continue to do so until the LAPD Chief apologized and reinstated him. He went on a reign of terror beginning with the murder of the daughter of an LAPD captain who served as his defense counsel at the review board hearing of his case. Later, he shot at officers in their patrol cars, killing some."

"How awful," Kate said.

He nodded and resumed. "The killer cop was later tracked and surrounded in a cabin at Big Bear Lake in the mountains of San Bernardino. Many police departments in the area, including mine, joined in the hunt and were part of the force that trapped the guy. Cops were nervous; discipline broke down. Some fired at anything moving or thought to be moving. I was hit by what the military calls "friendly fire."

"Oh my god," Kate said.

He finished with a flourish. "In the ensuing firefight, the cabin burned down and the guy shot himself rather than surrender. End of story."

"Yet you still limp."

"A reminder that's all. I'm not in much pain to tell the truth. May be limping out of habit now. One way to avoid dancing at which I'm inept."

"You did fine last night especially those hip gyrations."

"I had great motivation."

They lapsed into silence, finished eating then chatted for a half hour or more and promised to meet again; this time for an official date. Neither anticipated the trouble ahead.

Chapter 24

Susan Wilson, an English teacher at Hull High School, was raising two children alone, a thirteen-year old daughter Victoria and a ten-year old son, Jason. They all attended mass regularly, Susan assisting the Ladies Sodality cleaning and hosting fund-raisers for Catholic charities and local Catholic Youth Organization events; Victoria a member of the CYO leadership group, Jason an altar boy.

As a single parent and teacher, Susan understood the temptations facing teenagers and monitored her children's activities and screened their friends. She encouraged colleagues at the middle school to contact her regarding any risky or suspicious behavior of her children, like the use of drugs, having seen the dreadful life changing effects on some of her students.

On the Monday morning following the Hull High School reunion, Susan basked in the glow of her rendezvous with Johnny O'Shea until a call by the middle school principal shattered her mood. Police caught Victoria and two friends smoking marijuana in a neighborhood adjacent to the school. Furious, Susan grounded Victoria for a month and confiscated her cell phone, a device she provided her in case of emergencies. Susan ignored her daughter's pleas to keep the phone, and locked it in a drawer in her bedside table.

Two days later, while grading papers in the evening, she tried to call a coworker with a question on the assignment both had given but discovered her cell phone battery dead. She had no landline, a cost saving measure but sometimes inconvenient, like now. She remembered Victoria's phone and knew the passcode, one of the conditions set down when providing it to her daughter.

She retrieved it, called her friend and intended to return to her grading but the marijuana incident unnerved her. She abhorred spying on her kids but would do whatever it took to keep them safe. She decided to check the contents of the phone accessing Victoria's email account, the password also a condition of phone use, and scrolled through the messages. A couple of the user names unknown to her turned out to be classmates exchanging homework assignments or girl discussions about "hotties" at school.

Susan examined messages both sent and received and found three emails to a familiar address, Father John O'Shea's. Assuming them to be CYO business, she opened the first one and became nauseous, sat down, her heart racing. In a note to O'Shea, entitled "To My Favorite Priest,"

Victoria included a risqué picture. In the back and forth exchange, O'Shea praised her beauty, how nice she smelled, how soft her skin.

Susan broke down, sobbing, shoulders shaking, legs numb. She dropped the phone, picked it up again, images flashing through her mind of she and Johnny together, picturing her daughter with him, kissing, caressing, coerced by that slick talking rat bastard.

The contents of the other two emails devastated her. Victoria expressed her love for O'Shea, described her excitement when he touched her. The girl included another picture, this time dressed in sexy lingerie and bending down to expose budding breasts above a low cut bra.

Susan deleted the emails, inspected the rest of the phone, found nothing similar. She sat down in a chair in her bedroom and cried until the tears dried up. She intended to call the police but in her haste had destroyed the incriminating evidence. Plus, she didn't want to expose her daughter to the small minds that would attach horrible labels to her.

She did not sleep that night, wracked by physical and emotional pain. By morning she resolved to take action.

She was not a woman to be betrayed.

Part Two

Murder

Murder is an inherently evil act, no matter what the circumstances, no matter how convincing the rationalizations.

Bentley Little
The Ignored

Chapter 25

Telegraph Hill
Fort Revere
Hull, Massachusetts

Two hundred French sailors and marines died on this hill during the American Revolution, killed by smallpox. They were buried on the hillside below what is now Fort Revere once a coast artillery battery protecting Boston Harbor and now an abandoned relic. Rumors persist that the spirits of those dead warriors haunt the intricate passageways and gun crew quarters of the fort built above their remains. Visitors report seeing shadows, unattached to human forms, dancing on the walls of rooms and in tunnels and hearing unexplained noises and whispered voices in French. Ghost hunters have prowled the fort in hopes of capturing these paranormal images.

But the man now lying face down on the dank floor of one of the fort's concrete bunkers was no ghost; the back of his head was caved in and matted with dried blood. A stone the size of a softball, and flecked with blood, rested about a foot from his right arm. The stench of urine and decay permeated the air in the stifling confines of the graffiti covered room. Although it was September, the fickle New England weather served up temperatures in the eighties with humidity to match. Sweat oozed from the pores of the cops and medical personnel jammed into the small room adding to the rank odor.

The crime scene will be a nightmare to process. The abandoned fort, left to decay for years, is now under the auspices of the state park system but still a mess. The concrete bunkers and steps leading to the former gun emplacements are crumbling, grass grows in the wide cracks and graffiti covers almost every inch of wall space. The people who come here as tourists, history buffs, kids playing at war or lovers seeking a bit of privacy and a spectacular view of Boston and the outlying islands, leave behind all sorts of refuse and bodily fluids. The two teenagers cutting class who stumbled on the body came up here to smoke a joint. A cursory glance around reveals others have been here and done that.

The dead man's pants and underwear, pulled down to his ankles, suggested a sexual tryst though Hull Police Chief Randy Hundley didn't buy it. He shook his head and whispered, "no way" loud enough to be heard by Vince Magliore who was standing next to him. Magliore would have preferred sunning himself at the beach on a day masquerading as summer but deferred to the entreaties of his friend to accompany him here.

Chief Hundley continued to shake his head and mutter when Magliore poked him in the ribs. "No way what?" he asked.

"No way is this guy up here in this rat hole getting laid. No way!"

He pronounced "here" as "he-ah" of course since there are no "r's" in the language of New England.

The guy he was referring to, the dead guy was a boyhood friend of both Hundley and Magliore and also a Roman Catholic priest.

Or was until someone bashed his head in.

Chapter 26

Hundley and Magliore escaped the fetid bunker to seek some fresh air. They scrambled up a grassy embankment, avoiding crumbling stairs and stood in an open field on the edge of the parking lot where emergency vehicles and police cars sat at oblique angles to each other. The bright sun offered little relief from the heat.

A small crowd had gathered drawn by the commotion caused by multiple vehicles with lights flashing and sirens blaring. The subdued crowd murmured when the chief of police and an unknown person emerged from below. They made no move to draw closer riveted in place by the mere presence of two Hull police officers standing before them, arms crossed.

Magliore and Hundley moved further away from the gathering and stood on the edge of an incline with their backs to the group.

Out of earshot, Magliore asked, "Who kills a priest?" The question was less incredulous now than it might have been prior to the child abuse scandal that rocked the nation and the world. No one could measure the depth of anger by a victim or parent seeking revenge.

"Any ideas?" Magliore prodded as Hundley stared transfixed into Hull Bay, his fists clenched, his jaw tight, his lanky six-foot plus frame stooped, giving him a frail, diminished appearance, beaten down by the scene of death here.

His voice strained, he answered: "I can't think of anyone angry enough to kill Johnny. Some old timers didn't like or understand his sermons but he brought many people back to the Church awed by his charisma; young girls and women as you might guess."

No need to guess. Father John O'Shea was a three-sport star in football, basketball and baseball in high school, a member of the national honor society, senior prom king, brash, a free spirit, adored by the girls, envied by the boys. Hundley's wife, a cheerleader, had dated him.

"Must admit," Magliore confessed, "I hated him in high school but swear I didn't kill him."

"Good. We can eliminate you as a suspect," Hundley retorted, his mouth twisted into a weak smile, eyes reflecting pain, not amusement.

Johnny O'Shea was thirty-eight years old with a thick head of black hair, an unlined face and an athletic build. A charmer in his youth, he broke many a young girl's heart when he opted for the priesthood instead of marriage and a family. Given the scene here though, Chief Hundley thought, maybe he chose to serve God and still enjoy earthly pleasures like some of his colleagues. His behavior at the reunion with Susan

Wilson and rumored dalliances with other woman lent credence to that possibility.

Yet, Hundley didn't believe O'Shea dumb enough or reckless enough to seek sexual gratification in this old fort. Forget you might encounter others with similar intent up here—others who might recognize you. The uncomfortable, dreary, foul smelling dirty concrete would be an erotic turn-off.

Whatever his purpose in coming here, it wasn't sex.

Magliore read Hundley's thoughts. "Johnny was smart and fastidious about his grooming, the last one out of the locker room after showering, combing his hair, applying tons of deodorant and after-shave. If he did have an affair, an assignation, romp, whatever, he'd do it in a clean place, far from Hull where there are no secrets."

"Fastidious, assignation," Hundley mimicked suggesting these words beyond his buddy's comprehension.

"Hey, I'm a college grad, you know," Magliore protested.

"Yeah! And you also know there are some secrets in this town."

Chapter 27

Magliore, well aware of Hundley's secret, one the chief wished to keep from the townspeople and his wife, resented having been pulled into Hundley's drama and now feared Johnny O'Shea's death would worsen his predicament.

Ignoring Hundley for the moment, he looked out over the town. The landscape hadn't changed much since his youth although the island below him, a former army Nike Missile Defense base, was now plastered with upscale condominiums.

The jagged shoreline peeled right and wound its way back toward the center of town revealing moored boats and some bay front beach. Hull is a narrow spit of land jutting into Massachusetts Bay, a twenty-minute boat trip to downtown Boston. You can drive its length after Labor Day in about twenty-five minutes. Magliore could see from his perch on the hill the narrow point across from the yacht club where as kids they tried to throw a baseball from the Atlantic to the bay. He couldn't remember if anyone succeeded.

"Hey! Did anyone ever make that throw from the Atlantic to the bay?"

"Are you nuts," Hundley responded. "I've got a murder to solve, need your help, and you're thinking about throwing baseballs."

Magliore ignored the jab, folded his arms across his chest, and squinted in the bright sun. "I still want to know."

Hundley dropped his eyes to the grass and hesitated before answering. "Yeah. Buster Nolan."

Magliore smiled remembering their boyhood pal. "Big son of a gun. Is he still in town?"

The question was met with silence so he turned toward Hundley. The chief had his head bowed and his hands clasped in front of him. "Killed in Afghanistan. Buried in the cemetery here."

The response rocked Magliore. He liked Nolan. He frowned but before he could speak, Hundley said. "Karen and I have plots here too when the time comes."

Not something Magliore wanted to hear. He chided his friend. "That time's a long way off pal. A long way off."

Magliore fell silent. His protest forced him to consider his own future. He hadn't planned ahead. He had no will and no one to read it anyway. His parents were gone. He had no siblings, no spouse. Cops would bury him, he guessed, in California, not Hull. He continued to look out over the town without seeing. He shivered despite the heat; engulfed by loneliness.

Chapter 28

"Hey man where have you gone?"

Chief Hundley's question jolted Magliore back from his brief reverie. "Sorry Randy," he said. He reached into his pocket took out a small container of pills and popped two in his mouth.

Facing Hundley he lied, "Thinking about the old days."

Hundley noticed the movement with the pills as he had when they first met across from the Dunkin' Donut shop but didn't address it. "OK! I know you'd rather be elsewhere but help me out here."

"All right," Magliore said, "I'm not convinced the prospect of sex lured Johnny here. But he did dress to conceal his identity; black jeans, a black Red Sox T-shirt, tennis shoes and a baseball cap. No Roman Collar. If you're a priest here for a legitimate reason, not worried about being seen, why not dress the part?"

"OK. I'll concede the point," Hundley said, "but why meet someone in secret at all?"

Before Magliore could respond, a Hull police officer doubling as a detective on the small force joined them. He regarded Magliore with disdain unsure why the chief permitted the guy to be here; his expression understandable given Magliore's unprofessional attire. He wore a San Diego State Aztecs ball cap backwards, a white polo shirt with the University logo over the left breast pocket, grey cargo shorts and black Nike running shoes, no socks; the shirt and shorts wrinkled, the shoes frayed.

The detective dismissed Magliore with a nod and spoke to Hundley. "Chief, the vics cell phone, wallet and watch are missing. Might have been a robbery gone bad."

"Are we sure he owned a cellphone?" Magliore interjected eliciting a frown from the detective, no answer.

"He did," Hundley assured him. "He called people while driving all the time. I warned him more than once to knock it off, dangerous and against the law. He blew me off. 'Doing God's work,' he'd say."

"Sounds like Johnny. Never a stickler for rules."

"Yeah," Hundley said. "If his valuables are gone it might be a robbery, nothing more. The watch was expensive, an ordination gift from his parents."

"Doesn't explain his presence here, pants down. Someone he knew, a parishioner perhaps, enticed him up here. That person or person's killed him and posed him to make a statement either to highlight his sexual proclivities or to hide the real reason. We find out why he came here, we find the motive and identify the killer."

The Hull detective who dismissed Magliore as an interloper earlier thought that reasoning made sense. So did Hundley.

The search for that motive would take them on a wild ride, further soil the reputation of Father John O'Shea and shock the town to its core.

Part Three

The Investigation

Murder may pass unpunished for a time, But tardy justice will o'ertake the crime.

John Dryden
The Clock and the Fox

Asking questions is an essential part of police investigation.

Anthony Kennedy
Supreme Court Justice

Chapter 29

Father John O'Shea's death captured the media's attention as only horrific events can.

The Boston Globe's front page screamed, "Murder in Hull." The Quincy Patriot Ledger, a newspaper covering the South Shore, proclaimed, "Priest Slain." Talking heads on the local TV channels hinted at the salacious details surrounding the discovery of O'Shea's body. There are few secrets in a small town.

On the day after the murder, Vince Magliore met Chief Randy Hundley in his office at noon grappling with how to proceed. The Hull PD was not authorized to handle a murder investigation but not because it lacked the personnel. The department had over twenty sworn officers, including a lieutenant and two detectives. Massachusetts's law dictates only Boston, Springfield and Worcester, may investigate homicides. In the other smaller cities and towns, the County District Attorney coordinates and investigates murders within his jurisdiction. So as they spoke, state police detectives, assigned to the Plymouth County District Attorney's Office swarmed over Fort Revere in search of evidence while others examined O'Shea's residence. The state's lead investigator would determine the extent to which the Hull police would participate in the probe; a prospect neither Hundley nor Magliore relished. State and federal agencies tended to dismiss the ability of the locals.

Hundley, in uniform, his feet up on his department issue metal desk, leaned back in his wooden swivel chair, hands behind his head, eyes riveted on the ceiling, deep in thought or studying some contour or spot seen by him alone.

Magliore sat in a straight-backed metal chair in front of Hundley's desk dressed in a short-sleeved striped polo shirt, jeans and new white Nike running shoes he bought for the trip back to Hull. His right leg twitched, the result of three cups of Dunkin' Donuts coffee consumed before he arrived.

The two men sat in silence until Hundley dropped his feet to the floor and faced Magliore. "This was a set-up, Mags. Whoever did it wanted us to focus on the sex angle and away from the real reason for O'Shea's murder."

"Maybe it is what it is," Magliore said. "Intelligent people do stupid things. Some of our presidents, for instance."

Hundley's face flushed aware of how his own indiscretions resulted in blackmail. Magliore could have cited him as an example.

"I'm playing the devil's advocate here, buddy." Magliore assured him. "I agree with you. As a local kid, a priest, Johnny knew of the current media attention on the Catholic Church. If he did fool around, like I said before, I doubt he would have chosen a public place like Fort Revere to engage his passion."

Hundley kept silent.

"Don't get me wrong," Magliore said. "We can't ignore the sex issue. Yet the crime scene doesn't support the theory of an angry lover. O'Shea was struck from behind. If he's lying on top of some gal, and no woman I know is going to lie on that floor," he emphasized, "she couldn't hit him like that. If she picks up a rock and strikes him, the blow would be to the side of his head."

Hundley nodded, accepting that reasoning.

Magliore paused before continuing: "If O'Shea was killed during the act, which I doubt, someone else did it, jilted lover perhaps, jealous husband or boyfriend? O'Shea's not going to stand around with his pants down so his lover can get behind him and whack him on the head. And why would she?"

Magliore let his explanation sink in and said. "Could be an enraged parent of a molested kid. He kills the good padre and strips him to expose him to the world as a scumbag. Then the question becomes: On what pretext did he or she lure Johnny to the fort?"

Hundley's head bounced up and down like a bobble head doll in agreement.

"Any indication John was fond of children?" Magliore asked pursuing the irate parent angle.

Randy blanched. "About a month ago an angry father brought his fifteen year old daughter in to file a complaint. Said Johnny groped the kid when he drove her home after a CYO meeting."

"Did you investigate it?"

Randy lowered his eyes. "No. The day after the dad came in with the girl, the mother showed up to drop the complaint. Claimed the kid misjudged Father O'Shea's action— that he had been reaching for something in the glove compartment of the car and his hand brushed her daughter's leg. The girl thought about it overnight and changed her mind about pressing charges. The mother insisted the girl would not testify against Johnny if we went forward."

"Reaching for something in the glove compartment. Wonder who thought that up?"

"Pretty lame," Randy conceded. "Though it might be the truth. Can't fathom the guy was a pedophile."

Hundley sat back in his chair and raised his eyes to the ceiling again: "There have been rumors Father John had an eye for the ladies, married parishioners, nothing involving kids. I gave him the benefit of the doubt regarding the girl."

Magliore thought but did not say: Hadn't that been what the church did for years? Giving these guys the benefit of the doubt before shuffling them off to new parishes when the heat turned up. Still, he didn't want to condemn the man without proof. If not a pedophile, there could still be a sex related reason for his murder.

"OK. We're back to the jealous husband or boyfriend," he offered.

Hundley stroked his chin. "Like you said. Whoever killed Johnny was sending us a message, literally and figuratively by posing him with his pants down."

"Do you have the names of the women rumored to be having a relationship with Johnny?"

"Yeah."

"Let's go talk with them."

"Wait a minute, Mags, this isn't our case; the state's taking the lead. We could piss off a lot of powerful people if we charge ahead, like the district attorney. I'm not interested in making enemies at that level."

Magliore understood Randy's reluctance to alienate those at the top of the police pecking order. Procedure and chain of command were inviolate in law enforcement like the military. But he also believed they owed it to O'Shea's family to help find his killer and maybe clear the air on the sex innuendo. They both knew and liked his parents. They'd eaten at their home; slept over on backyard camping trips.

Magliore played the friendship card. "You want me to help you because I'm your friend and you're being blackmailed. Johnny was our friend. Don't we owe him something?"

Randy shrugged in resignation. "OK. Let's go chase some rumors."

Chapter 30

While Magliore and Hundley pursued the rumors about Father John O'Shea, Roger Finch met with his brother in their conference room. Steaming mugs of coffee rested on the table in front of them but neither had touched the liquid. Both gazed down at the table deep in thought.

Roger unfolded the morning edition of the Boston Globe and showed Adrian the article on the right hand side of the front page below the fold. The headline in bold type noted the murder of Hull priest, Father John O'Shea.

"I've seen it," Adrian said, shaken, lifting his mug in trembling hands. "You don't think" he started to say then left the question hanging in the air like a balloon dancing on the wind but destined to fall back to earth.

"I don't know what to think. Our new associates are not angels but I can't believe they're capable of murder," Roger lied. He had seen the murderous looks in the eyes of Rudolpho and his bodyguards. To challenge them was to court disaster. He would continue the façade with his brother as long as possible. He held out hope the priest's murder was unrelated to their new partners; in his gut he knew otherwise.

Roger sipped his now cooled coffee and took out his cell phone, dialed the number for Rudolpho Gonzales and when he answered, put the phone on speaker.

"You're on speaker phone sir," Roger said. "My brother is here with me."

"Yes my friend. What can I do for you?"

"Well, uh, we saw the newspaper about the murder of Father O'Shea in Hull."

"Yes," Rudolpho said again, making Roger work to get his question out.

"Well, uh, uh," Roger stammered. "Please don't take this wrong. We told you about the priest when we asked you to speak with Carter Fitzgerald, our CPA."

"Yes."

Roger groaned, droplets of sweat forming on his forehead. "Well, did your associates talk with the priest?"

A long pause on Rudolpho's end led Roger to conclude the connection had been terminated. About to redial, Rudolpho's voice penetrated the silence, startling both brothers, causing Adrian to spill his coffee.

"My associates did speak with the priest and at the place where he was killed, this Fort Revere. To ensure privacy."

Roger wiped his brow with the back of his hand. He didn't attempt to pick up his coffee cup.

"Señor," Rudolpho said, "as I told you before we are businessmen. My associates explained that to the padre and, how you say, stressed it was in his best interests, and of this Mr. Fitzgerald, he not speak ill of our company; any irregularities discovered were simple mistakes and would be corrected, pronto.

"The padre understood and agreed to convey our explanation to Mr. Carter Fitzgerald. They did not harm the padre in any way, I assure you."

Roger took two deep breaths to regain his composure. "Thank you sir. I appreciate your candor. And so does Adrian."

"I do sir, I do sir," Adrian interjected, his voice an octave higher than normal.

"Very well, gentlemen," Rudolpho said. "I am glad I could answer your questions. I look forward to our continued arrangement."

"As do we sir," Roger said and ended the connection by punching the off button on his desk phone.

"Well?" Adrian asked.

"Well nothing," Roger responded. "We have no choice but to trust him."

An uneasy silence ensued, neither brother inclined to voice any misgivings. They had no exit strategy to release them from the alliance they had forged with Rudolpho Gonzales. When you make a pact with the devil, you may wind up in hell.

Chapter 31

While Roger and Adrian Finch spoke with Rudolpho "Little Hammer" Gonzales, Chief Hundley and Vince Magliore visited the parents of Johnny O'Shea to begin chasing down rumors. Neither relished the task nor expected any great revelation or much cooperation for that matter.

Johnny O'Shea's mother and father lived on Ralph Crossen Circle in Hull in a three story old colonial home showing its age. The L-shaped porch, wrapping around the front to the right side, needed paint. The lawn was weed-infested, peppered with rocks and other detritus. One rain gutter was missing. The neglect surprised both Hundley and Magliore. Mr. O'Shea had been an inveterate handyman when they were kids, his house and grounds one of the finest looking on the block.

They walked up the steps of the house to the front door and Hundley rang the bell. After a few moments, Mr. O'Shea opened the door wearing a grey sweater, black slacks, and frayed slippers. Once an imposing figure well over six feet tall with broad shoulders and mitts for hands, he appeared frail. His hair matched his sweater, his shoulders stooped. Deep lines creased his face around the mouth and eyes. Age spots dotted his forehead.

"Don't look so amazed Mags," O'Shea said, noting the astonished expression on the younger man's face. "The years are not kind to many of us."

Magliore's face flushed. He felt foolish and exposed. "Sorry Mr. O'Shea. I didn't mean to offend you. I'm not usually so transparent."

A weak smile creased O'Shea's face as he stepped aside to invite them in. They entered a large living room. Mrs. O'Shea sat on a well-worn brown couch in a sitting area in front of a floor to ceiling stone fireplace. She forced a smile but did not get up. She too had aged but remained an attractive woman. Her brown hair, no doubt colored was cut short and framed a narrow blemish-less face; her hazel eyes bright and clear.

Hundley opened the conversation. "We are so very sorry for your loss. Johnny was a great guy and friend. He will be missed."

Mrs. O'Shea dabbed her eyes with a hitherto unseen handkerchief. Mr. O'Shea also teared up. He sat by his wife and put his arm around her. "I know this is more than a condolence call," he said. "Ask your questions."

Hundley nodded. "Can you think of anyone who might have wanted to hurt Johnny?"

Neither parent responded, their faces blank.

Hundley coughed and danced around the question both he and Magliore dreaded. "There were some rumors about Johnny's behavior.

That he, uh, might have had improper relationships with some women, married women."

"Johnny did no such thing!" Mrs. O'Shea shouted, straightening her back and twisting her mouth into a scowl. "He was a priest, for gods-sake. He would never break his vows. Never!" She slumped back in the couch. Mr. O'Shea patted her shoulder.

Hundley, shaken by the outburst, rocked back on his heels, but pressed on. "I understand you're upset," he said. "But we need to follow up on all leads. We want to find the person who murdered your son, our friend."

Neither parent responded and after an awkward silence, Hundley and Magliore again expressed their condolences and showed themselves out of the house.

Back in the car, Magliore said, "That went well."

Hundley choked out a laugh. "They're both in denial. Did you notice Mr. O'Shea didn't join in when his wife snapped at us? His eyes gave him away. He knows more than he's willing to admit."

More secrets.

Chapter 32

Rumors devolve from secrets and secrets sometimes reveal truth...or not. Small towns are full of them—rumors and secrets. Neighbors talk to each other. Stay at home moms learn things by peering out the window, gossiping with friends at the hair salon and super market or from trolling social media where every Facebook post, tweet or email is taken as gospel. Some of the stuff may be true most is exaggerated at best. Cops must determine the truth. And the way to do that is to investigate the rumors and gather evidence to support or refute them. So Chief Randy Hundley and Vince Magliore visited the homes of the ladies rumored to have had flings with Father John O'Shea to ask difficult and embarrassing questions. Not an easy or pleasant task and they expected pushback.

The first woman they interviewed was Erin Dougherty, a private duty nurse who provided home care for aging adults. They caught up to her at the home of Mrs. Mary Haggerty, an eighty-five year old who required help with the daily tasks most take for granted. Haggerty lived on Atlantic Hill just off State Park Road on the site of the old Atlantic House, once the most famous hotel in New England. World-renowned actress Sarah Bernhardt and Wallace Simpson, the Duchess of Windsor, once stayed there. Part of the hotel's foundation was used in the construction of Haggerty's home, a fact, no doubt, unknown to any of those meeting there today.

Erin Dougherty sat in Mrs. Haggerty's living room on a couch covered by an old brown furniture wrap. She was in her late thirties; bleached blond hair cut short, clear complexion, soft brown eyes. She wore a modest multi-colored dress cut a couple of inches below her knees.

Hundley and Magliore sat opposite her on two wingback chairs also adorned with brown covers. Hundley apologized for the intrusion. "We're sorry to bother you while you're working Erin, but we need to talk with you. You know Mags don't you?"

"By reputation," she said and offered a forced smile; her lips stretched tight, no teeth showing.

"Well, ah, we're investigating the murder of Father John," Hundley explained. "Mags is a homicide detective in California and has more experience in this area than I do. He's assisting with the investigation."

Erin didn't respond. She looked at Magliore and her eyes met his before she turned away.

Hundley's discomfort showed as he led the questioning. "Well, ah," he stammered. "We understand you do volunteer work with the Ladies Sodality."

"You know I do Randy."

"Well, ah, yes. Ah! In doing so you worked closely with Father John at times right?"

Erin understood why Hundley stumbled over his questions so she cut to the chase. "I wasn't sleeping with him if that's what you're implying. Although, God help me, I was tempted."

Hundley's head snapped back as if she'd slapped him unprepared for such candor. "Ah! I'm sorry Erin. We had to ask. Rumors."

Dougherty twisted her hands in her lap. "Of course there are rumors. Handsome men attract the ladies no matter what their vocation. Many women vied for his attention. Some, I suspect, would have hopped into bed with him at the drop of a hat if he asked."

"Did he ever approach you?" Magliore interjected.

She continued twisting her hands. "He flirted. I flirted. No sweaty clinches in the sacristy. Just flirting."

"Was your husband Bill aware of any of this?" Hundley asked.

"Bill, God bless him, is a plumber. All he knows are pipes and wrenches. He goes to mass with me on Sunday's because it makes me happy. The church or its priests don't interest him."

"What if he did know?"

She considered the question for a moment before answering. "He wouldn't believe it."

She got up signaling the end of the conversation and walked them to the door. As Hundley opened it, Magliore posed a final question. "Can you tell us if anyone did have an affair with Father John?"

"Talk to Elaine Richardson," She said. "But not with her husband around. He's a hot-head."

Chapter 33

Hot heads commit murder but usually in a moment of passion. They lose their temper, use their fists or grab whatever weapon is handy. They don't lure someone to a remote location for the kill. Perhaps whoever enticed Father O'Shea to Fort Revere did not intend to harm him but when talks or threats failed to frighten him grabbed a rock to do the deed.

But why did O'Shea turn his back on him?

Elaine Richardson and her husband lived on "C" Street in the middle of town. To get there, Hundley chose the scenic route along Beach Avenue although the high protective sand dunes on the ocean side of the road limited the view from the car. The dunes, now seeded with hardy grass, had been constructed to shield the homes across the road from the damaging flooding caused by Nor'easters and hurricanes. Some of the former summer cottages have been transformed into magnificent winter homes with great views of the ocean, part of the town's resurgence Selectman Carter Fitzgerald touted at the class reunion and that he insisted would be aided by the new redevelopment plan.

As Hundley turned onto "C" Street, he pointed to a three-story house on the corner, #201 Beach. "Know who was born there?"

"Enlighten me," Magliore said, rolling his eyes.

"Joseph P. Kennedy Jr., older brother of JFK."

"What are you? The town historian." Magliore responded, not impressed.

"I am the police chief, you know."

Magliore kept silent until they stopped in front of the Richardson place. "You think ole' Tucker knows a famous member of the Kennedy Clan once lived on his street?"

"From what I hear, on some nights, Tucker's lucky to remember he lives here."

They both laughed but kept their expressions professional as they exited the car and walked up the three front steps of the Richardson home. The chief rang the bell that was answered within seconds by a young man who appeared to be in his early twenties.

Hundley knew the boy who had had minor scrapes with the law as a youngster. He was a slender version of his dad and about as subtle. "Hi Russell," Hundley said. "Is your mom at home?"

Russell ran his eyes over Magliore as if questioning his presence. "This is Vince Magliore," Hundley said, responding to the unanswered query. "You may have heard of him."

"Some kind of jock hero, big deal."

Magliore resisted the urge to grab the kid by the stacking swivel and shake the living shit out of him. He let the remark pass without comment.

Hundley's reddened face showed the kid pissed him off too, but he remained calm. "We need to talk with your mother, Russell. Please tell her we're here."

The kid turned from the door and went to the foot of a set of wooden stairs leading to the second story of the house. "Mom," he shouted. "The cops want to talk with you."

Without turning around, he walked away toward the kitchen leaving both men standing there. "Courteous young man" Magliore said to Hundley who rolled his eyes as they stepped inside.

Elaine Richardson came down the stairs and both men stared wide-eyed. She wore a pair of tight white shorts leaving little to the imagination and a blue blouse revealing ample cleavage. She must have been a child bride if she was the mother of a twenty-something kid thought Magliore. He guessed her to be in her mid-thirties.

She smiled with the knowledge of her effect on the gawking men. Two dumb shits with their mouths hanging open.

"Hi Randy," she said as she held out her hand to him. "Introduce me to your friend."

Randy, tongue tied for a moment, stammered, "Ah! This is Vince Magliore, a high school friend and a homicide lieutenant from California. We're investigating the murder of Father O'Shea."

"Wow! Why in the world would you come to see me?" she said, holding her smile though it now appeared strained.

Before he could answer, Richardson interrupted. "I'm sorry. Where are my manners? Would you like something to drink?"

"No thanks, Elaine. May we sit down?"

"Of course," she said and led them to a couch and matching chairs. Randy sat on the couch beside her; Magliore took a chair in front and to her left.

Hundley, still shaken by Elaine's appearance, deferred to Magliore to ask the first question. "I hope we don't offend you, Mrs. Richardson. We need to explore all possibilities."

"Please call me Elaine. Mrs. Richardson sounds so formal."

"OK, Elaine," Magliore said. "We have reason to believe Father O'Shea was not faithful to his vow of celibacy."

This time Elaine Richardson laughed. "You can't prove that by me."

"Our information says otherwise."

She laughed again, not offended but scanned the room to confirm they were alone. Satisfied, she said, "Johnny and I had some fun together, all flirting, no real action."

She leaned forward ensuring both men an unobstructed view down her blouse. She enjoyed their discomfort and took pleasure in teasing them.

"I did a striptease for him once when we were alone in the sacristy," she confessed. "He was aroused but wouldn't go beyond kissing and fondling. It was a kick to do that with a priest."

Her admission didn't faze Magliore. He'd seen and heard it all in his years as a detective. "Was your husband aware of this?"

"Hell no," Richardson blurted. "He'd kill the both of us."

As soon as the words escaped her mouth, she tried to correct the impression her words conveyed. "Wait a minute. That was a figure of speech. Tucker can lose his temper sometimes throw things. But he's never raised a hand to me and wouldn't kill anyone."

"Can you be certain?" Randy pressed.

"Absolutely," she responded. "Better yet, Tucker was in Cleveland on business when Father John was killed. Check it out."

"We will, of course," Randy confirmed and both men got up to leave.

Elaine Richardson walked them to the door and as she opened it said, "You know, I wasn't alone in having fun with Johnny O'Shea. He played around with many Catholic women in town. Despite the rumors and gossip, though, I'd be very surprised if he had sex, intercourse, with any of them. He wouldn't break his vow of celibacy."

As they returned to their car, Magliore wondered if the rules defining celibacy had changed. Maybe flirting and fondling were permitted under some new Vatican Council Decree though he doubted it.

Once ensconced in the car he turned to Hundley. "Did you notice both Erin Daugherty and Elaine Richardson described their intimacy with Johnny as 'just flirting' as if they had agreed on that term?"

Hundley gripped the steering wheel and stared straight ahead. "Maybe it is what it is, Mags. Don't read more into it."

Magliore slapped his forehead. "Wow, Chief. Can't refute that logic."

Chapter 34

On the way to their next interview, Magliore Googled celibacy, which Webster's dictionary defined as "abstaining from marriage and sexual intercourse." Perhaps Johnny O'Shea interpreted that to mean other types of sexual activity were OK, endorsing the teenage concept that anything short of intercourse was not sex.

Magloire and Hundley questioned two other women rumored to have had dalliances with O'Shea. One denied any physical relationship with her priest and appeared embarrassed by the suggestion escorting them out of her house almost as soon as they arrived. The other, however, was not deterred by the strict Catholic concept of celibacy admitting to "touchy feely" moments with her pastor, 'no in and out stuff.'

It became clear Johnny O'Shea liked the ladies and discretion was not in his vocabulary. Any one of a number of irate husbands or boyfriends angered by a priest groping their partner could be a suspect. The investigation of his murder promised to be messy and embarrassing to many. And another thought bothered Magliore. If Johnny O'Shea played around with adult women, did his net ensnare younger ones as well? Was he a child molester? If so, add angry parents to the list of suspects.

As they drove back to the police station after their interviews, Hundley remained quiet, distracted, eyes riveted on the road ahead. Magliore respected his privacy and amused himself by gazing out the window as they drove down Nantasket Avenue, a road he once traveled often. They passed Strawberry Hill, without its former landmark water tower, the hill naked without it. In the Kenberma neighborhood, the aroma of coffee and muffins wafted in the air from Weinberg's bakery, one of the few businesses in the area Magliore recognized. Most of the others didn't exist in his day. Perhaps a sign of the economic times where small businesses struggled to survive and a renewal plan offered the best hope for a town's resurgence.

They passed the area leveled decades ago for redevelopment; the one Selectman Carter Fitzgerald believed would soon be a cash cow for the town. On their left, a vacant lot replaced former homes, a gas station and a delicatessen. On the right, a green area with some benches supplanted homes and some small shops, one of which, Magliore remembered, had been a shoe repair joint.

The Nantasket Resort Hotel occupied the space where the famous Surf Ballroom operated. The nightclub attracted many of the top bands and singing groups of the time like Sony and Cher, Frankie Avalon and Jimmy Morrison and the Doors. Legendary DJ Arnie "Woo Woo" Ginsberg spun records there for screaming teenagers and rocked the place with his signature train whistle.

Magliore leaned back in his seat and closed his eyes. The Surf in its heyday, like Paragon Park, attracted large crowds to Nantasket Beach, though the glamor of the old days was gone and would not return. He doubted Carter Fitzgerald's redevelopment project would have a similar impact though no doubt it would provide some stability and income to a town desperate for help.

"Remember the Surf Ballroom?" Magliore mused as he opened his eyes.

"No! And neither do you; before our time," Hundley said.

"I know but I still remember it. Like General Patton who recalled fighting the Romans as a Carthaginian. He believed in reincarnation. Maybe I rocked with Fabian."

Hundley regarded Magliore with a jaundiced glare. *He's popping too many of those damn pain pills.*

He said: "Don't lose it now pal. We need to solve a murder."

Magliore returned Hundley's stare and winked.

Chapter 35

Karen Hundley opened the door before he could knock.

She stood in the doorway with a smile on her face and a drink in her hand; appearing disheveled. Several strands of her dark hair flared up and out, her sleeveless blue blouse wrinkled and pulled half out of her short gray skirt. She listed to her right like someone on a sailboat leaning into the wind; the glass of wine in her hand not her first despite the early afternoon hour.

"Hey Mags," she said in a voice booming through the empty house. "Come on in, have a drink."

She turned and weaved her way down a short hall to a breakfast nook adjacent to the kitchen. Magliore closed the door and followed regretting his agreement with Randy to stay with them.

"Sit down, sit down, my friend," her voice reverberated off the walls too cheerful for the situation.

She poured two glasses of wine in the kitchen and brought them to the table. She sat in a chair to Magliore's right and turned so that her body faced him. She crossed her legs and as she did so, her skirt rode high up on her thighs flashing white.

She smiled as she caught Magliore gawking and raised her glass. "Here's to you my friend," she said and took a big swallow. She slammed the glass down so hard Magliore feared the table might crack or shatter.

"Oops!" she giggled.

Magliore was uneasy, reminded of the intimate hug she gave him at the reunion her thighs pressing into him.

He moved to get up when she reached over and put her hand on his arm: "Sorry if I'm making you nervous, Mags. I've had a little too much to drink as I'm sure you've guessed."

Magliore sat back in his chair, her hand still on his arm. "What's wrong Karen? This is not like you."

He hadn't seen her in years, had no idea whether this was like her or not. Might be the reason Randy dipped his wick elsewhere or maybe the result of him straying, he thought.

Her eyes welled up. Dismissing the question, she changed the subject: "Wasn't that awful about Johnny?"

"Yeah. Did you keep in touch after high school?"

"Both Randy and I did after he returned to town as our priest. We're Catholic, we go to mass. I worked at the church with the Ladies Sodality."

"Why would anyone want to kill him Karen?"

She gulped more wine and sat back in her seat. She gazed out the window, lost in thought perhaps deciding whether she should tell him what she knew.

"There were rumors," she said finally and put her head down on the tabletop, the conversation over.

Chapter 36

Fifteen-year old Melissa Cannon lay face down on her bed crying. Something she had been doing for the last hour. The news of Father John's death shattered her. She cried out of both loss and fear. Father John was dead, her Johnny, so handsome, mature. Not like the pimply-faced boys at school who wanted just one thing. Like that would ever happen, as if.

Melissa served as secretary on the Catholic Youth Organization's leadership council, which met once a week in a classroom at the Memorial School. Father John drove her home after each meeting always dropping other kids off first. He treated her as an adult, questioned her about schoolwork, offered advice about what classes she should take to get into college, praising her for being true to her faith, staying drug free and remaining chaste.

Sometimes, he would pat her knee and rub her back when he took her home. One time, when she wore a short skirt, his hand strayed to her upper thigh. She got wet fantasizing about it later and hoped it would go further.

One night after a CYO meeting, Melissa, wearing another tiny skirt, went into the bathroom and removed her panties before getting into Father John's car for the ride home. She noticed him stealing glances at her legs and detected a bulge in his pants. She squirmed in her seat forcing her skirt to her waist.

When they were alone, Father John praised her looks. He patted her leg and Melissa grabbed his hand and moved it higher so he could sense her nakedness. He let it stay there for a moment before withdrawing it.

Later, Father John pulled the car down a side street off Nantasket Avenue. He expressed remorse for his behavior and told her this must never happen again. He kissed her on the cheek and she put her head on his shoulder where it remained until they reached her home.

The intimacies didn't stop with that night despite Father John's protests to the contrary. Melissa didn't let them and he didn't mind. Parked at the curb on deserted streets, he stroked her arms and legs and fondled her breasts. She once used her hand and mouth to satisfy him.

Melissa's fantasy world collapsed when, after one CYO meeting, Father John informed her they must stop. As a man of the cloth, he would confess his sins and do penance. She and the other kids would have to find other transportation home after meetings.

Melissa was devastated and as fifteen-year olds are inclined to do, lashed out to punish the priest for rejecting her. After school, she confessed to her mother he had touched her inappropriately when driving her home. Furious, her mother dragged her to the police station to file a complaint.

Her father went into a rage when informed of the incident, cursing the church and its priests, denouncing the police for their inept handling of the information and vowing to kill O'Shea.

Melissa recoiled; shaken by her dad's reaction unaware a priest had molested him when he served as a young altar boy. Nevertheless, she changed her story offering a new explanation of what occurred. She said Father John had been reaching for something in the car glove compartment and his hand brushed her leg. She said she was mad at him for not driving them home anymore. She begged her dad to drop the complaint. He complied but wasn't fooled. He knew better.

Now, sobbing on her bed, mourning the loss of her first love, she worried her father had made good on his threat to harm Father John.

Chapter 37

The call from Bobby Jennings, a baseball teammate at Hull High, surprised Magliore.

The two shared a couple of stories at the class reunion but before that had not seen or spoken to each other in years. Jennings claimed to possess information about the murder of Johnny O'Shea and suggested meeting out of town. They settled on the Atlantica Restaurant in Cohasset Harbor. Magliore suspected the dinner would be on him.

He walked into the Atlantica around 5:00 p.m. There were few other diners present and he spotted Jennings at a window table for two, munching on some breadsticks, a bottle of beer on the table in front of him. Magliore waved off the hostess, pointed toward Bobby and mouthed, "I'm joining him." She nodded and followed with a menu.

Bobby raised his bottle in greeting, did not stand or offer his hand. Magliore slipped into a chair opposite him; the hostess slipped the menu on the table and asked for his drink order. He selected a California Merlo.

Outside, the sun was setting and shadows from moored sailboats and powerboats danced on the ripples of water made by a yacht sliding through the small channel, an Idyllic scene and one reminiscent of many New England coastal towns. Magliore turned from the window and focused his attention on Bobby Jennings who resembled a refugee from the seventies; shoulder length blond, stringy hair hiding his ears, sideburns reaching to his mouth and a moustache drooping below his jaw. He wore an open necked blue shirt with a gold chain adorning his neck. He needed a shave and a haircut; Magliore didn't suggest either.

"What do you have for me, Bobby?" he asked.

Before Jennings could answer, the waiter, a young man in his early twenties arrived with Magliore's wine and requested their food order. Jennings selected steak and lobster, one of the most expensive items, while Magliore, without inspecting the menu, ordered a scallop casserole, sure they had it. They did.

The waiter left.

"Why call me, Bobby?" Magliore asked. "Any information about the murder of O'Shea needs to be shared with the state police investigators or Chief Hundley."

Bobby laughed. "When I tell you what I have, you'll understand."

"The clock's ticking man."

Jennings hunkered down, leaned across the table to ensure he couldn't be overheard, eyes darting left and right. "You know O'Shea was a player?"

75

"If you mean, he liked the ladies, yes, I've discovered that."

"Well, one of the ladies he liked was Karen Hundley."

Magliore rocked back in his chair as if punched. Cops are seldom surprised by anything. This was different. "Don't shit me Bobby, are you sure?"

"I am."

"How?"

"I seen them together."

Bobby apparently hadn't paid much attention in English class but Magliore ignored his grammatical faux pas and challenged his claim. "What? They invited you in for a manage a trois?"

Bobby laughed again, took another swig of beer and leaned in. "My mail route includes the Hundley's. I seen O'Shea's car parked out front three or four times. Once, when I was about to drop the mail in the box on the porch, I heard giggling and laughing inside and peeked through a window near the front door. The blinds don't cover it. I seen Karen sprawled on her back, on a couch, skirt up to her ears and O'Shea up to his...ears."

Magliore wanted to punch Bobby and wipe the smirk from his face but you don't shoot the messenger, as they say. Many thoughts and questions went through his mind; he voiced just one. "Did Randy know?"

The waiter came with their food at that moment and they both fell silent until he left. The scallops smelled good but Magliore had lost his appetite. Bobby had no such problem and cut a big piece of steak and stuffed it in his mouth. Magliore waited until he finished and asked again. "Did Randy know?"

"Half the town did. The man wasn't all that careful, his being a priest and all."

"You're aware of the consequences if Randy suspected or knew, right?"

Bobby, irritated, raised his voice. "Why do you think I'm here telling you and not the state guys? The chief would go to the top of the list of suspects."

Chapter 38

Magliore was livid.

The news from Bobby Jennings cast a shadow on his newfound friendship with Randy Hundley and doubt on Hundley's veracity. He fumed in his car outside the Atlantica until he called the Chief and requested they meet for a drink in Hull.

They met at the Red Parrott Restaurant, a two-story structure on Hull Shore Drive a stone's throw from the beach. Hundley sat inside at an upstairs table by a window with a wonderful view of the ocean. On a typical gray New England evening with a light rain falling, the Atlantic surf pounded the rocks protecting the sea wall from erosion and the white spray blew several feet in the air.

Magliore slid into a chair opposite Hundley who raised his Adams draft in a greeting. Magliore ordered a Blackstone California Merlot from a young waiter who appeared as soon as he sat down.

The waiter trotted off, giving the two men privacy.

"So," Randy began. "You wanted to meet. You got anything on the murder or my blackmailers?"

"I do but you're not going to like it."

"Why?"

Magliore ignored the question and asked one of his own. "When were you going to tell me?"

"Tell you what?" Hundley said with a half-smile, his sharp blue eyes revealing his concern. Before Magliore could answer, the waiter returned with his wine and retreated again when both men said they would stick to drinks.

Magliore waited until the young man was out of earshot before continuing. "When were you going to tell me about your wife and Johnny O'Shea?"

Hundley leaned back in his chair, swigged some beer from the bottle and scanned the room to be sure none of the locals or guests could overhear their conversation though only a handful of people were in the restaurant. Magliore suspected Hundley was buying time before answering.

"That's bullshit Mags," he said after the brief pause, "I wouldn't blame her but I'm certain she didn't have sex with Johnny. They had a thing in high school. He broke her heart. Maybe the reason she wound up with me. I'm grateful she did."

"So grateful you're cheating on her."

Hundley put down his beer, clasped his hands together on the table, dropped his eyes and frowned. "You don't know the whole story."

Magliore, amazed, balled his fists and leaned forward. "I don't know the whole story. What's going on man? You ask for my help then withhold information. Level with me or I walk."

Hundley put up his hands in a gesture of surrender and shrugged. "Two things Mags: One, Karen did not fuck Johnny O'Shea. She flirted like some of the other women, her nature, but wouldn't betray the family, the kids. Second, I'm begging you to keep searching for the blackmailers. You find them, I'll tell you everything. I can't right now. Trust me please."

"Your trust level is not high with me, Chief. I've got an eyewitness who places them together in your house, on your couch."

"What eyewitness?"

"Bobby Jennings," Magliore blurted without hesitation. "Says he saw them when he delivered the mail."

Hundley laughed attracting the attention of a couple sitting two tables away. Chastened, he lowered his voice. "Bobby Jennings is a nut case, thinks the FBI, NSA and CIA are spying on him, put tin foil up on the windows of his house to block their radio waves. He doesn't watch television or own any electronic devices. He's pissed I didn't investigate his claims. He wanted me to station an officer in his house as protection. He's trying to get back at me through Karen."

Magliore had no comeback. Even if Bobby weren't operating with a full deck his claims could spell trouble for Hundley. "You're aware if Karen and Johnny did have a thing, and the state guys find out, and they will, you go to the top of the list of murder suspects. Karen might join you."

"Neither one of us had anything to do with it. Bobby's blowing smoke up your ass, I swear."

"I'm the one who should be swearing. You're holding back important evidence from me. You dragged me into this. What's going on?"

Hundley took another swig of beer. "I'm not thinking straight these days. My relationship with Karen is in the toilet; has been for a long time. My fault, I admit, the blackmail thing, followed by Johnny's murder. I hoped you could help solve these fast and save my butt. I like this town, like this job and love Karen in my own way."

Magliore clenched his teeth, glared at his friend, then relaxed his jaw. "If you want my help, man, the bullshit stops now."

"I understand."

Magliore had to believe Hundley would be honest in the future. If not, he'd walk, resume his vacation and put all this bullshit behind. Yet he wasn't ready to do that. He had his doubts, but hey, he was a nice guy and a pushover when it came to friends, even those he hadn't seen in years.

Later events would lead him to question the decision to stay involved.

Chapter 39

"Who kills a priest?"

That was the question posed by the lead state detective in the O'Shea murder, Ed "Big Cat" Catebegian, a former little All-America football player at Colby College in Maine and a professional who had a "cup of coffee" career with the Patriots and two other teams. Big Cat, an intimidating presence at six feet six, 265 pounds, shoulders as wide as a Mack truck, shaved head, scar on his right cheek, engulfed the one chair not behind Chief Hundley's desk and spit tobacco juice into a plastic cup.

Magliore, leaning against a wall, grimaced while Hundley rolled his eyes and studied the ceiling.

Big Cat ignored their obvious disdain for his habit. "So did the padre diddle little boys?"

Hundley returned his gaze to Catebegian. "No evidence to support that."

"Little girls then?"

"Nope."

"How about big girls or big guys?"

"Possibly. Mags and I interviewed some female parishioners rumored to have had sex with O'Shea. A few admitted to some groping and kissing, no intercourse. We believe them."

Big Cat twisted in his chair and inspected Magliore. He spit into his cup and narrowed his eyes, confused. "Who is this yahoo?" he asked, his confusion understandable. Magliore looked and dressed less like a cop than a gym rat. The muscles of his neck flowed through his shoulders and arms forming a triangle of power. His grey cut-off San Diego State football jersey, clinging to his thick frame, revealed six-pack abs like those on the muscle bound models of Men's Health Magazine. His backwards ball cap, cargo shorts and Nike running shoes completed his unprofessional appearance.

"He's a homicide lieutenant from California on vacation. He grew up here, knew the victim. He can help."

Big Cat spit again, studied the juice in his cup, and relented, but with one caveat. "He's your responsibility Chief. He screws up, interferes in any way, it's your ass."

Big Cat's bulk concealed a quick wit and keen intelligence. He understood cooperating with the Hull police could speed things along but he chafed at Hundley's less than insightful responses so far and he worried about the California beach bum. Yet, he spread his hands wide in defeat returning to his original question. "Why was the priest whacked if child abuse is not the motive? A jealous husband or boyfriend?"

"My gut tells me the sex angle is a red herring," Magliore interjected

"You got a theory? I'm all ears," Big Cat said, as everyone laughed; his ears, a prominent feature of his anatomy, spread out from his head like the wings of an Eagle.

"Well," Magliore said. "Perhaps he was killed for what he knew. Somebody afraid he wouldn't keep the seal of the confessional. If someone confessed a crime, in a small town like this and if that person was a regular churchgoer, O'Shea would know him or her. That person could lure O'Shea to Fort Revere on the pretense of further discussion of the matter. Catholic doctrine allows a priest to talk face to face with a penitent if the penitent chooses to do so."

"How come you know so much about Catholic doctrine and is penitent even a word?" Big Cat said a grin spreading on his face.

"I once studied for the seminary."

"No shit."

"Yes shit!"

Big Cat spit into his cup. "OK. What you suggest is a possibility. Though an angry spouse or boyfriend is more likely given what we now know about the Catholic priesthood."

"Exactly what the perpetrator wants us to think."

"Perpetrator!" Catebegian's laugh convulsed his whole body, threatened to collapse his chair and spill tobacco juice on his clothes or the floor. "OK! OK!" he said when he got control of himself. "I'll keep an open mind and I expect you guys to share whatever you find out--as soon as you find it out."

"You're OK with us conducting a parallel investigation?" Hundley asked.

"Yup! But don't fuck me over or you'll find out what two-hundred and sixty-five pounds feels like on your chest."

Chapter 40

Neither Hundley nor Magliore wanted Big Cat sitting on their chest or anywhere else. They had created doubt about the motive for O'Shea's murder but how could they prove their new theory?

With Catebegian gone, Magliore slumped down in the seat vacated by the big man swearing the man's bulk had expanded it. "OK," he said. "What does a priest do if a penitent confesses to a crime?"

"Again with the penitent? You should have been a priest."

"Yeah! And you should have been a cop."

Hundley smirked. "Funny, ha, ha. In answer to your question the priest advises the person to go to the police."

"And if that doesn't work?"

"I assume the priest must remain silent."

"Right. But Catholic doctrine regarding the confessional allows a priest to seek advice on a question of conscience although he can't reveal the name of the penitent."

"You did learn something in the seminary."

Magliore chuckled; the seminary had other benefits too. Women were eager to drop their pants when they discovered he studied for the priesthood. It baffled him that it was such a turn on. He chalked it up to another facet of mysterious womanhood.

Dismissing the thought, he said, "What we need to determine is who John would go to for guidance."

"What about another priest?"

"Maybe. But as the sole priest in Hull, he'd have to go elsewhere like Hingham or Cohasset and they would know him."

"So who?"

"How about his boss?"

"The Pope?"

"Yeah! Randy. He'd dial up Pope John, or Paul or Phil or whoever the guy is. Or is it a woman now?"

"You're an asshole?"

Magliore ignored the shot and got serious. "The local parish priest must have a supervisor, somebody under the Archbishop of Boston."

"How do we find out who that is?"

"Let's Google the Catholic Church Hierarchy in Massachusetts."

"Google. You continue to amaze me. You aren't exactly Mr. Technology."

"Hey! Just because I think "Twitter" is something old ladies do when they find something funny, doesn't mean I can't find my way around the Internet."

Randy rolled his eyes but fired up his computer!

Chapter 41

God bless Google, or perhaps Al Gore, Magliore thought, still feisty after his exchange with Hundley. Gore invented it didn't he? Or was it the Internet? Didn't matter.

In their search, they discovered the Archdiocese of Boston encompassed five counties, 289 parishes and 2,465 square miles. To assist in governing such a large area, the Archdiocese was divided into regions presided over by vicars or auxiliary bishops. The most reverend Daniel Conner, auxiliary bishop of Boston with a residence in Weymouth, supervised the south region, which included Hull.

Hundley called the bishop's office and secured an appointment when he explained the reason. Weymouth is about a fifteen or twenty minute drive north from Hull. With traffic heavy at eight in the morning, it took them thirty-five minutes. A male secretary, a young priest who appeared to be fifteen years old, ushered them into the bishop's office.

The office was huge, with mahogany paneled walls. A floor to ceiling bookcase covered the wall to their left. A picture of the current pontiff hung behind the bishop's desk while on the wall to their right were a half-dozen others of the bishop meeting with the Archbishop of Boston, Senator Ted Kennedy, the governor of Massachusetts and a few other dignitaries Magliore could not identify. The bishop's desk was clear except for a telephone to his right and an in/out box on his left. A slight odor of cigar smoke mixed with air freshener was detectable as they got further into the room, no doubt an effort to conceal the dirty deed.

What else might he try to hide?

The bishop, in red cassock and small red skullcap, did not stand to greet them. He gestured with his arm for them to sit in two padded straight-backed chairs in front of his desk, like two schoolboys about to be chastised by the principal, a position Magliore had been in more than once—unjustly of course.

Connor appeared to be in his late sixties, salt and pepper hair cut short, no sideburns. He was plump not fat, his red face round, with deep lines around the eyes and mouth. His green eyes fixed his visitors with a stare challenging them to be quick.

Randy Hundley spoke first: "Thank you for seeing us on such short notice, Excellency."

The prelate raised his hand, palm outward as if offering them peace like he would while saying Mass. "How can I help you? I know nothing about the murder of Father O'Shea, rest his soul."

"Well," Hundley said. "We have a theory Father O'Shea's murder may be connected to something he heard in the confessional."

"Stop right there," Connor protested. "The seal of the confessional is absolute. The priest can reveal nothing told to him. He cannot do so even to save his own life or the life of another or aid the course of justice, such as reporting a crime, which I suspect you are suggesting here."

"Please be assured," Magliore said, "we would never ask that. We do know if a priest needs guidance from a more experienced confessor to deal with a difficult case of conscience, perhaps in a situation where a serious crime has been or is about to be committed, he can do so if he first asks permission of the penitent."

The bishop pursed his lips in what passed as a smile. "I see you have done some homework on this," he said. "In the circumstance you describe, though, the priest may not reveal the identity of the penitent."

"We understand," Magliore acknowledged. "We only ask if Father O'Shea sought your advice. It might confirm our suspicions."

The bishop bowed his head, placed his hands together in front of him as if in prayer and frowned. "I'm sorry to say I did not speak to him regarding anything like you suggest. In fact, we hadn't met in quite some time."

Disappointed, the two men stood. "Thank you for your time, Excellency," Hundley said as Connor moved to escort them out. At the door, he paused. "You know, now that I think about it," he said. "Two days before his murder Father O'Shea scheduled a meeting with me. He didn't give a reason and we never met. I didn't connect that with his death"

Hundley and Magliore perked up. Their eyes locked; a glimmer of hope.

Chapter 42

They left the Bishop's office and stopped at a McDonald's in Weymouth near the Fore River Bridge.

"If they made Happy Meals for adults," Magliore said, "I'd order one." Now certain O'Shea scheduled the meeting with Bishop Connor to seek his advice regarding a confession.

Hundley wasn't convinced. "Don't be so smug. The fact Johnny wanted to meet with Connor doesn't tell us anything. Maybe it didn't have anything to do with a confession at all. Maybe he wanted to convince the Bishop the rumors of his whoring around were untrue or he wanted to discuss church architecture. Who knows?"

"Johnny hadn't met with the Bishop in a long time and two days before he's killed, he asks to see him. Coincidence! Bullshit."

Both men stopped talking to eat. Hundley devouring his burger and fries, Magliore nibbling on a fish sandwich adhering to his unstated philosophy: When in New England, opt for seafood, even from a fast food joint. He broke the silence. "So where does that leave us?"

Hundley shrugged. "Back to sex as a motive; a jealous husband or boyfriend or parent. Johnny diddled big girls, why not little ones? Boys even as Big Cat suggested."

Hundley sat back in his chair, focused on something outside the window and sipped his coke. The muscles of his face drooped, the dark rings under his eyes more prominent, the hand holding his drink quivered.

Magliore let him sit like that for several minutes before breaking into his reverie. "OK, what suspects do we have if sex as a motive is back in play?"

Hundley remained transfixed.

"Hey man," Magliore said raising his voice.

"What? What?" Hundley stuttered.

"What the hell's the matter with you? Are you on another planet? Do we have any suspects if sex is the motive for Johnny's murder?"

Hundley turned away from the window, clear eyed again. "Sorry, Mags. Didn't mean to zone out. We need to take another look at Elaine Richardson's husband, Tucker, from everything I hear he's a loose cannon, quick to mix it up, especially when he's soused. Let's check his alibi."

"Let's do it," Magliore said, as if girding up to take the field for a football game.

Chapter 43

Tucker Richardson's alibi did not check out.

A state police inquiry discovered Tucker had been in Cleveland for a four-day conference conducted by his employer but he flew back to Boston two days early and one day before Father O'Shea's murder.

"Tucker's got some 'splaining' to do," Big Cat said in a poor imitation of Desi Arnaz punctuating his comment by spitting into his ever present plastic cup. They were at the Hull Police Station but Chief Hundley was occupied trying to resolve a dispute between two homeowners in Kenberma so Catebegian and Magliore set out to see Tucker Richardson at the Home Depot store in Rockland where he worked.

They arrived at 1:35 p.m. One of the cashiers directed them to the lumber section. Tucker stacked plywood, two-by-fours and fence posts and made precision cuts for customer projects. A co-worker in lumber told them to check for Tucker in a nearby break-room. He wasn't there. A sign on the lone door in the room leading to the outside said "Patio. Smoking Permitted."

Magliore and Catebegian pushed through the door and found Richardson seated alone at a wooden picnic bench covered by an orange umbrella emblazoned with "Home Depot" in white block letters. An ashtray on the table overflowed with cigarette butts.

Richardson was smoking and drinking a diet coke, which by his bulk revealed the "diet" part wasn't working. He looked up when the two men invaded his space, took them for potential clients and said, "How can I help you gentlemen?"

Catebegian flashed his badge and Richardson dropped his welcoming smile. Big Cat sat opposite him while Magliore chose to stand.

Big Cat opened the conversation. "We have a few questions, Tucker, about the murder of Father John O'Shea."

"I don't know nothing about that," Richardson said, his grammar no better than his effort to diet.

"We think you do Tucker. Witnesses overheard you threaten to kill O'Shea if he messed with your wife and you lied about being in Cleveland for four days. You were back in town before he was killed."

Tucker took a drag of his cigarette, washed it down with coke and turned away for a moment.

"I didn't kill the bastard, I swear. But I'm not losing any sleep over his death. The scumbag hid behind his collar. He fucked my wife and many others from what I heard."

"You came back early from the conference Tucker, didn't tell your wife and didn't go home," Big Cat said ignoring the rant. "Where were you?"

Tucker took another drag of his cigarette, stubbed the butt out in the ashtray and scanned the area to ensure privacy. "I got something on the side. Her name is Estelle. She lives in Hingham. She'll vouch for me."

Big Cat and Magliore both grimaced. "You're cheating on your wife and are pissed she might be doing the same thing?" Magliore said.

"Damn right," Tucker said. "She's a woman. Men got needs."

What could you say to that? They took Estelle's contact information and left Tucker sitting at the picnic bench.

The man was easy to dislike, but despite his bombast and disagreeable nature neither Magliore nor Catebegian thought him guilty of O'Shea's murder. He didn't possess the skill or finesse to lure O'Shea to Fort Revere. He was more apt to charge into the sacristy or church and pummel the priest with his fists.

Tucker would charge in somewhere but it wasn't a church.

Chapter 44

Tucker Richardson was drunk, not an uncommon phenomenon. He had been at Jo's Nautical Bar since it opened, a couple of buddies having come and gone.

He was not happy, also not a rare occurrence. The cops harassed him at his work because his wife put out for that fucking priest and they suspected he wacked him.

"The bitch got me in trouble because she couldn't keep her knees together," he fumed at the man across from him as they sat at their usual table.

His companion had heard it all many times, turned away, rolled his eyes, careful not to let Tucker catch him. He didn't want trouble.

"I'm going to teach the bitch a lesson she'll never forget," Tucker said, standing and throwing several bills on the table.

"Let me drive you home man," his friend implored, reaching out to grab his arm.

Tucker broke free. "Fuck it," he said, attracting glares from other patrons familiar with his brutish behavior and language. He flipped them his middle finger as he stormed out.

He stumbled to his car in the parking lot, used the remote to gain access and fell behind the wheel. After three attempts, he put the key in the ignition, started the car and screeched onto the street, dust from the unpaved lot billowing behind.

Tucker smirked. No one at the bar knew he had a handgun and rifle in the trunk. "I'll show that bitch," he screamed. "I'll show her."

Chapter 45

The 911 plea came into the South Shore Regional Communication Center serving the communities of Hingham, Cohasset, Norwell and Hull, at 9:01 p.m.; the call made by a frantic woman in a home on Bluff Road in Hull. A man with a gun, the husband of one of the women attending a book club meeting, barged in threatening everyone. The woman making the call was in the bathroom when the man came in and still cowered there, door locked. She could hear the man shouting orders to the frightened women. She identified him as Tucker Richardson.

Drunk as a skunk.

Two police cruisers dispatched to the scene received rifle fire from the home as they arrived, front and side windows shattered, no one hit, officers forced to take cover behind their vehicles and call for back up. Bluff Road was L-shaped and both patrol cars parked parallel to the house on the stem of the L.

The sergeant on duty called Chief Hundley, who was sipping a glass of wine after having dinner at home with his wife Karen and guest, Vince Magliore.

"Sir we have an active shooter and possible hostage situation on Allerton Hill," the sergeant reported, his voice tinged with excitement and anxiety.

Hundley found the information difficult to process. *Christ, first a murder and now this.*

"What do we know?" he said regaining his composure.

"The shooter, identified as Tucker Richardson, is intoxicated and holding his wife and a bunch of ladies hostage near as we can determine. He fired at Officers Collins and Roebuck when they rolled up. No one hit."

"OK! Notify the State Police. Request a Special Tactical Operations Team (STOP). Also, get paramedics there in case this goes sideways."

"Yes sir."

"I'm on my way; contact Patterson and Villapango. Order them to suit up with appropriate weapons and send them to the house."

"Yes, sir."

Hundley hung up the house phone and faced Magliore and Karen, their after dinner drink interrupted and not likely to be resumed soon.

"You heard my side of the conversation?"

They nodded.

"That asshole Tucker Richardson has gone off the deep end. He's got his wife and some other women hostage. Shot at my guys, the dumb fuck. I'll kill him myself."

FRANK J. INFUSINO JR.

"Randy, please be careful," Karen said hugging him.

"I'll get my piece and join you," Magliore chimed in.

"No way, Bro. You can't participate. Stay here with Karen. I need you to do that for me."

His stare and set jaw told his friend not to fight him on this.

Magliore understood. He'd have done the same in Randy's position. "Keep your head down, buddy," he said.

Chapter 46

Inside the house Tucker Richardson herded the women upstairs to a bedroom and fired through the open window when the cops arrived, smiling when the car windows shattered.

"Tucker, what are you doing? Stop this," Elaine Richardson shouted at her husband. "Are you crazy?"

"I'll show you how crazy I am," Tucker retorted. "Take your clothes off."

"What?"

"Take your clothes off, whore. You didn't have any problem stripping for a goddam priest. Show everyone what ya got."

"Tucker please!"

"Do it," he screamed and slapped her face.

Elaine recoiled against a wall and slipped to the floor, tears streaming down her cheeks.

The other women wailed and cowered in fear sliding to the floor beside Elaine.

"Get up," Tucker demanded. He fired a shot from a handgun into the wall above his wife's head. "Up now," he repeated and fired another round in the same place.

Chief Hundley arrived on Bluff Road, heard the shots and saw the front door pulled open, a woman screaming and vaulting down the stairs where she fell in a heap.

Hundley and his two officers ran to the woman's side, ignoring the possibility of being fired upon from above.

"Roebuck come with me. We can't wait for the STOP team," Hundley directed as he charged into the house remembering the flack the Sheriff's department took at Columbine High School when they waited outside while two gunman killed teachers and classmates. He wasn't about to repeat that.

Once inside, he and Roebuck clambered up the stairs on their right, which led to the second floor. Hundley signaled Roebuck to stop when they reached the top. They could see Tucker Richardson, back to them, waving a handgun and shouting.

Hundley made a split second decision to rush through the door and tackle Richardson. Caught off-guard Richardson fell hard, his head smacking the hardwood floor, his gun discharging once again; this time into the floor. Furious, Hundley smacked Richardson's head to the floor multiple times rendering him unconscious. Officer Roebuck pounced on Richardson and handcuffed him.

The ladies still cowered on the floor. Elaine Richardson, ordered to disrobe by her raving husband, sat hugging her knees in an attempt to cover up, humiliated. "Get a blanket from one of the patrol cars to drape over her," Hundley ordered Roebuck.

"Oh Randy," Elaine sighed as she stood and moved into his arms. "Please hold me."

Hundley understood her fear and humiliation. He embraced her and whispered soothing words as he stroked her hair. Roebuck arrived with a blanket accompanied by two paramedics who escorted the other women downstairs to examine them for any injuries.

Officer Collins, having turned the woman who escaped the house over to the paramedics, joined Hundley and Roebuck in the room. Richardson moaned, announcing he had regained consciousness. "Have the paramedics check him out and then throw his ass in jail." Hundley directed.

Tucker Richardson would later be charged with attempted murder of police officers, kidnapping, hostage taking, spousal abuse, firing a weapon in public and illegal possession of a handgun. Hundley debated adding more charges but backed off. The chain of events stunned him. He was sure the murder of Father John O'Shea set this bizarre incident in motion. His tranquil town now reeled from a murder and a home invasion shoot out more characteristic of troubled cities with gangs and rampant crime.

He could not know this was just the beginning.

Chapter 47

Tucker Richardson's meltdown and subsequent arrest made him a prime suspect in the murder of Father John O'Shea. Yet, Vince Magliore wasn't convinced. There was no way O'Shea would have turned his back on a drunken out of control Richardson and he suspected a bumbling Richardson would have left incriminating evidence at the crime scene had he been there. Although other husbands or boyfriends cuckolded by O'Shea were still possibilities, they hadn't yet found any women who admitted having intercourse with their priest lessening the likelihood a lover or spouse would be spurred to murder. Considering this, Magliore returned to a motive they had considered but not pursued.

Perhaps child abuse rather than sex between consenting adults prompted the killing. With that in mind, Magliore researched, online, the Catholic sex abuse scandal and found no shortage of information. The results stunned him. He stared at his laptop computer screen in disbelief. One of the articles he pulled up gave an overview of the scandal nationwide: over four thousand U.S. priests accused of sexual abuse, two-hundred seventy in the Archdiocese of Boston alone, almost every parish on the South Shore, Hingham, Holbrook, Marshfield, Norwell, Cohasset and Hull, affected.

The inclusion of Hull astonished him. While he followed the stories of abuse on national television and in the newspapers, he presumed the scandal bypassed his hometown. It hadn't.

Christ.

Four Hull priests in the late sixties and early seventies molested young boys. Three in tandem accosted an eight-year-old altar boy, while another took a child to his family home in Canada to exploit him.

These boys would be adults now and might have children of their own. One victim, now an adult, wrote to the Archbishop of Boston detailing the mental anguish he and others grappled with their entire lives. There was no escape from the horrible effects of the betrayal committed in the name of God. Some of the victims, unable to live with the guilt committed suicide, delved into drugs or became violent.

This last point stuck with Magliore. If the victims of the Hull priests, now adults with children of their own, still lived in town or nearby, the stories and rumors of O'Shea's sexual exploits might have stirred old memories and thoughts of revenge, victims then, aggressors now. O'Shea, of course, hadn't been their abuser so long ago; he just represented the hated group.

Magliore called Chief Hundley's cell phone. He answered with one word, "Hundley."

"It's me," Magliore said.

"No shit Mags. I have this new-fangled technology, caller ID."

"Good for you, asshole. Do you want to know why I called?"

"Can't wait."

"I have a new theory on O'Shea's murder."

"Enlighten me."

"Did you know four Hull priests molested a couple of young boys in the late sixties?"

"Yeah vaguely. The Boston Globe broke the news and named names."

"Right. At least one eight-year old altar boy was abused and later sued the Archdiocese."

"OK!"

"The kid would be an adult now with kids of his own. Rumors of Johnny's escapades circulated widely, as we discovered. If this boy, now man, thought a priest was at it again, putting kids through what he experienced, he might be angry enough to want to stop it, permanently."

A few minutes passed before Hundley's reply: "Sounds plausible."

"Can you find out if the victim, or victims, reported the abuse to the Hull police?"

"That was over forty years ago. Our files weren't computerized. They might be in boxes stored away somewhere or non-existent."

"You better find them pal. Those records may identify our killer."

Hundley broke off the connection.

Chapter 48

Three days later, Magliore walked into the Chief's office and found Big Cat ensconced in a chair facing Hundley's desk sipping coffee and devouring a donut, his usual "see food" diet plan, see food, eat it.

At least he wasn't spitting tobacco juice into a paper cup.

"Our search of the records turned up something," Hundley said, grim faced.

"What?" Magliore asked.

"In 1970, the parents of an altar boy who claimed a priest fondled him reported the incident. An officer investigated, couldn't substantiate the kid's account. The pastor at the time declared the story preposterous, a child's fantasy."

"The same pastor later identified as having held down an eight year old boy while he and two others groped the kid."

Hundley nodded in the affirmative.

Big Cat, having polished off his donut, joined the conversation. "What happened?"

"The report was filed, no action taken. Priests were inviolate in those days, nobody wanted to take action against them nor could they believe them guilty of such unholy behavior."

"Christ," Magliore said, "Was the boy identified?"

"Yup," Hundley said, rubbing his right hand front to back over his head. "Phillip Cannon."

"Cannon, the father of the girl who claimed O'Shea molested her and later recanted?"

"Must be," Hundley said.

"What girl. What claim," Big Cat sputtered; his voice an octave or two higher like a woman discovering a mouse in the room.

Hundley filled Catebegian in, then directed his comments to Magliore. "Cannon lives in Hull Village not far from Fort Revere. He has motive and opportunity. The rocks scattered around the fort gave him the means."

"We better go see him," Big Cat said to Hundley. "You drive, I'll do the talking."

Did they have their man?

Chapter 49

The Cannon's lived in a two-story structure on Spring Street close to a Methodist Church and across from Hull's First Town Hall and School, a distinctive red building circa 1848. The field behind the building was often flooded during the winter for skating and where Hundley and Magliore played ice hockey.

Hundley pulled up at the curb and the three lawmen walked up the long walkway to the front door. The chief rang the bell but Catebegian stepped forward. A tall, slim woman in her mid-fifties with graying hair cut short opened the door on the third ring. She took a step back when confronted by the men, her eyes wide, a questioning look on her face.

She peered around Big Cat to Randy Hundley. "Can I help you chief?" she said, no doubt hoping for some reasonable explanation for this unwelcome intrusion.

Randy stepped beside Catebegian. "May we come in Lois? We'd like to speak with Phillip. This is Lieutenant Catebegian with the state police and Vince Magliore, a consultant. We're investigating the murder of Father O'Shea."

Lois's face blanched at the mention of Johnny O'Shea. "Why would you want to talk with Phillip, for heaven's sake? He's not a church goer and doesn't, didn't," she corrected, "know him."

"That may be, Lois," Randy said carrying the conversation. "But we do need to speak with him."

She moved aside, annoyed but compliant. The contingent of men stepped into a large uncluttered, attractively decorated living room. A fireplace and bookshelf dominated one wall with two long couches in front of the fireplace, one blue with a multi-colored pattern, the other a plain tan. A low coffee table with artificial flowers on top rested between the couches. A blue striped stuffed chair nestled beside a floor lamp completed the array of furniture. Pictures with a maritime theme dotted the walls.

As if on cue, Phillip Cannon came down the stairs from the second floor and shocked everyone when he blurted, "Wondered how long it would take for you to come?"

Cannon was slender like his wife, mid-fifties, pushing six feet. He had a narrow face, straight nose, thinning grey hair. He dressed in dark slacks, a short-sleeved blue dress shirt, and black shoes. He motioned everyone to sit.

Hundley and Big Cat took the tan couch, Magliore the stuffed chair. Cannon and his wife sat opposite them on the other sofa.

"I didn't kill him," Cannon said. "I thought about it many times, as you might guess, planned it even, couldn't do it. The bastards would win again if I did." He rubbed his hands together and sat back, his mouth twisted into a scowl.

"I'm sorry about what happened to you, Phil," Hundley said. "I didn't know. But why hate Father O'Shea?"

"I despise all of them for what they did to me and other children. They're all predators, still doing it despite what the church says. O'Shea had designs on my daughter. She didn't fool me with her feeble story."

"Where were you the night of the murder, Phil? We have to ask," Chief Hundley pressed.

"I don't have a great alibi if that's what you're getting at. Here watching TV with Lois. Lame but true."

"He didn't do it, he didn't," Melissa Cannon shouted as she all but jumped down the stairs, having eves-dropped on the conversation.

Husband and wife both stood at the outburst as Melissa rushed into her father's arms. Phillip Cannon peered over his daughter's head and shrugged.

"We'll need to talk to you more at the station, Phil," Hundley said, eager to move the discussion to a less charged venue.

"I understand," Cannon said.

Mrs. Cannon escorted the three lawmen to the door. "He's innocent Randy," she said, "you know that. He's a gentle, good man."

As they walked to their car, Magliore tended to believe Mrs. Cannon. He also knew gentle men could be pushed to violence, given strong motivation; like the prospect one of their children had been abused.

Chapter 50

"I lied," Melissa Cannon admitted that night at dinner. "I loved Johnny. We were soul mates. We did things."

"What things?" Phillip Cannon demanded, throwing his cloth napkin down on the table, glaring at his daughter. "Did you, did you," he sputtered, "have sex with him?"

Melissa sobbed wiping her tears away with the sleeve of her blouse. "Not really."

"What do you mean, not really, you either did or didn't," Phillip persisted, his voice rising with every word, his jaw tight.

Mrs. Cannon seized the moment, got up from her chair, went to her daughter and placed her arm around her. "Let's go into the parlor and talk dear."

Melissa buried her head in her mother's lap and squeezed her around the middle. She sniffled and got up.

Lois Cannon and Melissa sat together on the couch, Philip Cannon opposite in a stuffed chair. "Answer my question Melissa," he prodded. "Did you have sex with the man?"

Melissa tried to explain: "I did him with my mouth and hand, he touched me, that's not sex. I couldn't get into trouble."

Mrs. Cannon pulled her daughter close, devastated. "Oh honey," she said, crying along with her daughter, fearful of her husband's reaction. He had a temper, something she didn't share with the police.

Phillip Cannon moved to the edge of his chair. "I knew it. I knew it. The bastard took advantage of you. He was a scumbag like all the rest."

"Don't say that daddy," Melissa said between sobs. "I loved him, he was going to leave the priesthood to be with me. He made me feel like a woman."

Phillip Cannon rested both arms on his knees and dropped his head to his hands. "We need to call the chief," he said in a voice just above a whisper, "and set up an appointment. He needs to hear this."

Mother and daughter held each other and wept.

***

The next morning the Cannon family showed up at the Hull Police Station at 8:30 a.m., the exact appointment time established the night before. An office clerk escorted them into a small conference room where they were joined five minutes later by Chief Hundley, Ed Catebegian and Vince Magliore, all of whom carried cups of Dunkin' Donuts coffee,

Magliore pleased Big Cat didn't have a chaw of tobacco stuffed between cheek and gums.

The three law enforcement officers sat on one side of the rectangular conference table, the Cannon's, with Melissa in the middle, opposite. They declined offers of something to drink.

"Melissa has something to say," Mr. Cannon announced after everyone was settled.

Melissa hung her head and spoke in an almost inaudible voice. "I lied before when I said Father O'Shea didn't touch me in my private places. We loved each other. We did things."

Hundley kept his tone soft, non-threatening. "Did he force you, Melissa?"

"No, no," she said, trying to explain but keeping her head down. "I teased him. It wasn't his fault, it wasn't."

Magliore and Catebegian kept silent. The Cannon's knew Hundley. They'd be more relaxed with him asking the questions.

"OK, Melissa I'm not going to ask you what kinds of things you did only if you had intercourse. Do you understand?"

She dipped her head and after a short pause, confirmed they hadn't, relief evident on the faces of both parents.

"OK," Hundley said keeping the same gentle tone. "Did Father John have a relationship with any of the other girls?"

"He wouldn't do that, he loved me, he loved me," she wailed, shoulders shaking, tears flowing.

Hundley waited until the girl calmed down before speaking: "You can take Melissa out now, Lois. I'd like to speak with Phil."

Lois Cannon helped her grieving daughter up and grasped her shoulder as they shuffled out of the room.

"I didn't know, Randy, I swear," Phillip Cannon said when the door closed. "Not until last night. I suspected the truth about the car incident, didn't press her. She's a teenage girl, fragile. I gave her space."

He leaned forward, resting both arms on the table and cradling his chin in his hands.

"What would you have done had you known?" Magliore asked.

Cannon frowned and closed his eyes, didn't respond. The tension in the room was palpable as the question hung in the air like the blade of a Guillotine about to plunge.

A minute, then two passed before Cannon opened his eyes, sat up straight and broke the silence. "Killed the bastard."

The three lawmen shared knowing looks. Cannon's frank admission convincing them he didn't commit the crime.

One more suspect eliminated.

Chapter 51

Derek Gordon and Donald Green, the boys who found the body of Father John O'Shea at Fort Revere huddled together in the high school cafeteria. Typical teenagers, their efforts to act and dress differently, defiant of expectations, left them appearing much like many of their peers, as grungy as they could risk.

Both boys sported faded rock T-shirts, Gordon's a white Rolling Stones Classic Distressed Tongue, Green's a black Led Zeppelin; their worn blue jeans ripped and torn in as many places as possible without being obscene.

Gordon was thin, and wiry with unkempt brown hair cascading to his shoulders. His narrow face showed the beginnings of dark stubble. Green's sunken cheeks and scraggly mustache, coupled with his dirty blond imitation Afro gave him a wild appearance. Both had the reputation of being "potheads."

They sat at a table near the wall mural painted by students depicting town and school life. Ironically, an illustration of the observation tower at Fort Revere hovered over them.

Donald leaned in to his pal and whispered although the cacophony of other student voices drowned out his voice. "Do you still have it?"

Gordon grinned, took a cell phone from his pocket and placed it on the table.

"Jesus. Put that away man. We're going to be in deep shit if they find out we stole it from the dead guy," Donald snapped.

"You should see and hear some of the stuff man," Gordon said.

"Like what?"

"Pictures, voice-mail from women, some girls, one of our teachers."

"You're shitting me man," Derek said, his eyes wide.

Gordon pushed the phone across to his friend. "Check it out."

Green snatched it and shoved it in his pocket looking around to ensure no one noticed. He needn't have worried. The other students were too busy gabbing and horsing around to bother worrying about anything Gordon and Green might be doing.

Nevertheless, they left their seats in the cafeteria and went into the hallway for more privacy. Gordon acted as lookout as Green scrolled through the pictures on Father John's cell. Two of the female students were in his math class and he almost dropped the phone as he came upon a revealing pose by one of his teachers, dressed in high heels, black stockings, red panties and nothing else. The text with the picture said: "Eat your heart out."

"Wow," Green said, his face flushed, the bulge in his pants noticeable to his buddy who offered a knowing smirk.

"Listen to the voicemail messages," Gordon said.

There were a couple of suggestive ones from girls and women Green didn't know and one he did, his English teacher with the terrific body. She described in intimate detail various parts of Father O'Shea's anatomy and what she liked doing to them. A wet spot appeared on the front of Donald Green's pants as he listened.

He ignored two voicemails from Carter Fitzgerald, the selectman guy asking to meet because he had a problem and might be in trouble and one from some other dude requesting to meet at Fort Revere; the significance of that lost on the boys excited by the salacious sex stuff. Their thoughts centered on ways to exploit the knowledge they now had of their very sexy, vulnerable English teacher.

Their plan, if they had one, never happened though it did assist the police investigation of the murder of Father John O'Shea.

It didn't save the boys from a suspension.

Chapter 52

Swaggering back to class after lunch, Derek and Donnie couldn't keep their newfound knowledge to themselves. Outside of their classroom, they called a group of friends over to show them the explicit photo of Mrs. Wilson, their English teacher.

The cluster of boys, awestruck by the image, did not see assistant principal Heleana Drossin sidle up. She confiscated the phone without a word and marched everyone to her office.

"Now what's so interesting?" she asked. Holding up the phone to the chastened boys. A few snickered but a withering glare from Drossin quashed their momentary brashness. No one answered or met her gaze.

Drossin, a soft-spoken woman in her late thirties, had been a co-administrator at Hull High, her alma mater, for ten years. Her easy manner belied a strong will and unwavering ability to get the truth from wayward youngsters. She could cower students with a stare if the situation required it.

She took the softer approach with Derek and Donald who, despite their persona of defiance, were easily cowed. They confessed to swiping the phone from Father O'Shea's body. Drossin, appalled, called the Hull police who arrived within forty-five minutes in the persons of Chief Hundley and his new sidekick, Vince Magliore.

"You boys are in serious trouble," Hundley warned before he had even taken a seat in the assistant principal's office. "Tampering with evidence in a murder investigation is a felony and could earn you jail time. Your age won't save you," he lied.

The boys, already chastised by Ms. Drossin, abandoned their swagger and blabbed in unison before Hundley raised his hand and sent Derek out of the room. Never interview two suspects at once, classic interrogation strategy 101. Separated they would have greater difficulty getting their stories to sync. Play one off against the other. It worked with hardened criminals; a no brainer with a couple of scared kids.

Donnie sat beside Ms. Drossin, head down, hands clenched between his knees, tears forming in the corners of his eyes.

"OK, Donald," Hundley said "did you take anything else from Father O'Shea's body?"

"No sir."

"Are you sure?"

Donald hung his head. "We took his wallet. To get money to buy weed."

Hundley glanced at Magliore. Any robbery motive shot. He focused back on Gordon.

"You're testing my patience, young man. You lie again and you're toast, understand?"

"Yes sir," the kid said keeping his head down.

"OK. Did you take anything else?"

"No sir. We freaked out. The phone and wallet were lying on the ground; we grabbed them and ran. We didn't stop running till we got to school and told the principal about Father O'Shea. I'm sorry. I don't know why we took those things. Stupid, I guess."

"You're sure you didn't take them from his pockets?"

"No way. We wouldn't touch a dead body. Too creepy."

"OK, Donald. Now think real careful. Did you see anyone else around?"

Ready to say no, the kid's eyes widened, remembering. "Wait. Some guy left a message on the phone asking Father O'Shea to meet him at Fort Revere."

"What?" Hundley and Magliore shouted together.

The kid braced for another salvo of questions, but the lawmen sent him out of the room. Hundley turned the phone on, selected voicemail, found Fitzgerald's messages and one from an unidentified man and put them on speaker. Both of Fitzgerald's were requests to meet because he feared he was in trouble. The other message was more intriguing. The man spoke with a slight accent. "Father O'Shea we must meet. It is a matter of utmost importance to your parishioner, Mr. Fitzgerald, who is in grave danger. We must meet in private. Please come to Fort Revere tonight at ten o'clock. Do not ignore this, señor."

The message was left on the afternoon of O'Shea's murder no doubt by his killer. The caller may have blundered by his use of the term "señor" giving a clue to his ethnicity or used it to throw suspicion on Hispanics. An unlikely probability since the Latino population of Hull was miniscule and any assailant from that group would be easily found.

Nevertheless, a piece of the puzzle fell into place. They now knew why O'Shea went to Fort Revere. The man on the phone who obliquely threatened Carter Fitzgerald lured him there. And if that guy was the murderer, he left incriminating evidence behind, lying beside O'Shea's body. No professional would do that unless something or someone panicked him. If someone had been there, they hadn't come forward.

At least they now had more to go on. State forensic scientists would examine the phone to determine if they could extract anything useful about the caller. In the meantime, they needed to contact the one person who might hold the key to unlocking this mystery.

"Let's visit Carter Fitzgerald," Hundley said to Vince Magliore.

Chapter 53

Carter Fitzgerald lived on Beacon Road on Allerton Hill in a huge brown clapboard tri-level home with a spectacular view. On a clear day like this one the Boston skyline was visible along with many outlying islands like Georges, home to Fort Warren, a one-time Civil War fortress and prison, now a state park. Magliore and Hundley roamed the island as kids before it was rehabbed and opened to the public. In those days, they were forced to hide their outboard motor boat from the harbormaster who frowned on uninvited guests.

Neither man discussed their boyhood escapades as they climbed the stairs to Fitzgerald's home. Hundley, as usual, rang the bell, no answer. They stared through the windows but detected no movement inside. Magliore walked along the elevated porch and found no one sitting on any of the chairs arranged around a table and barbecue grill. Additional rings and a few raps on the door proved futile.

"Not here," Hundley said in understatement.

"No shit, Clouseau. Now what?"

"We call him and set up a meeting at the station."

"Works for me," Magliore said. They stood for a while enjoying the view before getting into Hundley's cruiser and leaving.

***

They wouldn't meet with Fitzgerald, not then, not ever. Father O'Shea's murder both frightened and alarmed him. He thought a short vacation on the Cape would do him good, time to think, plan his next steps. He might be perseverating over nothing. He grew up with O'Shea, liked him, trusted him yet knew the padre hadn't changed in some ways from the high school kid who attracted girls by the dozens and moved on from one to the other when he tired of them. He suspected Johnny's murder had more to do with his irresponsible sexual behavior than anything involving his own troubles. At least he hoped so although he had a nagging feeling he was fooling himself.

He left Hull two hours before Hundley and Magliore showed up at his door, intending to stop in Plymouth for dinner then drive to his hotel in Hyannis. He could be there by early evening. He told no one of his intentions though he planned to contact Kathleen Maxwell once settled in, perhaps persuade her to join him. He could hope.

It took him an hour to reach Plymouth with traffic. He chose to eat at the East Bay Grille on the waterfront, selected a window table and ordered a glass of Cabernet. Deep in thought, he didn't notice the two men in a booth behind him, men who followed him from Hull and had been watching him for days.

Greater vigilance might have saved him much grief.

Chapter 54

Magliore and Hundley returned to the chief's office with O'Shea's cellphone and wallet in an evidence bag. Both would be examined for prints later though the chances of that being fruitful were slim. The boys who took the phone, their friends, the assistant principal and untold others handled the device. Despite TV programs showing forensic labs performing miracles in discovering fingerprints from myriad surfaces, Hundley knew from multiple classes taken that on surfaces touched by many people fingerprints overlay each other and getting one identifiable print from such a mess was a long shot. They might be more successful with the wallet.

Hundley handed it to Magliore while he checked the contents of the cellphone. They both wore latex crime scene gloves.

"Well," Magliore said, "At least robbery can be eliminated as a motive for the murder."

"Yeah, small favors. Find anything of value in there?"

"You just gave me the damn thing."

"Sorry," Hundley said, putting off his inspection of the phone while he watched Magliore paw through the wallet.

"Not much here," Magliore said. "Driver's license, Clergy ID, Dunkin' Donuts gift card, a Bank of America credit card, twenty bucks. I suspect the boys took some money to support their cannabis habit but doubt Johnny carried much cash. Didn't need it. Like some cops, priests get offered a lot of freebees."

He put the wallet back in the evidence bag on Hundley's desk, sat back, arms folded and waited for Hundley to search the phone.

No password was needed. Hundley pulled up the email account and first scrolled through received messages. He didn't skip any as he moved from the most recent to the more dated. Four from Susan Wilson, the classmate who had been all over O'Shea at the reunion and an English teacher at the High School, caught his attention. They were sexual in nature and provided a lurid account of the sex acts she had performed with him in the rectory, the church, his car, a hotel room in Boston and on the grass under the stars at Fort Revere.

"So O'Shea did have sex at Fort Revere," Catebegian noted as he came into the office and peeked over Hundley's shoulder.

"Yeah," Magliore responded, "but not in a foul smelling, clammy, concrete bunker."

"Maybe he wanted to experiment. He and his lover did things to each other and in locations I've only imagined."

"Does your wife know?"

"Fuck you," Big Cat retorted.

"This is a very productive conversation," Hundley chimed in "but now Sue Wilson is a person of interest. The jealous lover motive."

"You know her?" Catebegian asked.

"Yeah," Magliore answered cutting Hundley off. "She was one of our classmates. Dated Johnny in high school for a time, clung to him like a cheap suit at our reunion."

"So talk to her," Catebegian directed.

"We intend to," Hundley said then read aloud two messages to O'Shea from Carter Fitzgerald requesting to meet. Then he opened one from Elaine Richardson, one of the ladies they interviewed. Her message hinted at a romantic encounter between the two at her home when Tucker, her husband, was away. No salacious details like Wilson's and might be a flirtation as she claimed but it raised new questions.

"Johnny was a player," Magliore commented. "Possibly involved with other women who didn't send him emails."

"Yeah," Hundley said, "but the recording indicates Johnny was enticed to the fort by someone with an Hispanic accent, because of something relating to Carter Fitzgerald. My bet is that's why he was there, and ultimately killed, and not because of some sexual liaison."

"I'm getting a headache," Magliore complained as Catebegian leaned against a wall, arms folded, eyes raised to the ceiling.

Hundley smirked, directed his attention back to the phone and accessed the picture file.

There were twenty-five pictures stored in the phone several with O'Shea and the CYO kids in front of the Memorial School and St. Anne's church; one of O'Shea with his arm around Melissa Cannon and another younger girl, others of O'Shea and a couple of female parishioners at a fundraiser of some kind. The last photo showed Susan Wilson flaunting her body in sexy Victoria Secret lingerie.

Hundley flashed the pictures to Magliore and Catebegian. "Would you keep these photos and emails on your phone if you were a priest?"

Magliore responded. "Nope. If I were a priest I wouldn't possess them in the first place. Nevertheless, we need to interview Susan Wilson and talk with Elaine Richardson again. Her email here suggests more to her relationship with Johnny than she admitted. Can't fault her for stepping out on that buffoon Tucker, though."

Hundley concurred. "Right. I can condemn her for the choice in lover although the onus is on Johnny. He chose the wrong calling.

"I'll look through the phone more after lunch," he continued. "My mouth's watering for the pizza at the All American Grill in Hingham. We can speak to Susan and Elaine tomorrow. Our office manager will set up times with both.

Hundley would not interview either of the women and Magliore's irresponsible behavior, fueled by his dependence on prescription painkillers, threatened to get him kicked off the investigation.

Chapter 55

The house phone on the bedside table jerked him awake interrupting a recurring dream of late—ghostlike figures in military uniforms chasing him through the tunnels of Fort Revere. They hadn't caught him yet and he feared what would happen when and if they did. He rubbed his eyes, cleared his mind of those thoughts and answered the phone. "Hundley."

"Sir. Officer Faulkner."

"This better be good Larry. My clock radio is showing me it's 2:30 a.m. And I emphasize AM."

"Understood sir. But we have a situation."

"What kind of situation?"

"Well sir. I was cruising the Alphabet Streets and found a car had plowed into a sand dune at the end of L Street on the ocean side, motor running, door ajar."

Faulkner paused.

"Go on," Hundley said.

"I searched the area and located a man about ten yards from the car lying face down on the beach."

"I'm still wondering why you called me instead of hauling the guy to jail."

"Sir. He had a badge on him. He's a lieutenant from California. Name's Vince Magliore. Heard the name around the station, understand he's working with you on the O'Shea murder."

Hundley's heart skipped a beat at the mention of Magliore's name. He hesitated before responding: "You did the right thing Larry. Sorry I got on your case."

"Not a problem sir."

"Is he drunk?"

"No sir. Passed the Breathalyzer test but he's disoriented and keeps passing out on me. I suspect he overdosed on something. There was a plastic pill bottle on the car seat, empty, no label or doctor info."

"OK Larry. Bring him to my house please. He's staying here."

"Yes, sir."

Chapter 56

Hundley, in his bathrobe, sipped a cup of freshly brewed coffee in his kitchen when a soft rap on the door alerted him to the arrival of officer Larry Faulkner. He put his coffee down on the counter, walked down the short hallway to the front door, opened it and found Faulkner, face contorted, struggling to hold up a tottering Vince Magliore. Hundley stepped forward, wrapped an arm around Magliore's waist and, along with Faulkner, dragged the near deadweight of Magliore down the hall, through the kitchen and into the family room where they plopped him down on a couch in a sitting position. He promptly slid sideways planting his face into a cushion.

Faulkner stifled a laugh, the scene reminding him of an old Three Stooges movie.

Hundley stood, hands on hips, shaking his head at the prone Magliore, whose loud snoring reverberated through the room. He turned toward Faulkner and thanked him for handling the situation discretely.

"Let's keep this between us Larry until I sort things out. Magliore was wounded in the line of duty and is on pain pills. He might have taken too many or mixed them with something else causing a bad reaction."

"Understood sir," Faulkner said. He half raised his hand in a salute, thought better of it, turned and walked back down the hall to let himself out.

"What's going on?" Karen Hundley asked, startling Randy as she came up behind him, a cup of coffee in hand. She had slipped on a pink robe over her nightgown. She glanced from Magliore to her husband with a quizzical look on her face.

"Larry Faulkner found Mags passed out on the beach near L Street. He ran his car into a dune, left the door open and the motor running."

"My god. Is he drunk?"

"Faulkner says no."

"What then?"

"He's been taking pain meds for his leg wound. I've seen him pop them like candy. Don't know for sure, I never asked, but if it's something like Oxycodone, extreme drowsiness or sleepiness is a side effect."

He rubbed his chin then continued. "I searched through his belongings after Larry called and found five plastic bottles, unlabeled, containing blue pills. A common street name for Oxycodone is 'Blue Kickers.'"

"My god, Randy. That stuff's real dangerous."

"Yeah," Hundley said, shaking his head. "In some cases abuse can be fatal."

"What are you going to do?" Karen said, tears streaming down her cheeks.

"Get him some help," Hundley responded, putting his arm around his wife and looking down on the snoring Magliore. Both sadness and concern gripped him. Sadness for his friend who was fighting his own demons, concern for himself because he counted on Magliore's expertise to extract him from the quagmire of his own making—blackmail.

You've got to pull yourself together pal.

Chapter 57

Vince Magliore awoke alone and in pain, his mouth dry, his head pounding and his eyes unfocused. It took a few minutes for him to comprehend he was on a couch at the Hundley's. He remembered nothing from the previous night let alone how he got here. He tried to stand but a lightning bolt shot through his brain and he fell back on the couch, sweat pouring down his face, hands trembling.

He rested his palms on his knees and considered a second attempt to get to his feet. He had no other choice. The prospect of lying down nauseated him. Chancing it, he sprang up and forward and into the kitchen while a snare drummer beat a constant rhythm in his head. He grabbed a glass from a cabinet and quaffed drink after drink of water. The cool liquid cleared his head and he noticed his car keys resting on the counter, no recollection of how they got there.

He set his glass in the sink and staggered down the hall to the bathroom. He stripped, stepped over the side of the tub, pulled the plastic curtain closed and started a shower, letting the hot water pummel his body until he was refreshed.

He exited the tub, shaved while standing naked in front of the mirror above the sink, splashed some after shave on his face and shuffled into his bedroom where he slipped on a pair of jeans, a polo shirt and Nike running shoes, no socks.

He sat while lacing up his shoes, leaned back in the lone chair in the room and reflected on his predicament. Last night's blackout endangered his role in the investigation of Johnny O'Shea's murder, something he once resisted but now accepted, even embraced. And while he hadn't done much to investigate the blackmail of Randy Hundley, he intended to pursue that as well.

The painkillers he popped every day, he suspected, were now used less to manage his pain than to support an addiction. If he continued, the result would not be good for himself or for those around him. He resolved to quit but still reached into his suitcase and stuffed a container of pills into his pocket. He didn't relish going cold turkey.

He returned to the kitchen, snatched his keys from the counter, walked to the front door and opened it. His rental car was sitting by the curb parked there by someone unknown to him. Bewildered but realizing he could be in deep trouble, he decided his next move was to drive to the Hull Police Station to convince Chief Hundley to let him continue working the O'Shea murder.

And he hoped Ed Catebegian wasn't aware of his meltdown.

Chapter 58

The reception area in the Hull Police Station is small with bench seating on the left as you enter and a wire cage on the right housing the receptionist/office manager and a records clerk. Sometimes an officer or two could be found in the enclosure doing paperwork or checking computer information.

When Magliore entered the building, the receptionist glanced up and an officer checked him out but neither seemed to regard him with more than the customary glance when someone enters a room unannounced. Magliore took it as a sign that his previous night's escapade had not made the rounds of the department.

He was buzzed through a door next to the cage and ran into Chief Hundley standing in the hallway studying a file in his hand. Hundley's face darkened. He motioned Magliore into his office with a jerk of his head.

Once inside, Hundley closed the door and shoved Magliore into a chair. He leaned against the edge of his desk, arms folded glaring at his friend. "What the hell's going on Mags? You have a death wish or are you just an addict?"

Magliore sat with his head in his hands, elbows on his knees and kept his head down when he spoke. "They're prescription drugs for my leg. I had a drink. Miscalculated. Took the pills too soon is all."

"Bullshit. I've watched you pop them whenever you feel like it," Hundley said. "You're hooked. You're going to kill yourself, screw up this investigation and take me down with you. I'm going to tell Big Cat you've been recalled to California. I can't risk having you around anymore. I'll find a way to deal with my own situation. You haven't been much help on that anyway."

Magliore sprang to his feet. "Don't do this Randy, please. I'm dealing with more shit than my leg. I need to keep focused on things other than my problems. At first I thought I could just lie around on the beach or take long walks. But that's not me. I can help with the blackmail stuff and with finding O'Shea's killer. You know I can."

He reached over the desk, grasped Chief Hundley's shoulders and stared into his eyes. His voice quavered: "Give me another chance, man. I'll do anything you want. I swear."

Hundley broke away from Magliore's grip and circled around to the front of his desk. He rummaged in the right hand drawer for a couple of minutes and pulled out a business card that he handed to Magliore. It was for a Mavis Fisher, a psychologist who worked out of a mental health clinic on Derby Street in Hingham.

Magliore blinked and held the card in a trembling hand.

"You can stay on one condition," Hundley said. "See Mavis. She'll help you get clean and deal with your other problems, which I suspect, and you know, are related anyway. She's one of the best. I'll check with her to confirm you made an appointment. Blow this off and you're outta here. "

Magliore took a deep breath and bowed his head. "Thanks man," he said, his voice low and trembling. "I'll see her as soon as she can get me in."

"Don't fuck this up, Mags. I don't want to face Big Cat's wrath."

At that moment, a thunderous voice echoing through the building jolted them to attention.

***

Ed Catebegian was berating one of his subordinates, his face red, brow furrowed, teeth clenched, jaw thrust forward while he bounced up and down on the balls of his feet like an enraged drill instructor chewing out a raw recruit. The object of his wrath, state detective George Jones, stood at attention, his thumbs along the seams of his trousers, eyes locked on a speck on the wall behind Catebegian.

"Are you telling me," Big Cat shouted, "we've had O'Shea's computer in our custody since the day of his murder? Are you telling me that detective?"

Jones continued to focus on the wall and answered meekly, "Yes, sir."

"Explain that to me detective," Catebegian said, inching his face closer to Jones.

"Miscommunication, sir. We thought the Hull officer with us was going to report the seizure of the computer. He thought we were going to do it. No excuse sir."

Catebegian screwed himself up to his full six-foot five inches about to unleash another volley on the hapless Jones, when he stepped back. *What am I doing? I'm in charge of the investigation. I knew we searched O'Shea's place. I should have asked for a report. My fault. Stupid.*

"Where's the device now, Jones?" he said, the fire gone from his voice.

"In the conference room, sir." Jones said, red faced, "on the floor in a corner." He expected another harangue from Catebegian at this lapse in chain of custody but his commanding officer spoke in a calm, measured tone. "Is it password protected?"

"Yes, sir."

114

"OK. Give it to the techies and let me know as soon as they gain access. Can you do that detective?" Big Cat asked, his frustration evident but his demeanor more professional.

Jones hustled from the room glad he still possessed all of his appendages.

***

Father John O'Shea had lived in the rectory located a couple of houses down from St. Anne's Church. The residence belonged to the Archdiocese as is typical since clergy are often transferred from one parish to another. That could be problematic for investigators because fingerprints or items retrieved there might belong to visiting priests slowing the investigation or careening it in directions not pertinent to the case.

In the end, the detectives discovered little of value in the house except the laptop computer whose passwords were easily breached by a state police technical expert. O'Shea, neither security conscious nor creative, used "FatherJohn1," to get into the computer and "JohnnyO202" to open his email. It could have been a sign there would be no incriminating pictures or emails present since other priests would probably use it—or it could be another indication of his reckless behavior?

The former turned out to be true, no spicy emails or photos like those on O'Shea's phone. One email confirmed his meeting with Bishop Connor set on what turned out to be three days after his murder.

A Carter Fitzgerald message thanked him for his advice but did not elaborate. Another from a Cohasset priest sought to arrange a combined outing with the Hull and Cohasset CYO leadership teams. Harmless stuff

Magliore and Hundley joined Catebegian after his tirade directed at detective Jones. The big man glanced from one to the other without comment. They both hoped his silence indicated he had not been informed of Magliore's indiscretion.

Chapter 59

Big Cat, Hundley and Magliore reviewed the data on O'Shea's computer together.

The priest had two folders on his desktop one labeled "Church Business," and one "Personal."

The lawmen first checked "Church Business" and discovered a schedule for the day of the murder.

5:30 am Wake up, morning routine, breakfast
6:00 am Mass—Talk with Ladies Sodality
7:30 am Holy Hour, Office. Readings and Morning Prayer from Liturgy of the Hours
8:00 am Meeting with Carter Fitzgerald; work problem
9:00 am Office--catch up on e-mails and phone calls
10:30 am Hospital and nursing home visits
12:00 pm Lunch, Midday Prayer
1:00 pm Meet with Jeff Singer and Regina Evans; upcoming wedding
2:00 pm Meeting: Mrs. Gilroy, complaint about sermon
3:00 pm Office---prepare Sunday's homily
4:00 pm Afternoon break--coffee, exercise at Gym
5:30 pm Evening Prayer
6:00 pm Dinner
7:00 pm CYO Meeting, Memorial School
10:00 pm Prayer and retire for the night

Nothing suggested O'Shea anticipated going to Fort Revere. Only the meeting with Carter Fitzgerald tied in to their investigation.

On his future calendar, he planned to see Bishop Connor, no reason listed. Magliore and Hundley speculated he intended to discuss his options regarding the seal of the confessional.

"Might be worth a follow up with Fitzgerald," Magliore suggested.

"Yeah if we could find him," Hundley said.

They moved on. O'Shea died before the meeting with Bishop Connor and the other calendar citations were not pertinent to their investigation.

Under the "homily" category, they did find one dedicated to the abuse scandal. In it, O'Shea urged parishioners not to judge all priests by the actions of a few. He didn't mention the actual number of priests accused. It was doubtful his flock would consider over four thousand priests, a few. Nevertheless, he made a forceful argument for understanding and urged prayer and thought for those abused. O'Shea handled the delicate subject skillfully ending with a plea that everyone support the Church's effort to root out all who would destroy their faith.

The man had Hutzpah.

*****

The Homily

My dear parishioners, we all know bitter feelings still exist because of the horrible revelation some clergymen committed unforgivable acts against our blessed innocent children. That this behavior persisted for years and was covered up in some instances revolts us all.

We in this church, emissaries of God, have taken steps to prevent this from ever happening again. You must help us in this endeavor, be vigilant, listen to your children.

And despite your pain and revulsion, I ask you to find it in your hearts to forgive those who have transgressed and you not judge all priests by isolated reprehensible behavior. Pray for these men so they might repent but more importantly pray for the children who have suffered and continue to suffer.

So my dear men and women let us move forward keeping Christ always in our thoughts. Let us work together, laypeople and priests, to accept the Church's teaching so we may live a life of happiness and grace.

Let us pray.

Magliore raised his eyebrows. "Wonder how that went over?"

"I heard it," Hundley said. "Mixed reaction; some liked it, others were skeptical or bitter. One woman made a loud comment about 'people in glass houses' that sort of thing. Two couples in the back walked out."

"OK." Catebegian jumped in. "Let's not get sidetracked. We're looking for evidence to help us solve a murder not to debate Catholic doctrine or the behavior of the clergy. We're interested in one priest here and what he did or didn't do to get himself killed."

He then opened the folder labeled "personal."

Chapter 60

The first items opened in the "personal" folder were mundane. Emails to and from his parents, correspondence with priests from nearby towns regarding steps to attract more parishioners, planned social functions, children's fairs and the like. Things the three men thought belonged in the Church business folder but they weren't there to quibble over O'Shea's method of filing or to understand his thinking.

The one folder raising some concern contained a photo album identified as CYO Leadership. It consisted of school type headshots, mostly girls, some in cheerleader uniforms. Three of the leadership girls posed in bikinis displaying much skin.

"The good padre liked the girls," Catebegian said. "I'd be pissed if my daughter posed for a picture like that. Might take my concern to O'Shea."

Magliore, remembering his encounter with the young girl on the beach who was not embarrassed when she inadvertently exposed her breasts to him, didn't see evil intent in the photo. "I can tell you from experience, this is a sign of the times. Nothing fazes these kids anymore."

Hundley knew there was some truth to what Magliore said but wasn't ready to give O'Shea a pass based on all the sexual content they had uncovered on his phone and the innuendo from witnesses they had interviewed. "We can't ignore what we've seen, Mags. It's pretty incriminating and a motive for murder by pissed off husbands or boyfriends. Some parents might not be as restrained as Philip Cannon if they suspected improper behavior with their daughters."

Hundley's comment set Magliore off. "All this is bullshit," he said, his voice reverberating off the walls. "Some guy, maybe an Hispanic, requested a meet with O'Shea at Fort Revere; something to do with Carter Fitzgerald. My money is on that as the reason Johnny went to the fort and the reason he was killed. We're spinning our wheels on this sex stuff."

Hundley recoiled and thought, but did not say, the Oxycodone might be affecting Magliore's behavior. His friend was headed for trouble.

Catebegian stared at Magliore, sizing him up. He crossed his massive arms on his chest and scowled. "I don't know how you yahoo's investigate a crime back in the land of fake boobs and fake tans. In Massachusetts we practice "due diligence." Follow every lead, every suspect. You don't like that, walk."

Magliore hung his head as if the school principal had just chastised him. "Noted your eminence," he said.

Big Cat and Hundley fought the urge but both broke down and guffawed. It would be the last time they laughed together.

Chapter 61

The two men sat scrunched down in a battered blue Dodge Charger with Red Sox caps pulled low on their foreheads. They parked at the corner of Nantasket Avenue and George Washington Boulevard. They had occupied this spot for the last two hours to ensure getting a position affording them an unobstructed view of the Dunkin' Donuts shop across the street. They were waiting for their target to arrive. He came to the shop every morning between 9:30 a.m. and 10:00 a.m. then walked across the street, sat on a concrete bench, drank his coffee, ate his donut and lost himself in thought.

The driver of the car sipped his own coffee purchased in Hingham while his partner smoked cigarettes in rapid succession and stuffed them in the overflowing ashtray. He swiveled his head from side to side, looking, waiting. "Where the hell is he?"

"Only 9:35 *Por el amor de dios*. He'll be here."

"I don't like it. We're not getting paid enough for this," smoker said, lighting up another.

The driver ignored him and kept his eye on the donut shop; his patience rewarded when the target showed up five minutes later. "He's here man," he said and turned the engine over.

Their man completed his purchases, exited the shop and stepped into the street.

The driver edged his vehicle away from the curb and when he calculated the time was right, gunned the engine. The Charger's rear end fishtailed and the tires squealed as it barreled into the man caught in the middle of the road.

The man was thrown onto the hood and fell off to the right as the Charger accelerated away. A woman on the sidewalk screamed and fainted. Three men rushed out of the donut shop to assist her and the poor soul sprawled on his back in the street.

Chief Randy Hundley's legs and arms were splayed and his eyes closed.

Chapter 62

Magliore, old school, didn't answer his cell at lunch.

It pissed him off when half the people in a restaurant carried on loud phone conversations when he sought to enjoy his food or talk with a companion. Some times and places should be sacrosanct when the electronic noise gets blocked out. So—he ignored the vibration in his pocket until he finished a lobster roll and fries, paid for his meal and stepped on to the sidewalk outside the Saltwater Diner.

He checked recent calls, the last three from the Hull PD. He dialed the number and waited a few seconds until connected. The man who answered sounded agitated. "Lieutenant. This is detective Dempsey. I've been trying to reach you."

"What can I do for you detective?"

"Sir! The Chief is down. It's...it's bad."

Dempsey now had his full attention. "What do you mean down?"

"Hit and run. By the Dunkin' Donuts on Nantasket Ave and George Washington Boulevard."

"Hit and run?"

"Yeah! No accident! Somebody ran him down."

"You sure?"

"Yeah. A couple of the regulars at the donut shop saw two men sitting in a car next to the Corner Café waiting for something. When the Chief crossed the street, they aimed the car straight at him and cut him down. Never slowed."

"Could they describe the vehicle?"

"Yeah! A blue Dodge Charger. Mass plates. Didn't get the number. We have an APB out on it."

"Where's Hundley now?"

"They took him to South Shore Hospital."

"Anyone notify Karen?"

"Yeah! She's on her way to the hospital. I sent a squad car to take her."

"Good. I'll meet you at the Dunkin Donut shop in five minutes."

"On my way, sir."

Magliore punched the end call button on his phone and stood on the sidewalk for a moment. The Chief blackmailed and run down; a priest murdered. Two horrific incidents in a quiet town like Hull where drunk driving and residential burglaries often top the list of crimes.

No way that's coincidence. No way!

Chapter 63

Magliore arrived at the accident scene in less than ten minutes. Nantasket Avenue, for about twenty-five yards, was cordoned off with yellow crime scene tape while Hull police officers kept people from entering the area.

Magliore parked his rented Ford Escape diagonally in front of the tape and jumped from the vehicle leaving the driver's side door ajar. Waving to Sergeant Dempsey, he attempted to duck under the yellow tape; two officers blocked his way. Lieutenant Dan Porter, Hundley's second in command, and now by virtue of Hundley's incapacity, acting chief, strolled up beside the officers.

"Where are you going Magliore?" he challenged, his jaw set, his eyes narrow, piercing.

"Randy's my friend, Dan. I'm assisting on the O'Shea murder. This is connected somehow."

"We don't know that. And until I receive contrary information, I'm in charge here. You're not cleared to participate in this investigation."

Magliore peered over Porter's shoulder to sergeant Dempsey who shrugged his shoulders not willing to challenge his lieutenant.

Magliore understood Dempsey's predicament and returned his attention to Porter. "Did anyone call Catebegian?"

"He's been notified and until he gets here and tells me something different, you stay behind the tape."

Magliore opted not to create a distraction or appear to be undermining Porter's authority. The man had a bug up his ass about him, Magliore reasoned though they hadn't said more than two words to each other since Magliore's arrival in town. He and Hundley worked the O'Shea case with the State police. Hull officers had only been tangentially included possibly the reason Porter now had his nose bent out of shape.

Magliore raised his hands in a sign of surrender. He got back in the Escape, yanked the door closed, started the engine and pressed the gas pedal to the floor peeling rubber and jackknifing onto George Washington Boulevard heading toward South Shore Hospital to check on Randy Hundley and do what he could to comfort his wife Karen. His eyes misted as he thought of his friend fighting for his life. He gripped the wheel so tight his knuckles whitened.

Magliore bristled at the treatment from Lieutenant Porter but he wasn't thinking straight. Wouldn't be much help right now anyway. He focused on Randy and Karen hoping for the best, fearing the worst. He shot through the red light at the pier missing a car pulling onto the boulevard by inches.

Jesus Christ. Get a grip; Randy was a tough SOB, he'll pull through.

Chapter 64

Magliore was wrong.

Chief Randy Hundley died at 5:05 p.m. the night he was run down never regaining consciousness. His wife Karen, grief stricken, had to be sedated and remained in the hospital overnight.

The next few days flew by. Cops take the death of a fellow officer personally and turn out in large numbers to honor a fallen comrade. Hull, Hingham and Cohasset officers stood guard at the funeral home for the two days of viewing. Hull police drove Karen and her two adult children back and forth to the wake. The procession from the funeral home in Hingham to St. Anne's Church in Hull included police from around the South Shore and the state. Ed Catebegian led a contingent of troopers. The motorcade stopped traffic for miles on most major highways leading into Hull.

The Church overflowed with attendees, many listening to the service outside on speakers set up to accommodate them. Uniformed officers from multiple departments stood along the walls in front of the stained glass windows in their dress uniforms, Big Cat towering over everyone.

During the service, three Hull officers eulogized their fallen leader, their esteem and empathy evident in their tearful remembrances. His son spoke from the heart, of his love and respect for his dad calling him his hero. His daughter brought tears and laughter from the congregation when she described his inept attempts to tie her bathing suit straps when she was a child, the top kept falling down, and to braid her hair, strands flying in all directions.

Karen Hundley, grief stricken, implored Magliore to speak in her stead. He limped to the podium on the altar, the pain in his leg more intense, unfolded a piece of paper and recited the first lines of a poem written about fallen officers:

"Somebody killed a policeman today," he read "and a part of America died." A muffled cough or two could be heard among those in attendance as he continued in his own words.

"Yes Randy died, and a piece of us died with him. We are not here to wallow in sorrow, rather to celebrate the life of a good man who, in addition to carrying a badge, was a devoted son, loving father, caring husband and loyal friend. We are all better off for having known him. His spirit will live on in those of us who carry on his work and in family members who loved and cherished him."

Magliore finished by reciting the last lines of the poem:

He answered the call...of himself gave his all,
And a part of America died.

"Rest in peace, Randy."

After the service, the motorcade proceeded to the Hull cemetery. Three local police cruisers parked on the access road near the gravesite, officers at attention by their vehicles. After the priest made his final comments, Interim Chief Dan Porter, in a hushed voice, spoke into his microphone. Seconds later, the patrol car radios blared a message from the dispatcher:

"All units stand by for roll call."

"Chief Randal Hundley."

Silence.

"Chief Randal Hundley."

Silence.

After a third call went unanswered, the dispatcher intoned reverently: "Chief Randal Hundley, we thank you for your dedication and service to the people of Hull and the citizens of Massachusetts. Rest in peace."

Another brief silence followed before the dispatcher finished with: "Chief Randal Hundley is 1042 forever; End of watch."

Randy Hundley was buried on the hill below Fort Revere where all of this drama began. His spirit joining those of the French sailors and marines buried nearby.

Chapter 65

Vince Magliore remained at the cemetery long after everyone else had gone. Tears formed at the corners of his eyes as he remembered the conversation with Randy on the grassy hill at Fort Revere on the day they discovered the body of Father John O'Shea. He'd chided Randy for having purchased a cemetery plot for he and Karen saying something like "that day is a long way off."

Suddenly, the impact of Randy's death struck him like a blow to the stomach. He doubled over, hands on knees, his body wracked by dry heaves, his abs pulsating in pain. He dropped to one knee and gulped air until he could regain his composure. He staggered to his feet, made the Catholic Sign of the Cross and vowed to avenge his friend's murder.

Two days later, Magliore drove Randy Hundley's two kids to Logan Airport. Despite their heartache, they could not be absent from their jobs for an extended period of time. They encouraged their mother to come to stay with them for a while. She declined.

On the way to the airport Donna Hundley asked Magliore to pull off the road and park at Wollaston Beach. They got out of the car and savored the ocean breeze, the Boston skyline visible in the distance. Tears streamed down the young girl's face as she held onto her brother's arm. He stood ramrod straight as men are supposed to do in situations like this, his face exposing an inner turmoil.

"Are you going to find out who killed my dad?" she asked Magliore, trembling.

"Count on it," he assured her, sounding more confident than he was.

Still shaken, she crossed and re-crossed her arms then spoke. "Why?"

Magliore knew no answer was going to absolve the hurt that tormented her, but he shared his theory. "I suspect it was because of something your dad was investigating. Maybe he was getting close."

"Close to what?" both kids blurted.

"Close to the reason for Father O'Shea's murder perhaps."

"I thought that was a sex thing," Donna said.

"That's one possibility, but, and this is still confidential, your father and I believed it related to something told to Father O'Shea in the confessional."

Their expressions reflected doubt. "I know," he said, "Just a theory. No proof yet."

Donna put her arms around her brother and they clung to each other for comfort. Magliore breathed in the salt air, invigorated, and enjoyed the Boston skyline.

When Donna and her brother broke their embrace, her eyes bore into Magliore, pleading; "Catch the bastard, Mags. Catch the bastard."

Magliore touched the distraught young woman on the arm, shook hands with her brother and they all got back into his rental car and drove toward Logan Airport.

The investigation of Randy Hundley's murder would take many bizarre twists, the final one shocking everyone.

Chapter 66

The first twist began with a phone call to Vince Magliore as he was having coffee and a bagel at the Dunkin' Donuts near the Nantasket Beach Resort. He glanced at the phone, didn't recognize the caller ID. No big deal but few people in the area had his number. He answered and a man identified himself as Corey Cahill, a detective with the Quincy PD. Corey with a "C" he stressed. He said he had important information to share about Randy Hundley's murder; Magliore never heard of him but arranged to meet in an hour at the All American Grill in Hingham.

He entered the restaurant and eyeballed a man sitting in a booth at the back. He wore an inexpensive off the rack grey suit with a muted blue tie held to his shirt by a tie tack in the shape of handcuffs; a cop.

Magliore caught his eye, walked to the back and slid into a seat opposite him. The man reached over and shook his hand, large mitts with a firm grip; square jaw, short brown hair, penetrating hazel eyes, skin smooth and tanned, straight white teeth.

"Thanks for coming," he said. "I needed to talk to you as soon as possible."

"You said you had some information on Chief Hundley's murder."

"I do," he said scanning the room to ensure privacy. He leaned forward and whispered, "I imagine you might be considering an irate husband as a suspect."

"How did you figure?"

"I'm aware Randy asked you to try and find out who was blackmailing him because of his affair."

"Didn't think that was common knowledge; he wanted to keep it quiet, for many reasons."

"I'm sure it wasn't common knowledge."

"I'm at a disadvantage then. Why would he take you into his confidence?"

Tears formed at the corners of the man's eyes. He caught himself and leaned back in the booth, his silent sad stare, revealing. At that moment, Magliore, stunned, knew.

Cahill read his facial expression—total shock. "Now you understand why he didn't identify his lover," he said, choking back his emotions.

Magliore, too shaken to respond, was rescued when a waitress came to their table. They gave her drink orders and she scurried away leaving menus.

"I can see you're struggling with this," Cahill said offering a weak smile.

"That would be an understatement," Magliore responded as the waitress brought him coffee and Cahill iced tea.

"Have you decided, or do you need more time?" the girl inquired.

"I'll stick with this for now," Magliore said. Cahill nodded and the waitress left.

"We met at a police conference in Boston about thirteen months ago," Cahill began. "We connected from the get go. After many drinks and the bar closed, Randy invited me up to his room. We tapped into the booze there and one thing led to another. In the morning, Randy confessed he had been fighting his thoughts and feelings for years."

Magliore sipped his coffee staring at Cahill, afraid to speak fearful of what he might blurt out.

"Did Karen know?" he asked when he regained his composure.

Cahill shook his head. "Randy promised to tell her, could never do it. He feared the impact on his kids and his standing in the community. Having a gay police chief might not sit well with the good people of Hull."

"Not to mention his wife," Magliore added.

Cahill recoiled from the obvious put down. His eyes bore into Magliore but he held his tongue.

Chapter 67

The two men sat in silence, Magliore struggling to process the bombshell dropped by the Quincy cop; Randy Hundley in a gay relationship somebody found out about; hence, the blackmail. He had been curious about that whole scenario. What could they hold over a police chief's head? Now it was clear but still not what they wanted. Something regarding the town, he suspected, and it began before the murder of Father John O'Shea. So were the two murders connected or coincidental. Magliore still had trouble believing in coincidence. He spoke first. "Why are you telling me this now?"

"Figured you would pursue the idea an irate husband killed Randy after finding out about his affair. Didn't want you wasting time going down that road."

"Any thoughts on who might have killed him?"

"No. He was investigating something going on in Hull, though he wouldn't tell me what."

"Did it involve Father John O'Shea?"

"Pretty sure it didn't."

"So what could be so important someone was willing to extort a police chief and later resort to murder?"

"More than a priest diddling some housewife," Cahill offered.

"How did these guys discover your relationship?"

"One of two ways, I think. Either someone we knew saw us together or...someone employed a private investigator to track Randy to turn up some dirt to use against him."

"Him and not you."

"Yeah! I'm still in the closet. You know how it is with cops, and nobody has approached or threatened me."

Magliore leaned back in the booth and considered that for a few minutes before speaking. "OK! No way some local yokel sees you guys together and decides on extortion as a next step. Or had the time, energy and resources to tail you himself."

Cahill agreed. "So somebody hired a PI."

"Got any on file?"

"I can provide the names of a couple here in Quincy. Some good guys, some sleazebags."

Magliore knew some "sleazebags" in the business, like Anthony Pellicano, a high profile Los Angeles private investigator, famous for his work with Hollywood celebrities, jailed for wiretapping and racketeering. He interfered in an extortion case Magliore was working. The two butted heads, figuratively not literally, although Magliore considered the latter option. He hoped there was no Pellicano on Cahill's list.

Chapter 68

Before he pursued Cahill's list of private investigators, Magliore decided he needed to keep Ed Catebegian in the loop. With Hundley gone, his inclusion in the investigation of Father John's murder and now the chief's was in jeopardy. Lieutenant Porter, acting chief, and not a fan, demonstrated his enmity by excluding him from the Hundley crime scene. Catebegian tolerated him because he respected Hundley's desire to keep him around. Porter might persuade the Cat to cut him loose.

Magliore called Catebegian, informed him he had uncovered some evidence that might shed light on Hundley's murder and requested a meeting. He suggested Porter be included.

Might as well start off on the right foot.

They met in a small conference room at the Hull PD. Catebegian sat on one end of a large rectangular table with Magliore and Porter flanking him. Porter's glare did not inspire Magliore's confidence. Big Cat was oblivious, his chaw puffing one cheek, his ever-present plastic cup on the table in front of him.

"OK." Catebegian ordered dipping his head toward Magliore. "Talk."

Magliore opted to start at the beginning. "When I got to town, Randy asked for my help. He confessed to being blackmailed and wanted me to find out who was behind it. Unofficially of course, because the news, if made public, would shake up the department and the town."

Porter sat up straight in his chair, a shocked expression on his face. Catebegian spit into his cup. Both waited for Magliore to continue.

"Randy was having an affair. The blackmailers found out somehow and identified his lover, had dates and times of their rendezvous."

Porter blanched. "Christ."

Catebegian spit again, his expression pained. "What did they want?"

"Randy claimed not to know though I doubted that. Not money. Who would take the chance to blackmail a police chief for a pittance? I'm convinced it was to warn him off an investigation he was conducting, something going on in town—a gut feeling. I have nothing to back it up yet."

Porter spoke up. "Did you identify his lover?"

"Yes."

"Well," Catebegian prompted.

Magliore hesitated, then forged ahead. "Don't kill the messenger."

***

Lieutenant Porter looked as if killing Magliore might be a good idea. He clasped his hands together on the table and waited for the other shoe to drop.

Catebegian glared, working the chaw of tobacco around his mouth ready to unleash a stream.

Magliore resolved to tell them straight out. "Randy's lover was another cop. A male cop."

Porter's knuckles turned white; his face reflecting disbelief. "No way," he blurted. "No fucking way. You're a piece of shit, Magliore." He clenched his fists and scooted to the edge of his chair as if poised to attack.

Big Cat straightened up. Even seated his bulk was imposing. He unleashed a stream of tobacco juice into his cup and locked eyes with Porter. "You better calm down, lieutenant or I'm going to kick your ass out of this room, remove you from this case, and write up a report that'll make it hard for you to find a job as dog catcher. Capiche."

Catebegian's rebuke stunned Porter. He took a deep breath, released it slowly and rolled his shoulders forward. He placed his hands in his lap and averted his eyes. "Understood," he whispered.

Catebegian focused on Magliore. "You're sure about this."

"Yes."

"How."

"Randy's partner contacted me."

Magliore used the term "partner" rather than the more emotional one of "lover," hoping to lessen the negative impact on his colleagues. When neither responded, he forged ahead. "His partner knew Randy sought my help in identifying the blackmailers. He didn't want me, us, spinning our wheels searching for a jealous husband or boyfriend."

"So what's this person's name?" Catebegian pressed.

"I can't reveal that, sir. He's a cop; still in the closet. He risked a lot contacting me. I promised I'd keep his name out of this."

Catebegian scowled and raised his eyes to the ceiling. He stayed motionless for several minutes. And when he returned his gaze to Magliore, his expression had softened. "OK, for now. And I emphasize for now. Circumstances may change this decision."

Magliore nodded, relieved.

"So what's our next step?" Porter asked, mollified by Catebegian's dressing down and striving to stay included.

Magliore recounted his discussion with Cahill and how they determined someone hired a PI to bird dog Hundley until they stumbled on to his secret.

"So who hired the PI?" Porter asked.

"Someone threatened by the chief's unofficial investigation is my guess."

"Back to this phantom investigation," Catebegian said, irritated.

"Not a hell of a lot going on in this town worthy of an investigation," Porter said.

"Noted," Magliore responded. "But if I'm right and we can discover the PI employed. We might be able to get to the bottom of this."

"Assuming there is a PI and this is not going to take us down a rat hole that will divert us from the real motive for the chief's murder," Catebegian retorted, punctuating his comment with another stream of tobacco juice.

Magliore overcame his revulsion to Catebegian's habit and promised to pursue this idea on his own if given the latitude.

Big Cat pushed away from the table, grabbed his cup and stood up. "Do it," he said and left the room.

Porter shrugged and left without comment leaving Magliore with his theory. He needed to find a PI in the haystack of PI's in the area trolling for clients—and preferably not a sleazebag.

Chapter 69

Cops define a sleazebag as an untrustworthy, immoral piece of shit. The description covered many individuals, from politicians to drug dealers. Magliore hoped Cahill's portrayal of the private investigators he referred did not reflect their moral character.

There must be a wonderful gentleman or two in the profession.

On second thought, who better to spy on someone engaged in adultery than a sleazebag? So he scratched out the first name on the list, Carlton Investigators, after reading the agency's website which highlighted corporate intelligence, executive protection, civil litigation and missing persons. No spying on married couples listed. The next seemed more promising. The William (Billy) Brown detective agency heralded its expertise as Marital Infidelity Experts with twenty-four hour surveillance capability.

The agency was located off route 3A on South Street north of the Fore River Bridge, surrounded by fast food joints, a car wash and a Dairy Queen. A nondescript lounge was within walking distance, possibly where Billy spent his lunch hour.

Magliore pulled into the lot in front of a low red brick building with darkened windows and a weathered black and gold sign attached to the roof identifying the place as The William (Billy) Brown detective agency. The constant use of "Billy" in the company name made him wonder if the guy was a "good-old boy" from the south or just a regular guy doing God's work.

He exited his car and opened the front door of the building. A secretary of indeterminate age with caked on make-up and reddish-brown hair smiled as he entered. Her cluttered desk held the remnants of several fast-food lunches, a stained coffee cup and a container with four pencils. A computer with post-it-notes adorning the sides and top also rested on the desk.

"How can I help you sir?" she asked in a losing effort to keep the smile affixed to her face. You can't smile and talk at the same time. Try it!

Magliore flashed her his California badge and put it back in his pocket before she could examine it. "Lieutenant Vince Magliore, homicide. May I speak with Billy?"

She didn't flinch at his use of "Billy," punched a button on the phone on her desk and announced his visit.

"He'll be right with you sir," she said after putting the receiver back in its cradle. "Please have a seat."

No sooner had Magliore plunked his butt into one of the two straight-backed chairs in the room, than the office door opened and Brown swooped in. He didn't present like a "sleazebag." An inch or two shy of six feet, hair trimmed, clean-shaven, wide shoulders, no paunch. He wore a blue dress shirt, matching striped tie, pressed grey slacks and spit-shined cap-toe black Oxfords. He smiled and walked toward Magliore, hand extended. "Billy Brown, lieutenant, come on in."

He stepped aside to let Magliore pass. The cramped office had a couch, glass-topped coffee table faced by two stuffed chairs and two padded metal ones facing a mahogany desk free of clutter save for a manila file folder, computer and telephone. The walls were bare except for a framed copy of Billy's PI license and a painting of the Boston skyline at night.

Brown sat in a black swivel chair behind his desk. Magliore took one of the metal chairs in front.

Brown was relaxed but puzzled. "How can I help you, lieutenant? Don't get many of Quincy's finest in here."

Magliore quickly dispelled any feelings of deceit Brown might later experience. "I'm not with the Quincy PD, Billy. I'm assisting the state police with the investigation of the murder of Hull Police Chief Randy Hundley."

Brown's eyes clouded over at the mention of Hundley's name. He sat up straight and rested his arms on his desk. "Why do you think I could help?" he asked not questioning Magliore's credentials; a sign he was caught off guard, more concerned about what Magliore knew than who he was.

"We believe you had the chief under surveillance on a matrimonial issue and the information you provided your client led to Hundley's being blackmailed and murdered."

"Wait a minute. I don't take the blame for that. Did my job. Assumed the wife hired me through an intermediary. Happens all the time. Lady doesn't want her hands dirty to avoid blowback in case the guy finds out."

"So who was the intermediary?"

Billy raised his eyebrows, laughed. "Right. I could lose my license, the trust of anyone looking to hire me in the future."

"This is a murder inquiry Billy. We can get a subpoena for your records."

"Better than me volunteering."

Magliore took a different tact. "Chief Hundley was my friend. We grew up together. He was a stand-up guy. I'm godfather to his son," he lied.

"They need closure on this. So does his wife. She's feeling guilty enough as it is. No one needs to know where this information came from or how it was obtained. You have my promise."

Brown relaxed. Leaned back in his chair, closed his eyes, considering his next move. After several moments, he got up and went to a freestanding metal file cabinet wedged in a corner behind his desk. He retrieved a brown folder, put it on top of the cabinet and walked toward the office door. "My secretary and I are going to lunch. Make sure the outside door is locked when you leave."

Magliore gave Billy time to exit the building, grabbed the folder, opened it and read the surveillance report on Randy's dalliance with Cahill. The client's name, or the intermediary as Billy called him, was Francis G. Prescott, Attorney at Law, Quincy, Massachusetts.

Magliore typed the name in his notes app on his IPhone, not a total techno-idiot as some of his colleagues suspected.

And Billy Brown, thought Magliore, was no Anthony Pellicano, no "sleazebag."

Chapter 70

Magliore Googled attorney Prescott's name, found his address on Hancock Street in Quincy and arranged a meeting later in the afternoon, explaining the reason to his secretary.

Next he called Ed Catebegian.

"Cat," Magliore said after the lead state detective picked up.

"Yeah," Catebegian responded, a man of few words.

"I got a lead on the client who solicited a PI to surveille Chief Hundley."

Magliore heard the crunch of an apple before Catebegian spoke again. "Yeah."

He must have been conserving energy to eat.

"He's an attorney. I've set up a meeting for four this afternoon. Can you meet me?"

Another crunch. "Give me the address."

Magliore did so and the connection ended; Catebegian's acknowledgement he would be there.

Hungry, Magliore stopped for lunch at "The Fat Cat" restaurant on Chestnut Street. He sat at the bar and watched a replay of an NFL game on one of the overhead TV's while he devoured a chicken wrap and onion rings, passing on the signature cocktails offered, settling for coffee. The food was tasty, price right, service excellent. Might even post an online review, he thought. Nah!

Sated, he drove the ten minutes from the restaurant to the Law Office of Francis G. Prescott and parked in front of the three story red brick building.

As he waited for Big Cat, he thought of Randy Hundley's relationship with Corey Cahill. Magliore's parents, third generation Italian, mother a devout Catholic, father less so, never discussed homosexuality at the dinner table or anywhere else. He doubted either one knew much about the subject and wouldn't discuss it if they did.

He wasn't much more advanced than his parents. The whole LGBT thing confused him with Transgender issues beyond his comprehension. He couldn't fathom how men and women grappled with that conundrum. His own attitude toward gays reflected the now discredited military policy, "don't ask, don't tell." Macho cops, some deep in the closet, to protect themselves, made gays the brunt of crude locker room jokes. Magliore never laughed; to his discredit, never stopped it either.

Not comfortable with homosexuality, he nevertheless believed everyone should be free to love who they love. He could imagine how

Randy wrestled with his feelings for Cahill and Karen; the blackmail an added weight to carry.

Before he could explore his thoughts further, Catebegian drove up, executed a U-turn and parked opposite Magliore on the other side of Hancock. He pushed his two hundred sixty-five pounds up and out of his car, retrieved his suit jacket from the rear seat and ambled across the street joining Magliore to walk into the building housing the law offices of Francis G. Prescott. They nodded to each other, didn't speak. Big Cat had finished his apple.

Chapter 71

The directory on the wall next to the elevator listed the Law Offices of Francis Prescott on the second floor. They rode up together, no other passengers, yet Magliore felt claustrophobic wedged beside the big man.

The elevator doors opened on a cavernous office reception area with floor to ceiling windows, two low hanging chandeliers and a secretary ensconced at an immense desk at the far end. Catebegian presented his credentials to the young woman who directed them to sit in two couches arranged in an L-shape near and below her elevated position. She pressed a button on her phone and announced their arrival to her boss.

A smiling Francis Prescott swept into the room before they could get comfortable sitting. He appeared to be in his forties, trim, well groomed, tailored Brooks-Brothers suit clinging to his slender frame as if glued on, his Oxfords polished to a reflective glow.

He extended his hand to Catebegian, then to Magliore, deferring to the huge hulk with a jacket and tie instead of his scruffy sidekick. "Come in gentlemen, come in," he said in a voice dripping with false cheer as if welcoming the IRS to audit his books.

He led them into an enormous office the size of an auto showroom; the walls adorned with paintings of landscapes, multiple law degrees and pictures of their host posing with dignitaries most unknown to Magliore except for one with Senator Edward Kennedy; popular, successful guy. He'd stonewall them without regret.

Prescott took a seat behind a massive mahogany desk, free of clutter save for a computer to his right and an in-box on the left. Catebegian and Magliore sat in two leather chairs facing him.

"How can I help you, gentlemen?" he said, making the word "gentlemen" sound like something to scrape off the bottom of your shoe. Magliore disliked the man from the get-go.

"We're investigating the murder of Hull Police Chief Hundley," Catebegian answered. "I'm detective Catebegian from the state police and this is Lieutenant Magliore."

Prescott pursed his lips and thrust his chin forward in his best imitation of bewilderment. "A tragedy, a tragedy," he said, referring to Hundley's murder. "I'm not sure how I could help though."

Catebegian responded in a booming voice forcing Prescott to fall back in his chair as if punched. "We think you can, counselor. You hired a private detective to bird-dog the Chief who was then blackmailed and murdered. We need the name of the client who hired you."

Prescott face became a zombie-like mask. "I'm sympathetic, of course. But you know I can't breach attorney client privilege. I'd be disbarred."

"We're talking murder, here counselor. Murder of a police chief."

"I understand. I understand. My hands are tied."

Catebegian stiffened, inched forward in his seat, fist balled, the muscles in his neck bulging, like an NFL lineman ready to fire off the line of scrimmage to knock an opponent on his ass. He regained his composure and stood up. Towering over Prescott, he leaned into the desk thrusting it back into the lawyer's lap. "We'll be back with a warrant," he announced and turned to leave.

Prescott jumped up and escorted them from the office without a word glancing sideways at his secretary, beads of sweat dotting his forehead. He stopped short of the elevators, did a quick turnaround and strode away from the two detectives no doubt relieved he still had all his body parts.

Once inside the claustrophobic box, Magliore spoke. "This guy is a high powered attorney. He doesn't take two-bit marriage infidelity cases. Someone with clout hired him. Someone with enough juice, and unsavory connections, to employ hit men."

Catebegian wrapped his massive arms around his chest. "So what's going on here, Mags? And how does this relate to Father John's murder? Doesn't make sense."

"Let's get a warrant and find out," Magliore said and hoped his comment didn't sound like an order. *No need to piss off the big man.*

Chapter 72

After visiting the Law Offices of Francis Prescott, Magliore returned to Hull and his temporary residence at the Hundley's where he had been staying since Randy's death. The kids were gone, back to their jobs. And they still didn't know if Karen was in danger.

The puzzle of Father O'Shea's murder and the deliberate hit and run of Randy had Magliore still twisting and turning in bed at 1:26 a.m. The red letters on the clock radio on the night table beside the bed lit up the room. He rested on top of the sheets in the guest bedroom, sweltering in the heat and humidity, no air conditioning. He wore a pair of boxer shorts. No pajamas for this macho man.

As he stared at the ceiling, a figure standing in the doorway of the room caught his eye. His Smith and Wesson M&P 9 was nestled under the pillow but as his eyes focused, he could see that backlit by the hall light stood Karen Hundley. She wore shorty pajamas to keep cool. Magliore tensed as she walked into the room and stopped a foot from his head. Her perfume filled his nostrils and his chest tightened.

Without speaking, she crawled over Magliore to lie on his right side. She put her head on his chest and snuggled against him. Through her tears she murmured, "Hold me."

Magliore stroked her hair and whispered, "It's going to be all-right" several times reassuring himself as well.

They fell asleep with Magliore's arm around her shoulders and hers across his chest.

***

Magliore awoke to the smell of coffee brewing and bacon frying, the nectar of the gods. The crumpled sheets beside him coupled with the lingering woman's fragrance reassured him last night's encounter had not been a dream.

He grabbed a towel, showered and shaved in the bathroom across the hall and limped to the kitchen, his leg frequently stiff in the morning. He dressed in a white polo shirt, shorts, no shoes.

Karen stood at the stove in a pink robe and matching fluffy slippers, her hair wet from a recent shower, her eyes bright; her skin glowing, looking great without make up.

She smiled when she saw him, turned, poured two cups from the coffee maker on the counter and handed him one.

"Sorry about last night, Mags. I'm still a little needy."

Magliore took a sip of the coffee and returned her smile. "No worries. As my Italian New York relatives would say, "forgetahboutit."

She giggled, filled two plates with bacon and scrambled eggs and led him to the glass-topped table in their family room. The table was in front of a sliding glass door that opened onto a wooded, elevated deck with a view of Hull Bay and a nature, camping area across the water called World's End.

They ate and drank coffee for a few minutes until Magliore got up, refilled their cups and returned to his chair. "Karen, can you think of anyone who might have wanted to hurt Randy?"

She took a deep breath before sharing her thoughts. "Randy was having an affair, I'm sure of it. We hadn't been intimate for a long time. He rejected my efforts to seduce him, acted distant, distraught. Desperate, I searched his pockets, checked his phone messages, and inspected his collar for telltale signs of lipstick or perfume. Found nothing. Attempts to talk went nowhere. He withdrew from me. Maybe his lover's jealous boyfriend or husband got mad enough to attack him." Tears formed in the corners of her eyes.

Magliore sipped his coffee, didn't respond.

"Do you know something Mags? If you do, tell me. He's gone. It won't make a difference now."

Wrong, Magliore thought. It would make a big difference to her, to the kids. She had a right to know, not his place to tell her though, at least not now.

"Karen. We're seeking any possible reason someone would want to hurt Randy. Could be an investigation he was conducting. Could be more personal, someone with a grudge against the police, or Randy in particular."

She pressed the affair angle. "So you don't think he was having an affair?"

"Not something we're pursuing right now," he lied.

"OK! OK," she said. "Randy used the small room at the end of the hall, near the front door as an office. He had been going in there a lot the last few weeks, to get away from me, to avoid confronting our issues. If he were investigating something he would have kept the documents there. He has a desktop computer too. He avoided keeping things on it though, feared hacking, like anyone would hack us."

Happy to move on from the infidelity issue, Magliore decided to search the room, certain Randy wasn't killed because of an affair, even of the homosexual variety. He was convinced the blackmailers wanted him to back off an investigation. The files in attorney Francis Prescott's possession held the key, he hoped, but Randy's notes or documents might be instructive so he began the search of Hundley's small office.

Chapter 73

Randy Hundley's office was a ten by ten room intended to be a bedroom and used as such when the children lived at home. The room had a small love seat against one wall and a desk and swivel chair pushed into one corner. A picture of old Paragon Park adorned the wall above the desk along with a photo of Randy, Karen and their two kids in an earlier time. A window to the street provided light and a limited view during the day. Something about the window bothered Magliore. He couldn't put his finger on what so he turned to the desk and addressed the problem at hand.

The desk, three drawers on the right none on the left, was black as was the mesh-backed swivel chair. An old model IMac computer rested on top of the desk. Magliore rifled through the drawers first, found nothing of substance. The top drawer held some blank note pads and a key, the second some computer cables and software disks for the IMac while the third had file folders designated, "repairs," "termite control," "flood insurance," etc. Magliore inspected them but the contents were as labeled.

Karen walked in after a few minutes, brought Magliore a fresh cup of coffee, and slumped down in the love seat to watch. "Find anything?"

"Nope. Desk is clean."

He reached behind the left side of the computer screen and pushed the on button that activated with an audible bong. "Maybe we'll have better luck here."

The computer screen emerged, a muted blue, no picture or design and no folders displayed on the desktop. Magliore frowned. "Did Randy ever use this thing?"

"Not much. Just for email."

"What email service did he use?"

"AOL."

Magliore clicked on the Safari icon and the AOL homepage appeared with the mail logo in the upper right corner. He opened it and was prompted to input a username and password. "I don't suppose you know these," he said turning toward Karen.

"I do. He surrendered them to me in a moment of weakness."

Magliore raised his eyebrows.

"I was giving him a blowjob and promised to bite if he didn't."

"T.M.I. lady. Just tell me please." Magliore said, flustered.

Karen giggled. "Married people do that you know."

"Yeah, yeah. I'm waiting."

"His user name is BigDogHPD1, the BD and HPD all caps she stressed and gave him the password: HHSCLAW1957. All capitals and the year the high school opened.

"Somewhat creative" Magliore mused, "but would take a hacker about thirty seconds to figure out."

"That's why Randy seldom used the computer and I'm sure he didn't put sensitive information on it."

Magliore input the username and password and discovered ten emails. Karen was right. Nothing explosive. Most were from school committee members concerning safety for high school football and basketball games and a couple from selectmen asking for security plans for the proposed redevelopment project. Two from Carter Fitzgerald inquired as to the feasibility of hiring a private agency for twenty-four hour protection. Thieves often raided construction sites and stole everything from tools to copper wire, he knew.

Magliore exited the email and took a deep breath. "Shit, I hoped we'd catch a break." He took a drink of coffee, closed his eyes and leaned back in the swivel chair. When he opened them, he reached into the top drawer of the desk and took out the key. "What's this to?"

"We own a safe deposit box at Rockland Trust for important papers like the mortgage contract, the trust for our kids, stuff like that."

"Important papers," Magliore repeated almost to himself. He stood up. "Let's go see what else Randy thought was valuable."

"OK. The deposit box is in Rockland; the local branch doesn't have them. Randy liked that it wasn't in town; thought it more secure."

On to Rockland as a famous football coach might say.

Chapter 74

The Trust Branch in Rockland was located on Union Street. It took them forty-minutes to drive the less than twenty miles on Route 228 North that was Main Street in Hingham, one of the most scenic in all of New England; many of the homes along the road dated back to the sixteen and seventeen hundreds. The Old Ship Parish House circa 1653 and the Ripley Homestead, 1692 were among the oldest. Magliore had made this drive many times and never ceased to marvel at its beauty and tranquility. As they crossed Route 53 at Queen Anne's Corner, though, he pushed those thoughts aside to focus on the less positive task ahead.

They pulled into the small parking lot adjacent to the Rockland Trust, exited Magliore's rental car and entered the building. Karen walked up to a cashier and requested access to her deposit box. The cashier, blond, mid-thirties, perky summoned the bank manager to escort them to the area where Karen would use her key in tandem with the manager to open the box. The manager left so they could examine the contents in private.

The box contained the mortgage and living trust papers Karen mentioned earlier and one other, a green file folder below the other documents. They extracted the folder, opened it and discovered several articles printed from the Internet, the first titled, "The Top 10 general contractors in Plymouth County Ma." The companies were located in Brockton, Duxbury, Rockland, Hanover, Bridgewater and Quincy. A second article listed the largest general contractors in Massachusetts with locations in Boston, Quincy, Everett and Milford while the next few pages highlighted websites for some of those companies. Randy had jotted notes beside each; by Finch & Sons Construction, he wrote, "see Big Dig."

The Big Dig, officially The Central Artery Tunnel Project, became the most expensive highway undertaking in U.S. history. It included the Ted Williams tunnel with entrance to Logan Airport, a new modern bridge over the Charles River and the Rose Kennedy Greenway that replaced the space previously occupied by the I-93 elevated roadway.

Multiple contractors and subcontractors worked on the massive endeavor. Problems dogged the project from start to finish with many the result of fraud. Some of the articles documented that fraud—practices like submitting false time and materials slips, using substandard materials such as leftover concrete and cheap, unsanctioned epoxy to hold tunnel ceiling tiles. Finch & Sons over billed by categorizing apprentice workers as journeyman and padding the time cards of such workers who were paid on the basis of time worked rather than a fixed sum.

The U.S. Department of Transportation, the FBI, and the Massachusetts State Police through the state attorney general's office investigated the suspected fraud. Finch & Sons was fined and banned from state funded projects for five years.

Randy's notes indicated his intent to call the state attorney general, the state police and Selectman Carter Fitzgerald who had championed Finch & Sons Construction for the Hull redevelopment venture. Nothing in the file indicated he had done so and none of the emails between he and Fitzgerald touched on that subject. If Randy had made those calls, Magliore reasoned, an insider friendly to Finch & Sons might have tipped off the company about the inquiry; hence the blackmail attempt to back him off.

"What's all this mean?" Karen asked. "And how does it relate to Randy's murder?"

Magliore deflected her question. "I don't know. Randy was doing his due diligence regarding Hull's redevelopment efforts; being protective. We'll do some more checking and see what turns up. In the meantime, I'd like to take this folder with me."

"Sure. But please keep me in the loop. I need to know if this had anything to do with Randy's murder."

"Count on it," Magliore said unaware or ignoring the possibility that by following up on Randy's research, he might now be at risk.

If they dared kill a police chief, they wouldn't hesitate to take him out.

Chapter 75

They left the Rockland trust and drove in silence back to Hull, each grappling with their own thoughts. When they arrived at the Hundley's, Magliore executed a U-turn on Clifton Ave and stopped the car facing toward Nantasket Avenue, turned the engine off and leaned back in his seat.

"Want to come in for coffee?" Karen asked.

"God no. My back teeth are floating from all the caffeine we drank this morning."

Karen laughed and turned toward him: "Mags. I'm confused."

"You're not alone kid. I'm certain there's a link between Father John's murder and Randy's. I just can't make it."

"What about this construction stuff. The notes he made. He never said anything to me."

Magliore wrestled with a dilemma. Should he keep silent about Randy's affair or at least give her that much. She caught his eye and suspected something was wrong. "What? Tell me Mags. You owe me that."

"Funny, Randy said the same thing when he dragged me into this mess."

She blinked, not following.

"I suspect the construction investigation led to his being blackmailed." Magliore said. "Someone wanted him to stop."

"What could they use to blackmail him?"

Magliore hesitated. The truth might ease her pain or make it worse. But seeing the depth of her grief, he opted to tell her.

"Randy had an affair, Karen. He was ashamed and worried that being exposed would hurt you and the children and cost him his job. He asked me to help, to find out who orchestrated the threats. The articles he accumulated on the construction fraud now make me suspect someone working for or being paid by one of the construction companies was behind it."

Karen had long suspected an affair but the reality of it devastated her. She moaned, her whole body convulsing, her head flopping from side to side seemingly unconnected to the rest of her body, signs of a seizure.

Magliore released his seatbelt, then hers and pulled her to him. Her chest heaved and she made guttural sounds while clinging to him. His shirt became wet with her tears.

Magliore stroked her hair and whispered it's "OK" over and over until she regained her composure and sat up. "I need to know who he was cheating with Mags."

"I don't know, Karen," he lied. "Randy never told me. And before I could even pursue it, Father John's murder diverted our attention and we spent all of our time investigating that."

"And you think the two murders are linked somehow?"

"I do."

"Did his affair have anything to do with it?'"

"No, no," he said grabbing her hand in both of his then stroking her arm. "Like I said, I'm sure the key lies in these notes on the building companies, especially the one chosen to work in Hull. I'm going to pursue that."

Karen wiped her eyes on her sleeve. "OK," she said. "You're coming back for dinner tonight right?"

"I shouldn't Karen. There are enough rumors circulating in this town. I'll find some other place to stay."

"Absolutely not. Randy wanted you here and so do I. I promise not to attack you."

Magliore moved his hand to her cheek. "OK. Providing you make something good for dinner."

She smiled, held his hand in both of hers for a minute before exiting the car and walking up the walkway to the front door.

As Magliore watched her go, his gaze fell on the window beside the door. He now remembered what had bothered him earlier. It opened into the office not the living room. All you could see was the small love seat barely large enough for two people to sit on. Only a contortionist would attempt sex on it. Bobby Jennings lied about watching Johnny and Karen have sex on a living room couch.

The little prick.

Chapter 76

Later that same day, Magliore parked his car at the curb on Hull Shore Drive and crossed the dirt parking lot and Nantasket Avenue to sit on a bench overlooking Hull Bay; a bench soon to be lost to the planned renewal project if Carter Fitzgerald had his way.

Living near water often provides the opportunity for introspection, personal or professional. Something Magliore needed having been sucked into the murder investigations of his two boyhood friends; he and the other detectives on the case ping-ponging from one motive to another, from blackmail, to sex, to robbery, to fraud, leaving little time for reflection especially of his budding relationship with Kathleen Maxwell, another layer of confusion.

There was also the secret he repressed with painkillers, a secret that could undermine not only his future with Kathleen but also his job and even his freedom. He fumbled in his wallet and found the business card Randy had given him after his overdose: Mavis Fisher, psychologist. He studied the card from every angle as if simply holding it would provide the help he needed. He shrugged and slipped it back into the wallet. Maybe later.

For the moment, he mentally pushed his problems aside and focused on the sunset, a marvel of nature. He was awed by the multi-layered phenomenon with red, pink, yellow and blue interspersed, the red broken up by cloud formations resembling distant mountains; boats on the water bathed in color, sailboat masts raised in salute.

Nature, awesome and cruel, nurturing and hostile, offered hope, sometimes pain. Man was as unpredictable as his environment, often as ruthless and with less reason. Someone had determined Father John O'Shea and Police Chief Randy Hundley should die leaving Magliore to uncover the rationale and manage the consequences. He didn't relish the task. He wanted to heal and grieve on his own.

He mourned the deaths of his two friends, links to his past, although they hadn't been part of his life for many years. That connection was now severed and could never be restored. Finding their killers might ease his loss and the sadness of those they left behind. That was not certain. And where Kathleen Maxwell fit in his reordered world, he could only guess.

He watched as the varied hues of the sunset faded with night soon to follow. He leaned forward to get up when a hand touched his shoulder and Karen Hundley scrunched down beside him slipping her arm under his and grasping his hand.

"Saw you sitting here when I drove by. Beautiful isn't it?" she said.

"Magnificent."

"Find out who killed Randy, Mags. For me, for us." She leaned against him and they sat huddled together until darkness fell.

Chapter 77

Magliore opted to follow up on the documents and notes found in Randy Hundley's safe deposit box on his own. He'd loop in Catebegian and Porter later.

He first called the state attorney general's office identifying himself as a homicide lieutenant investigating a murder in Hull neglecting to mention his tenuous status as an unofficial consultant.

The Massachusetts Attorney General is the topmost lawyer and law enforcement officer of the Commonwealth. The office is organized into six bureaus with the Criminal Bureau responsible for handling financial fraud and other violations of the public trust. Teams of state police detectives conduct the investigations initiated by the Bureau.

Magliore wasn't aware of the above organization so his call bounced around until connected to Captain Victor Cruz in the Criminal Bureau.

"How can I help you sir?" Cruz answered.

"My name is Vince Magliore, I'm a homicide detective assisting Lieutenant Ed Catebegian with the investigation of two Hull murders."

"You're working with Big Cat. Good man. That chaw habit is something else though."

"Couldn't agree with you more," Magliore responded and they both shared a laugh.

"What can I do you for, detective?" Cruz asked again using the grammatically incorrect sentence structure common to cops and others attempting to sound like ordinary "Joes."

"Are you familiar with the Big Dig fraud case a couple years back?"

"Not personally, this section handled it in conjunction with some federal agencies."

"I'm interested in one case involving the Finch & Sons construction company."

"How does that tie into your murder cases?"

"That's what I hope to determine. The company has been selected to do the redevelopment work here in Hull and Chief Hundley was looking into it, perhaps thinking their previous indictment for fraud might be too risky for the town to employ them."

"OK. I'll access the old files but it may take a while. We're swamped right now."

"I understand captain but we need your help. We're talking about the murder of one of our own."

"Point taken. I'll do my best to expedite things. Give me your contact information or should I send the files to the Cat?"

"No. No. Please send anything you find to me." He gave him Chief Hundley's house address and his own email account.

"Will do," Cruz acknowledged and ended the connection.

Magliore's call to Captain Victor Cruz put a target on his back.

Chapter 78

Kathleen Maxwell sat at the breakfast bar in her condo at the upscale Seaport at Marina Bay in Quincy. Her patio provided a magnificent view of the water and downtown Boston, which she now ignored. Her hand trembled as she thought about the murder of Father John O'Shea in Hull. She put down her coffee to avoid spilling it on herself.

My god. That had to be a coincidence. Didn't it.

Father O'Shea's murder occurred after he advised Carter Fitzgerald to go to the authorities regarding his concerns about the Finch Company. She suggested Fitzgerald wait, then told Adrian and Roger about their conversation. She knew about the accident that killed the Hull Police Chief but didn't suspect a connection. Her concern was the priest's death.

She took another sip of coffee, holding the cup with both hands. The Finch brothers were unethical, perhaps, not murderers. Yet some unsavory characters visited the office in recent days. Three men she had never met huddled with Roger and Adrian in the conference room yesterday. They dressed well but looked hard, mean, not your average businessmen.

What should she do? Was she imagining some conspiracy where one didn't exist? Was there a connection between the men and O'Shea? Ridiculous. She couldn't go to the police with no proof of anything. She feared discussing it with Roger and Adrian, not sure why.

Yet! She couldn't dismiss the nagging feeling something was wrong, no matter how she rationalized it. She had to tell someone. Get another perspective. She thought of Magliore. He was a cop. She could talk to him unofficially. Seek his counsel. She took her IPhone from the counter and punched in the number.

"Hey Kate," Vince Magliore answered. "What's up?"

"I need your help, Mags. I might be in a lot of trouble. Can you come to my apartment to talk? I'll ply you with pizza and wine!"

Despite her proposal of food and drink, Magliore detected the tremor in her voice. He tried to lessen her anxiety with a popular line from the Godfather. "As my friend Don Corleone would say, 'an offer I can't refuse.' See you in about an hour."

Chapter 79

Magliore got to Kathleen Maxwell's at 6:15 p.m. according to his Seiko wristwatch, cheap yet reliable. He located a spot in visitor parking, entered the massive, ornate lobby, perused the list of tenants and found her on the second floor. Eschewing the elevator, he took the wide steps two at a time and rang the bell to her apartment.

Kate answered the door on the third ring. She was dressed in tight blue shorts, a matching tank top and sandals, her red hair pulled back into a ponytail, stunning as ever. Magliore stood transfixed, unable to move.

"Are you going to come in or what?" she asked, a smile on her face, concern reflected in her eyes.

Magliore stepped inside. A small oak table, set for two, with four chairs arranged around it, nestled in a corner near the kitchen. Two wine glasses beside good china plates completed the setting. A Papa Gino's take-out box rested on the nearby bar.

Kate motioned for him to take a seat at the table and placed the pizza in the middle. She had ordered a supreme with as many toppings as possible crammed on top, the way to a pizza lover's heart.

Magliore lifted his wine glass. "To friends." They touched glasses and each took a sip.

Staring into her eyes, he said, "what's wrong? You sounded distraught on the phone."

She took another sip of wine before responding. "This is stupid, I know, but I may have had something to do with the murder of Father O'Shea."

Magliore sat up straight. "That's silly, Kate?"

"I know it sounds crazy," she said. Then described her meeting with Fitzgerald, his concerns about the company, his seeking the priest's advice along with hers, her subsequent report of her meeting with Fitzgerald to the Finch brothers and the distasteful looking "businessmen" talking with Adrian and Roger.

Magliore listened though not sure what to make of her story. "So you think there is some connection between these businessmen and Father John's murder?"

"That's just it," she said. "I'm not sure. Could Father O'Shea have been killed to keep him quiet about what's going on with the company?"

"Kate. You've read too many crime novels. Why would these men, whoever they are, kill Father O'Shea and not Fitzgerald? He's the one with evidence of wrongdoing. Like you."

He regretted the comment as soon as he said it. Kate blanched, tears streamed down her face, her body shook. "Oh my god, Oh my god," she choked.

Magliore leaped out of his chair, went to her side and wrapped his arms around her. "Kate! Kate! You're not in danger, trust me. Businessmen don't go around killing people. We believe Father O'Shea was murdered by a jealous boyfriend or husband enraged by his attention to their wife or girlfriend," he lied. *They had pretty much dismissed that theory, but no need to worry Kate.*

He opted not to tell her Carter Fitzgerald was missing or that he was investigating a possible connection between Chief Hundley's murder and the Finch organization of which she was a part. His cop instinct also told him there was a link between Father O'Shea's killing and Hundley's; too much of a coincidence.

As he thought about that he had a mini epiphany. He remembered the phone call, which lured O'Shea to Fort Revere and the Spanish accent of the caller. "Kate. This may sound like a strange question but do many Hispanics work for your company?"

Maxwell glanced at him sideways. "Yes, of course, like many construction companies. We have Latino laborers, maintenance personnel and custodial staff. Why on earth do you ask?"

Magliore shrugged and stonewalled. "Another case we're working on. Since you're in the business, I thought I'd ask, is all."

Maxwell, not convinced, didn't pursue it. They spent the rest of the evening drinking wine, eating pizza and joking about high school reunions. Later, after much vino, Kate took him by the hand and led him into her bedroom where she fell into his arms. He pushed her against a wall and they groped and stroked each other, the heat between them palpable. He pulled her tank top up and over her head and let it drop to the floor while he kissed her neck and the tops of her breasts. She ran her hands over his back and let her one hand drift lower.

He picked her up and she wrapped her legs around his middle as he maneuvered her to the bed where he placed her down gently on her back continuing to kiss her eyes, nose, cheeks and neck. He unbuttoned and pulled off her shorts exposing a black bra and panties. He reached behind her and unsnapped the bra; her small breasts firm, nipples erect. This time he would not hold back.

He straddled her and their bodies moved in unison to a rhythmic dance only they heard. Each shared the lead. They touched, probed and kissed as the phantom melody reached a crescendo and their emotions gave vent to unbridled passion. When the music ended with their energy spent, they fell asleep in each other's arms remaining entwined until after one-thirty in the morning when Magliore awoke, and despite her protests, chose to leave.

A mistake.

Chapter 80

Magliore exited the parking lot at the Marina Bay Condos and connected with Route 3A south toward Weymouth, Hingham and Hull. There was little traffic at that hour, a good thing, because he was buzzed from the wine and his intimacy with Kate.

He didn't notice the truck behind him until he crossed the Fore River Bridge. The damn guy had his Brights on and the glare reflected off his driver's side rear view mirror. He tried to adjust it but couldn't find the button in the unfamiliar rental car. He slowed to let the guy pass but the truck stayed behind and nudged closer.

The truck rode Magliore's bumper until both vehicles sailed across the Back River Bridge into Hingham, then jolted forward and slammed into him. Magliore's car fishtailed and caromed off the low center divider as he skidded by the 99 Restaurant on the right.

The truck banged into him again after he fought back into the right lane, sparks flying as the car's rear end collapsed toward the back wheels close to the fuel tank. The second impact thrust Magliore's car forward and provided some separation. But the rear frame scraped the wheels and slowed his progress. He pushed the pedal to the floor to escape the onslaught. The pursued and pursuer bolted through two red lights before the truck caught up. Instead of smashing into Magliore again though, the driver pulled alongside and swerved into the car forcing it into the guardrail. Sparks flew and the right side of Magliore's vehicle crumpled inward as it was sandwiched between truck and guardrail. Then, the guardrail ended and Magliore's vehicle plunged into the undergrowth bordering Broad Cove Lake. It rammed a tree head-on, the air bag inflated and Magliore lost consciousness.

***

When Magliore opened his eyes, the concerned face of Ed Catebegian towered over him. A quick glance left and right revealed he was in a hospital room.

"Where am I?" he asked. "And do I have all my parts?"

"Everything but your brain," Big Cat responded, a grin creasing his face. "You smell like a wino. You're lucky the Hingham cops didn't arrest your ass. And you're in the South Shore Hospital."

"Only had a couple of glasses of wine."

"Yeah, and I was only holding the funny cigarette for a friend."

"No sympathy for a fellow law enforcement officer injured in the line of duty."

"None," Big Cat said. "What happened?"

"Damned if I know. I left Kate Maxwell's and started driving home when some idiot drove me off the road."

"Did you cut him off or flip him the bird for some reason known only to your pea brain?"

"I swear I didn't."

Magliore put his head back on the pillow, his mind racing. Two guys were in the cab of the truck that ran him off the road. Could they have been the same two guys who killed Randy Hundley? Did they get on to him because he was investigating Randy's murder? And how did they know unless someone tipped them off. His head hurt as much from wrestling with the answers to these questions as from his injuries.

Catebegian noticed his spaced out look. "What are thinking, Mags? Spill your guts, in a manner of speaking." He chuckled, amused by his own joke.

Magliore repeated his concerns and Kate Maxwell's fears.

Now, neither man thought it funny…or not plausible.

They needed the warrant for attorney Prescott's files, which they hoped would reveal the client who hired him and subsequently PI Billy Brown to watch Chief Randy Hundley.

And whom they suspected tried to blackmail him.

Chapter 81

Magliore stayed in the hospital for a day suffering superficial cuts and bruises, no internal damage. Over Catebegian's protests, he ordered another rental car, a new Ford Escape, delivered by two affable young men from National. They didn't mention his catastrophic previous experience with one of their cars.

Nice guys.

He drove to Hull and parked in front of the comfort station at the end of Shore Drive, needing time to think. Plunging temperatures, strong winds and ominous grey clouds ushered in the month of October, the kind of day that touched the soul and led to introspection.

Magliore leaned against the rusting railing separating the station from the beach and gazed out at the ocean. A small cabin cruiser with a canopied top deck bobbed up and down in the rough seas, a man navigating, binoculars around his neck, both hands on the wheel, perhaps rethinking his decision to challenge the ocean today.

Magliore, in turn, had second thoughts about participating in the murder investigations of Father John O'Shea and Chief Randy Hundley. The attempt on his life unsettled him, brought back memories of the day he was shot during the manhunt for the murderous rogue LA cop. He convinced himself his actions that day were justified but keeping his secret ate at him, a reason he contemplated leaving the force.

The physical pain was not the issue; rather the games played by the mind. The cold sweats, the replay of his movements, wondering if he could have done anything different, saved the guy who died beside him in a hail of bullets. A cat had nine lives, not so a human. He dodged death twice now; might a third attempt succeed?

Two arms encircled him as he grappled with those questions, Kate Maxwell. He'd called her before leaving the hospital and asked her to meet him here. He had something to tell her.

Magliore turned to face her grasping both her hands in his. She took his breath away. She wore no make-up, or lipstick. Her red hair hung to her shoulders, framing her soft, angelic face. A white sweater, black slacks and pink Nike running shoes completed the picture of a very desirable woman.

Kate gasped as she inspected the lacerations on his face. "My god, Mags, you look awful. How do you feel?" She ran her fingers along his right cheek tracing the prominent sutures there.

"Like I could go another ten rounds," he responded with bravado. "Sorry they stopped the fight."

She smacked him on the arm; relieved he could joke about his appearance. "I'm serious you dope. You might have been killed."

"Walk with me," he said, not responding to her anxiety.

He held her hand and they navigated down a sand covered cement ramp to the beach and trudged across rocks and seaweed to get to flat, wet sand. The tide was out.

They walked in silence as far as Kenberma, where Mags had once manned a lifeguard stand for the town. They stopped and sat in the soft sand, their bodies touching. Maxwell put her head on his shoulder and he pulled her hand to his chest.

They sat like that for several minutes before Magliore spoke: "I'm thinking of resigning from the Anaheim PD. Not sure what I'll do. Something less dangerous, settle down, marry a wonderful woman, start a family."

She squeezed his hand, lifted her head from his shoulder and gazed into his eyes. "And who might that wonderful woman be?"

"Not sure. I'll find someone."

She smacked him again, harder than the first time. "You can be an asshole you know?"

He rubbed his shoulder and stared out toward the water. "Randy used to say that a lot."

She rested her head on his chest and wrapped an arm around him. She couldn't see his eyes well up.

Chapter 82

Magliore's car incident prompted Lieutenant Catebegian to accelerate the warrant for the files held by attorney Francis G. Prescott relating to the surveillance of Chief Randy Hundley. A sympathetic judge complied and Big Cat directed Magliore to meet him at the attorney's office in Quincy since he had other business in the city. He didn't elaborate.

Ushered into Prescott' office by a secretary, the two lawmen were once again greeted by the attorney with his Cheshire cat grin. "Sorry I had to put you through this process," he said with a less than convincing smile on his face. "Lawyer client confidentiality you understand?"

Catebegian nodded. Magliore glared.

"I'll help you in any way I can," Prescott asserted as he handed the file to Catebegian, who opened it, raised his eyebrows and passed it to Magliore.

"Why would a construction company CEO want to set up a surveillance of a town police chief?" Magliore asked.

Prescott shrugged. "I represent the company in many contractual agreements and sometimes contentious personnel issues. I didn't ask."

"You weren't curious?"

"Of course, but I don't make a habit of pissing off clients by questioning their actions."

"Even after Chief Hundley was killed?" Cat pressed.

"The media described it as an accident. I had no reason to think otherwise or make a connection between the surveillance and a mishap."

"Come on counselor, you're a smart man. Don't bullshit us."

Prescott sat back in his chair and folded his arms across his chest, finished talking.

"We'll get back to you counselor," Big Cat said, "If we have more questions." He got up from his chair, jerked his head toward Magliore in a sign to follow, turned and walked out. Magliore trailed behind like a little boy trying to keep up with his father.

They didn't speak again until they reached the sidewalk in front of the building, Catebegian clutching the file in his massive right hand. "I need coffee. A Dunkin' Donuts is not far from here. Follow me."

Magliore followed for about a mile or so on Hancock Street and pulled in behind Catebegian in a small lot fronting the donut shop. When they entered, Catebegian took a table in the back while Magliore got the coffee, black; two jelly donuts for the big man and a plain for himself.

Magliore put the coffee and donuts on the table and slid into the plastic chair opposite Catebegian who sat without speaking for a few moments with the file in front of him.

"Magliore," he began, and the California detective braced for bad news. Catebegian called him by his surname and not "Mags" when pissed.

"I'm rethinking my decision to keep you on board. Lieutenant Porter's right. You're not a cop in Massachusetts and you're a friend of the victim in the case we're investigating. Both should disqualify you."

"Cat, you're right," Magliore conceded. "But I found out about the surveillance on Randy and that got us to this point. Without that lead, you'd have bupkis."

"We'd have gotten there."

"Maybe."

"We're not amateurs, bud. Not as sophisticated as you big timers in California. But we get the job done, don't need your help."

The conversation was not going well for Magliore, pissing in Catebegian's soup not helpful. He backed off, pleaded. "Come on Cat. If it was your friend tell me you wouldn't do everything possible to help?"

Catebegian's took a sip of coffee, downed one of his jelly donuts, wiped his mouth and gazed out the window.

Magliore knew not to interrupt and soon Catebegian turned back to him. "OK! Don't make me regret this. You follow my lead and do everything by the book. I'll crush you like a grape if you don't. Capiche?"

Was Catebegian a closet Italian?

Magliore held back a smile careful not to let his relief show. He took a bite out of his donut and washed it down with a swig of coffee. "Not a problem, sir."

"As long as we understand each other," Catebegian retorted not fooled by Magliore's sycophantic use of the term "sir." He then wolfed down donut number two.

Chapter 83

They stayed in the donut shop with the Hundley file on the table between them, drank more coffee, gazed out the window and sat without speaking until Magliore broke the silence. "Carter Fitzgerald, a Hull selectman, did some work for the Finch Company as a CPA. He found something that disturbed him when he examined their records. Kathleen Maxwell told me he shared those misgivings with Johnny O'Shea and her. Johnny recommended he go to the police. She begged him to hold off. Now Johnny's dead, Fitzgerald's missing and Randy, whom I now think initiated his own investigation into Finch is also dead. The Company is the common denominator."

"Great theory. What's your proof?"

"Why else would they have a PI track Randy? The company was doing something illegal; Fitzgerald uncovered it and shared it with O'Shea in the confessional. That's why O'Shea planned to meet with the Bishop to explore his options regarding the seal of the confessional."

"Just speculation Mags. Makes sense though the surveillance alone doesn't prove they blackmailed the Chief or they had him wacked. Even if their books are hinky and their work in Hull endangered, it's a stretch, and a very long one, to think construction company CEOs engaged in multiple murders to conceal some creative accounting. They could pay a fine and be done. Doesn't compute."

"Then something beyond cooking the books is going on here. Something to kill to hide," Magliore suggested.

"We might be able to secure a warrant to examine their books but without Fitzgerald we wouldn't know where to begin. And these guys have had ample time to sanitize their records."

Magliore nodded, got up and ordered two more large coffees and another jelly donut for Big Cat, none for himself.

He brought the coffee and donut back to the table, sat down and gawked as Big Cat devoured the donut in one bite and washed it down with the coffee. "So what do we do now?" he asked

"We can visit the Finch Company without a warrant. Scare the shit out of them, force them to do something stupid."

It didn't work. Though unnerved and intimidated by Big Cat's bulk and imposing presence, the Finch brothers hung together and referred all questions to their attorney.

They were afraid of something or someone more threatening than the police.

Chapter 84

Frustrated by their visits to attorney Prescott and the Finch brothers, Magliore and Catebegian returned to the Hull Police Station still convinced there was a connection between the murders of Father John O'Shea and Chief Randy Hundley. Cops don't believe in coincidence. And in a town where a major crime is some drunk pissing on a neighbor's lawn, two murders within weeks of each other had to be linked.

Catebegian confirmed such a link when they met in Hundley's office after their return. Catebegian sat behind the Chief's desk holding a cup filled with tobacco juice leaning far back in the swivel chair, a dangerous act considering his bulk. Magliore worried the chair would collapse and nasty fluids would be spewed everywhere.

Two documents were spread out on the desk.

"Interesting reading?" Magliore inquired.

"It is. They found the blue Charger that ran down the Chief abandoned in the parking lot at the train station in Hingham. A search of the car turned up a cigarette butt under the front passenger seat. Our lab analysis determined it's a Fiesta brand manufactured in Mexico."

Magliore didn't comment but his eyes betrayed interest.

Big Cat savored the moment as a grin creased his face. "And out of all that crap in and near the bunker at Fort Revere our team also uncovered a Fiesta. DNA on both matched."

Magliore sat bolt upright, eyes wide.

"Yeah," said Big Cat, "someone with the same DNA smoked a Fiesta cigarette at both crime scenes. The DNA's not in the system though."

"No way that's a coincidence"

"Nope."

"These guys are not professionals," Magliore offered.

"Nope. No professional leaves incriminating evidence at one crime scene let alone two."

That fact was not necessarily good news. The state police, FBI and other federal law enforcement organizations had a database of known professional hit men or at least organizations that employed them. Freelance amateurs wouldn't be in anyone's system making the Fiesta cigarettes their most viable clue.

"Are Fiesta's sold in the U.S?"

Catebegian stroked his chin and spit a stream of tobacco juice into the ever-present cup. "My guys checked. You can buy them on the Internet and smoke shops might order them for you. Difficult to track down."

"Can we narrow it down to the South Shore area?"

"Long shot," Big Cat responded before spitting again.

Magliore cringed. "You got any better ideas? We have no other concrete evidence. Everything else is rumor or innuendo. Sometimes a Hail Mary pass connects. I've thrown a few myself."

Big Cat had been an offensive lineman, one of the "Big Uglies" as sportscaster Keith Jackson humorously but affectionately dubbed the huge men who toiled unnoticed by most football fans. He never threw or caught a pass but he also knew that a "Hail Mary" sometimes won games.

"I'll put some guys on it," he assured Magliore.

Chapter 85

The "guy" chosen to throw the Hail Mary pass was a woman, Theresa "Terry" Lopez, though soccer not football was her sport of choice. Lopez was new to the state police detective squad and a fluent Spanish speaker. She was in her early thirties, slender, with jet-black hair and soft brown eyes that belied her strength of character and competence. Her perseverance and work ethic won admiration from her colleagues and led Catebegian to select her for the difficult assignment.

Lopez wasn't thrilled with the task but as a newbie she knew not to complain or argue so she pressed on with "vigah."

JFK would be proud.

She first tried the corporate offices of the company that produced the Fiesta brand, Cigarrera La Moderna of Mexico City, reasoning they might track individual sales in the United States; they didn't, only bulk to tobacco companies. No info on online sales either.

She did discover two tobacco companies, Finck Cigar of San Antonio and R.J. Reynolds, operating as Reynolds American, the nation's second largest tobacco company, imported and distributed Fiesta's.

Lopez believed she would have more luck with R.J. Reynolds since they operated nationwide, so she called their main office in Winston-Salem, North Carolina. After three transfers, she reached a deputy director in Marketing, a Bernard Wallace.

"Mr. Wallace, "I'm detective Terry Lopez with the Massachusetts State Police. We're investigating two homicides in one of our coastal communities."

"Homicides," Wallace said, the skepticism evident in his voice. "How can I possibly help?"

"Well sir, we found a Fiesta brand cigarette at the crime scenes and we're trying to track down where that cigarette may have been purchased. We understand your company distributes them."

"Well, yes we do. We've handled that product since our merger with Brown and Williamson five years ago. But tracking an individual pack is impossible. In addition to smoke shops, our products are distributed to grocery stores, liquor stores and convenience stores. Wholesalers carry our major brands but I doubt Fiesta."

Lopez sighed. "I understand sir, but wouldn't a smoke shop be more likely to sell imported brands than the others you mentioned."

There was a short pause before Wallace answered. "True. We still would have difficulty narrowing down which store sold them. We send our products to distribution centers and then to individual stores."

"Where are your distribution centers located in Massachusetts?"

"Brookline and Springfield."

Brookline was closest to the South Shore so Lopez asked for and received a contact number for the manager of the Brookline office. She thanked Wallace for the help and broke the phone connection.

Before calling the number, Lopez had an idea to narrow her search. She fired up her laptop and Googled "Hispanics in Massachusetts," reasoning the purchaser of a brand like Fiesta was a Latino, a guess, yet worth a try.

To her surprise over 700,000 Hispanics resided in Massachusetts and accounted for 11% of the total nationally. In Massachusetts though, Mexicans ranked behind Puerto Ricans and Dominicans in numbers, slightly ahead of Cubans and Salvadorians. The largest number of Hispanics resided in Boston, of course, followed by Springfield, Worcester and Lowell. Another problem: 69% of the Hispanic population in Massachusetts was native born and 94% of all Hispanics in the state were of non-Mexican origin.

How many U.S born Mexicans would buy a cigarette manufactured in Mexico and would non-Mexican Latino's do the same? Shaking her head, Lopez realized her chances of success were minimal at best.

Nevertheless, she pressed on concentrating on the Hispanics in cities closest to Hull, doubting the killers came from as far away as Worcester or Springfield. So Boston, Bridgewater, Holbrook and Quincy were all in the mix; listed among the top one hundred cities in the state with the highest percentage of Hispanics. Bridgewater, Holbrook and Quincy had just over 2% while Boston had around 15%.

Armed with those statistics, Lopez contacted the Reynolds American tobacco distribution center in Brookline. The manager, Geno Alitori sounded annoyed by the inquiry.

"I know this is a long shot sir," she reassured the man, "but I'm focusing on the smoke shops in Bridgewater, Holbrook and Quincy that might sell Fiestas."

She wouldn't tackle Boston until later if necessary and thought smoke shops would be the place someone interested in a foreign brand would go rather than a supermarket or convenience store. All conjecture. The best she could do under the circumstances.

"Do you know how many tobacco shops are in those cities detective?" Alitori asked.

"Many I'm sure sir. Understand, this is a double murder investigation and we need your help."

After a prolonged pause, Alitori surrendered. "Very well, detective. It will take a little time to get that information."

"I understand sir. I'd appreciate it though if you could expedite the search. We need to apprehend the killer or killers before other murders occur."

"Understood," Alitori responded somewhat more engaged than he had been at the beginning of the conversation.

Lopez hoped he would stay that way.

Chapter 86

The next day, detective Terry Lopez received a call from Geno Alitori, manager of the Reynolds American tobacco distribution center in Brookline. "Detective. I obtained the information you requested. Are you ready to write these names down?"

"Thank you sir. I'm ready."

"Good. While there are hundreds of smoke shops in the region, the demand for Fiesta's is small and only the larger shops stock them, three in Quincy, four in the Bridgewater and Holbrook areas."

He gave the shop names to Lopez.

"I appreciate your cooperation sir," Lopez said. "This will help. I have one additional question though? Could someone walk into a smoke shop to buy a Fiesta and ask the clerk to order it online?"

"They could but the clerk or manager would reject such a request if they wanted to stay in business. It's a crime for them to do that because they must pay a sales tax on products sold. They would risk a fine and might even be shut down."

"Any individual could go online and order Fiesta's though, right?"

"Correct detective."

Lopez thanked Alitori and punched her cell phone off. Her last question identified the elephant in this whole process. If their suspect ordered the Fiesta's online, they'd come up empty.

Undaunted, Lopez scanned the names of the smoke shops Alitori provided. There were three Quinn's smoke shops, a franchise, two in Quincy and one in Brockton. The others, Discount Cigarettes and More, J&B Smokes, and Rockland Vape were in the Bridgewater and Holbrook areas.

Lopez began calling the shops and soon discovered why a Hail Mary was aptly named; prayers weren't always answered. Most of the shops indicated those who purchased Fiesta cigarettes were regulars, local families, day laborers, kids seeking something different; one, though, looked promising, a Quinn's in Quincy. The owner/clerk reported two Hispanic males, maybe Mexican, he wasn't certain, had come in four or five times during the last month and purchased Fiesta's. His description fit any one of a hundred Hispanic males, medium height, dark complexion, mustaches, long unkempt black or brown hair.

Not a great lead but Lopez decided to visit the store on Copeland Street in Quincy. Forty-five minutes later she arrived at the store, positioned on the corner of Copeland and Cross Streets. A green and white awning shielded the front.

Two clerks manned the large store; one, a young man of indeterminate national origin, wore a black T-shirt with "Lost Fog" emblazoned on the front. Lopez scanned the shelves, impressed by the store's inventory, everything to meet a smoker's needs, from cigars, to cigarettes to glass bongs and some items Lopez couldn't identify.

She approached the clerk wearing the black T-shirt and identified herself. The clerk smiled. "Yes ma'am, I talked with you on the phone."

Lopez was relieved she picked the right clerk. "Good. I'd like to ask you some questions about the two Hispanic men you described who bought Fiesta cigarettes."

"Yes ma'am," he said, a thoughtful expression on his face. "They came a couple of times. Only one bought anything, the Fiesta's. Never seen them before or since."

"Were they Mexican?"

"Couldn't say for sure. We get all kinds in here. They did speak Spanish to each other though."

Promising. "A store this size, with all this merchandise," Lopez observed, "You must have security cameras."

"We do ma'am, but they're on a loop. We don't keep them if nothing has occurred."

Of course, thought Lopez. "If I put you with a police artist, would you be able to describe them to him?"

"I'll try. And now that I think about it, one of the guys had this problem with his lip, tried to cover it up with his mustache; it didn't work."

"What do you mean trouble with his lip?"

"You know. His upper lip had been sewn together. It pulled his lip upward. A bad job."

"You mean a cleft?"

"Yeah, yeah. That's what you call it."

"OK. That could be helpful. A police sketch artist will contact you. Describe these men in detail, as best you can."

"Yes ma'am," the clerk responded.

Lopez shook the man's hand, gave him her card and walked out of the store.

The Hail Mary pass was still in the air wobbling toward its target.

Chapter 87

"I'm impressed," Ed Catebegian said to Lopez as he studied the drawings a police artist had made from the description of the suspects supplied by the smoke shop clerk.

"Yeah," Terry replied. "Typical Hispanic males though, except for that distinctive cleft."

Catebegian sat behind Chief Hundley's desk while Lopez occupied a chair in front. Big Cat had not yet relinquished the office and acting Chief Porter did not press the issue.

As they studied the sketches spread out on the desk, Magliore walked in, glancing at them. "You did great work on this Terry but, not to burst your bubble, these guys could be anybody, day workers, lots of them in Massachusetts now, working on a nearby job, probably gone now."

The rebuke didn't faze Lopez. "Noted. My gut says otherwise though."

Catebegian chimed in. "I'm with Terry on this. Let's put these out to the media. We might get lucky."

Magliore shrugged. "Worth a shot," he admitted.

***

The newspapers, T.V. stations, and the State Police website carried the sketches that evening with no accompanying story other than a brief statement explaining the men were persons of interest in two homicides and asking anyone who could identify them to call their local police department.

Four people recognized the drawings: Rudolpho "Little Hammer" Gonzales, Roger and Adrian Finch and Kate Maxwell. Their reactions differed.

Gonzales, catching the evening news while dining with his family, sprang up from the table and called his two associates. "Bring the car around in an hour," he said into his cell phone, "we have some business."

Adrian and Roger Finch also saw the sketches on the evening news. Their hearts sank. The two men served as maintenance workers in their Quincy office; men supplied by Rudolpho Gonzales.

Adrian, shaken, called his brother. "Did you watch the news tonight?"

"Yes," Roger said offering no other comment.

"This is horrible, horrible," Adrian stammered. "What are we going to do?"

"I don't know, Adrian. Those sketches could be anybody. No need to overreact."

"We've got to contact the police, Roger, report our suspicions. We're not murderers. We can't be blamed for this."

"No Adrian. Calm down. Do you want to go to prison, bring disgrace to our families? Lose everything we worked for? Let's think this through."

Confused, bitter, afraid, Adrian's whole body trembled. He'd always relied on his brother. He lacked the courage to act on his own. "OK, Roger. Meet you in the morning."

"Good. Have a drink. Relax. Everything will be OK. Trust me."

That trust resulted in dire consequences for both brothers but not from the source they feared.

Chapter 88

Kate Maxwell's trust in the Finch brothers shattered when she opened the Quincy Patriot Ledger the morning after the T.V. broadcasts and saw the drawings on the front page. One of the men, the one with the cleft, doubled as a custodian and maintenance worker in her building, cleaned her office.

She sat at her breakfast bar drinking coffee and staring at the paper, shocked, scared, trying to convince herself this was some horrible mistake, knowing otherwise, her earlier fears confirmed.

She told Adrian and Roger about Carter Fitzgerald and his priest, now the priest was dead. She couldn't reach Fitzgerald; he didn't respond to her phone calls and messages. She had no idea why the Hull Police Chief was killed, dreaded it was connected to all of this. She broke down and cried until she experienced dry heaves and rushed to the bathroom in a vain attempt to vomit.

Recovering after several long minutes of physical pain and emotional terror, she called Vince Magliore.

"Hey lady," he answered, "been thinking good thoughts about you."

"Mags, this isn't a social call. I need your help."

Magliore detected the tremor in her voice. "What's the matter, honey? What can I do?"

"Mags. The two sketches of the men wanted as persons of interest in the Hull murders."

"Yeah?"

"I know them. Well, one for sure. He works at Finch."

Magliore inhaled and then let it out. "Are you sure Kate?"

"Yes. Yes. I see him a lot. The man with the cleft cleans my office. I've never talked to him. Didn't think he spoke English. He just nods when he sees me."

Magliore didn't want to worry her. They weren't sure these men had anything to do with their cases.

"Kate. These men may not be guilty of anything. They're persons of interest as the bulletins said. We should err on the side of caution though. Say nothing about this to anybody. Especially your bosses."

"What should I do? I'm scared."

"I know. I know. Go to work as usual. You're absence might raise suspicion. We'll have some state detectives there as soon as possible."

"Mags, I'm so frightened."

"You can do it honey. You're strong."

FRANK J. INFUSINO JR.

After a brief pause, she answered. "All right. Send someone as soon as possible please."

"I will. Promise."

Maxwell needn't have worried. The two men wouldn't report to work that day.

Chapter 89

Two people who didn't see the sketches of the men wanted as persons of interest by the state police in the two Hull homicides were the men themselves. They didn't watch television, read newspapers or have access to a computer. Carlos Carterenez and Erick Ortega lived in a house in Quincy that housed male undocumented immigrants who provided much of the workforce at Finch & Sons construction. Their dwelling was a block from another sheltering female illegals like Angelina Suazo, who also toiled for Finch.

Carlos and Erick did not come to the U.S. seeking a better life. As soldiers for Jalisco New Generation Cartel (CJNG), they participated in wars against the Zetas and other gangs that left a trail of carnage in Guadalajara, Vera Cruz, Nueva Laredo and Tijuana. The gang conducted guerrilla attacks on the police and took credit for shooting down a Mexican army helicopter.

Carlos and Erick, veterans of these wars, sneaked into the U.S. aided by Rudolpho "Little Hammer" Gonzales to provide muscle whenever needed. They weren't hit men so much as ruthless thugs. Caution wasn't a requirement of a Mexican gang member since corrupt police often shielded them from arrest. So they threatened Father John O'Shea and killed Chief Randy Hundley leaving behind evidence tying them to both murders. Carlos enjoyed Fiesta cigarettes.

The men waited on the curb in front of the house, Carlos chain-smoking, to be picked up by their real employer for their next assignment. They smiled as the black sedan came down the street toward them.

Their smiles were short lived.

Chapter 90

Three days after the police sketches of the men wanted as "persons of interest" appeared in the media, the bodies of Carlos Carterenez and Erick Ortega, nude except for torn and ripped boxer shorts, washed up on the rocks at Wollaston Beach in Quincy.

A couple jogging made the brutal discovery, called 911. The first responders, Quincy patrol officers, set up traffic cones and strung yellow police tape between them to cordon off the remains. Detectives and crime scene investigators arrived minutes later.

Corey Cahill, Chief Randy Hundley's former lover, was the first detective on the scene. He identified the corpses from the published police sketches despite their ravaged torsos, their faces unscathed but for minor bruises and scrapes. Each had been shot twice in the head, once in the heart. Cahill notified Ed Catebegian by phone and Big Cat requested everyone back off until he got there.

Catebegian and Magliore arrived an hour later. They walked down to the water's edge where the first responding officers had dragged the bodies, not protocol but no one made an issue of it yet.

Cahill nodded to Magliore and introduced himself to Catebegian.

"Nice to meet you Corey," Big Cat responded taking a quick look around. "If these are our guys, I'll be taking over the investigation." His eyes bore into Cahill challenging him to object.

"No problem, Lieutenant. Glad to help in any way," Cahill said casting a sideways glance at Magliore.

Catebegian and Cahill all donned latex gloves and approached the bodies for a close examination. Magliore hung back visually inspecting the corpses, not cleared to participate.

Cahill photographed the index finger of each man with a digital camera, the image to be sent to the State police for processing and on to the FBI, who would run it through their new Next Generation Identification System (NGI) that contained millions of fingerprints of criminals or suspected criminals, including thousands of terrorists.

Catebegian inspected each prone man searching for any birthmarks or other abnormalities to help identify them. He nodded as he discovered a tattoo on the inside of each man's left arm; the initials in capital green letters CJNG. "Hey Corey. Recognize the tattoos?"

Cahill checked them, frowned and rubbed his chin. "No. Not a Quincy gang unless it's new. The 730's control Quincy."

"OK," Big Cat responded. He took a picture with his IPhone. "I'll send it to my guys. See if they can identify it.

"My CSI will be here soon to gather evidence. I appreciate your cooperation. We'll keep you in the loop and might need your help again."

"Not a problem, Lieutenant. I... we, want the people who killed Chief Hundley. These thugs may have done the actual killing but someone else had to be pulling the strings, don't you think?"

"I agree," Catebegian said glancing from Magliore to Cahill. "These two were just persons of interest, a long shot, or Hail Mary as Mags would say. By taking them out, someone confirmed their guilt. We find out who did that, we identify Hundley's killer and maybe Father O'Shea's."

"These dudes could have been the ones who ran me off the road. Couldn't say for sure," Magliore offered.

Cahill and Catebegian nodded but didn't comment. Cahill instructed the patrol officers to secure the area until the State Police CSI arrived and joined Big Cat and Magliore as they walked up to the parking lot from the beach.

The CJNG tattoo when later identified would further baffle the detectives.

Chapter 91

The Massachusetts State Police did not have the CJNG tattoo in their databank so they contacted the FBI and the Department of Homeland Security, federal agencies that track such data from street gangs to extremist groups. The director of the Boston Office of Homeland Security contacted Ed Catebegian with the information.

"What?" Big Cat was incredulous when told CJNG stood for Cartel deJalisco Nueva Generacion, a new and vicious Mexican cartel. "Why would that group kill a local police chief and priest?"

"Don't know, lieutenant, just providing you the info you requested."

"Understood," Catebegian said, thanked the man and broke the phone connection. He turned to Magliore and relayed the news.

Magliore sat in silence for several minutes sipping coffee and digesting the information. He then brought Catebegian up to date on his discovery of Hundley's cache of documents, Kate Maxwell's phone call about the two now dead suspects working at her office and the link between the two: Finch & Sons Construction.

"Yeah," and the Finch Company hired that jerk-off attorney, Prescott, to set up a surveillance of Hundley," Catebegian noted.

"So somehow Finch discovers Randy is doing a background investigation on the company, decides his probe might sour the Hull deal and hires these guys to take him out?"

Catebegian's expression conveyed doubt. "That's a huge leap, man. Construction companies may cut corners in many ways. I've never known any of them to engage in murder. No way."

"I agree. Yet somehow the Finch organization, either voluntarily or through coercion, got mixed up with the cartels, a slippery slope. You make a deal with the devil, you sometimes get the working end of the pitchfork."

Catebegian rolled his eyes at Magliore's feeble attempt at a metaphor, or was it a simile, or neither. He worked the chaw of tobacco around in his mouth preparing to spit.

Magliore winced in anticipation.

Chapter 92

Adrian and Roger Finch met with Rudolpho Gonzales in Adrian's office. They sat in straight-backed padded chairs, shots of whisky on the small coffee table in front of them. It was not the first drink of the day for either brother, steeling themselves for their meeting with "Little Hammer." Kate Maxwell was out of the office.

Roger smiled but his eyes twitched and his hand trembled as he hoisted his drink. "To our successful, and lucrative, association," he proposed as each man threw back a shot. Two of "Little Hammer's" associates stood flanking the door of the office.

"You asked for this meeting, señor," Gonzales said, staring at Roger. "What can I do for you?"

"Well, we, uh, we uh," Roger said, stumbling over his words, reluctant to offend Gonzales. "We are concerned about the death of the Hull Police Chief, very, uh, concerned."

Gonzales folded his hands on the table and stole a glance at the men by the door.

"A regrettable accident, I understand, nothing to do with us, señor. We are businessmen. We do not condone violence."

He appraised each brother in turn; his eyes narrow, his face grim, challenging, threatening.

"Of course not," Roger Finch said, hesitating for a brief moment. "I, uh, uh, wanted to bring this to your attention, is all. We have a big investment in the redevelopment project in Hull. Means a lot of money for all of us."

"I understand," Gonzales said and stood up. "Thank you for the whisky, señor, good quality." He motioned to his men and all three hurried out of the office leaving the door open.

***

Roger Finch got up and refilled his brother's glass and his own after the Gonzales entourage departed. Neither man spoke for several minutes until Adrian broke the silence.

"My god, Roger did you read the story in the Ledger about the cop investigating the Hull Chief's murder being run off the road in Hingham? Almost killed." He leaned back in his chair and closed his eyes.

Roger was the stronger of the two, older, worldlier, willing to gamble. He protected Adrian in school from bullies and from his father's wrath. He had prodded him to enter into the deal with Gonzales and wasn't about to let Adrian wimp out.

"Look. The chief's death and the incident with the detective are of no concern to us. We have a business agreement with an investment company, nothing more. What they do in their organization is out of our control. Whatever happened is coincidence, nothing to do with us."

"Coincidence," Adrian repeated. "Just coincidence." His voice trailed off as he turned away.

"That's right." Roger threw his head back downing the remaining liquid in his glass.

Adrian faltered trying to emulate his brother's bravado. His hand shook spilling some of the liquid.

They both would need more than swagger in the days ahead.

Chapter 93

Adrian Finch was drunk, a condition he had been in since meeting with "Little Hammer" Gonzales about the murder of the Hull Police Chief. Scared, he didn't share his brother's optimism. He felt trapped.

He was drinking alone in his office after 5:00 p.m. when he observed another cleaning woman enter the break room, not the same one he had encountered before. This one was older yet filled her uniform better, top and bottom.

Adrian threw back a whisky and poured another, his eyes riveted on the woman. He got up from his chair, bumped his hip on the desk, spilling liquid on his hand and the floor. He gulped the drink to keep from losing any more. He slammed the glass down and staggered forward, listing to the right, then the left. He yanked the door open and fell through it before the woman detected his presence. She was leaning over scrubbing the countertop, her back to him.

Adrian lunged and pinned her from behind, her knees slamming the cabinet doors under the counter, his hand clamped over her mouth stifling her scream. She tried to twist away but stopped when Adrian whispered in her ear. He spun her around to face him slapping her with such force her head snapped back, tears forming in the corners of her eyes, too fearful to cry out.

His breath reeked of alcohol, his face contorted into an angry mask. Pressing against her, he jerked her dress above her waist, excited by the sight of her white panties against brown skin. Aroused and keeping her constrained with one hand, he ran his other hand over her thighs, her buttocks and between her legs before pulling her underwear down. He opened his pants intent on penetrating her. She thwarted his attempts by twisting back and forth. He slapped her again and snarled, "Stop fighting bitch."

She recoiled from the danger reflected in his eyes. She stopped struggling and he thrust himself into her, not caring about any pain he might cause.

As the woman struggled, she reached behind her searching for a container of silverware close by. She knocked it over and fumbled until her hand settled on a knife. Grasping it she drove it into Adrian's belly, again, and again, and again until he slipped to the floor clutching his wounds and screaming.

Kathleen Maxwell, working late, heard the commotion and ran back toward the screams. She burst into the break room to find Adrian writhing on the tile floor blood oozing from his wounds, the cleaning woman standing over him, bloody knife clutched in her hand, her uniform streaked with blood.

"He attack me, he attack me," the woman said, shaking, tears cascading down her cheeks.

"Help me," Adrian croaked, thrashing around trying to stanch the flow of blood with his bare hands.

Maxwell pulled a strip of paper towels from the wall dispenser and knelt beside him, forced his hands apart and used her own to put pressure on the wounds. Kneeling there she noticed for the first time the zipper on his pants was down and his genitals exposed.

Realizing she needed professional help, Maxwell stood, grabbed the woman's shoulders and guided her to a chair beside a small table in the room. "Stay here, don't move," she said, in a voice as calm as she could muster. She retreated to her desk and called 911 from her landline. She gave the operator the address, floor number and circumstances and returned to comfort the hysterical woman and assist the whimpering Finch.

"He attack me, he attack me," the frightened woman kept repeating. "We are, we don't have papers, Mister Adrian, he touch us, hurt us, we can't complain or the *federales* take us away, send us back home."

Maxwell was shocked, unaware of Adrian's reprehensible behavior or that the company employed illegals. "How did you come to work here?" she asked.

"The Coyote's they take us across the border, charge us more than we have. We must work to pay them back. Many men here are like me."

Before she could say more the paramedics rushed in, moved Maxwell aside and administered to Adrian. They taped a compress to his wounds, took his vital signs, lifted him to their mobile gurney and sped out of the room as two Quincy police officers entered. The older man, a sergeant sat beside the frantic cleaning woman still shaking and crying. Kate Maxwell washed her hands and sat on the other side of the woman and put her arm around her shoulders.

The sergeant took out a notebook. "Tell us what happened ma'am," He asked.

"Adrian, Mister Finch, attacked her, she defended herself," Maxwell cut in. He..."

The Sergeant held up his hand. "I need to hear from this lady. I'll talk to you in a few minutes."

Maxwell opened her mouth to speak but the sergeant's menacing stare stopped her. "Please miss. You'll get your chance to talk."

Maxwell chastened, continued to drape her arm around the frightened woman's shoulders and grasped and held her hand with her own.

The sergeant took their statements, arrested the cleaning woman and told Kate she needed to come to the station as well.

"May I make a call first?" she asked.

"Do it in front of me please."

Maxwell punched in Vince Magliore's number and got his voice mail. "Vince please meet me at Quincy Police Headquarters. There's been an incident." She ended the call and the sergeant escorted both women out of the building.

Chapter 94

Magliore got Kate Maxell's phone message and notified Ed Catebegian who drove them to Quincy Police Headquarters. Once there, Catebegian flashed his state police credentials to put them in contact with the officers who had been at the scene of the stabbing. They were escorted to an area outside a conference/interrogation room where detective Corey Cahill and his partner, Brian Moore, a tall wiry man with thinning brown hair, were interviewing the cleaning woman. Kate Maxwell, sitting in the area, jumped into Magliore's arms when she saw him.

"No worries, Kate," he said, rubbing her back and shoulders and holding her close. He knew he shouldn't talk to her before she spoke with detectives so he guided her back to her chair. He whispered in her ear and joined Catebegian who knocked on the glass of the interrogation room to get the detective's attention.

Cahill opened the door and seeing Catebegian and Magliore stepped outside.

"We believe this is connected to Chief Hundley's murder, Corey," Magliore said. "The suspects we found dead at Wollaston Beach worked at the Finch Company. This woman may be able to provide information about them."

"If she does, this is part of our investigation, and I'll take over," Big Cat said. Cahill winced, not happy, but deferred and waved the men into the room. Once inside, they introduced themselves to Moore, Magliore again failing to mention his unofficial status.

Without preamble, Catebegian slipped two photos from a folder he carried and pushed them in front of the woman. "Do you recognize these men?"

She gasped and held a hand to her mouth. "Si. They work at Finch, like me. He, he was my boyfriend," she said pointing to Carlos Carterenez. "Rudolpho, want me to sell my body to make more money. Carlos, he say no, I am his girlfriend, he no want me going with other men."

"Who's this Rudolpho?" Catebegian asked.

"Rudolpho Gonzales, he is one who brought us here, make us work."

She described how she lived in a house in Quincy with five other women while Carlos and Erick resided nearby with other men. They all gave Rudolpho most of the money earned.

"Did the Finch Brothers know you came here illegally?" Magliore asked.

"Si."

The detectives eyed each other. Then Catebegian placed another photo in front of the woman. It showed the CJNG tattoos worn by both Erick and Carlos. "Is Rudolpho CJNG?"

"Si. Cartel deJalisco Nueva Generacion. Very bad man. He hurt our families if we don't do as he say. Everybody afraid."

"Thank you," Catebegian said and motioned the others to join him outside.

Once outside, the group moved to a corner of the large room away from Kate Maxwell.

"So Finch is employing illegals supplied by the cartel to keep profits up, costs down." Catebegian observed.

"Amazing," Magliore responded, folding his arms across his chest. "These guys cut corners on the Big Dig and wound up being fined and banned from state projects for five years. Now they have the balls to get involved in human trafficking,"

He glanced at Cahill. "Once they got the Hull redevelopment job, Chief Hundley investigated the company on his own, doing due diligence, didn't tell anyone. Somehow his investigation was exposed. The cartel used Carlos and Erick to take him out. Not sure how Father O'Shea fits into the equation."

"Let's ask the woman," Catebegian said and they reentered the interrogation room.

Chapter 95

The frightened woman cringed as the men confronted her again. Catebegian resumed his questioning without trying to console her. *She still might face charges for stabbing Finch although the scumbag deserved it.*

Catebegian put the pictures of Carlos and Erick back on the table. "Did these men hurt the Hull Police Chief?"

Her eyes opened wide, tears again formed at their corners. "Si. Rudolpho say he punish their families if they don't do this."

"Did they also kill a priest?"

"No, no señor. Carlos promise me. They no kill priest. They go to hell. They just scare him."

"Are you sure?"

"Si. Si. Carlos swear on the Virgin Mary."

"Why did they want to frighten him?" Magliore asked.

"I don't know señor. Rudolpho say do it. They do it. No kill him, señor, no kill him."

Cahill cut in. "Why did you stab Mr. Finch?"

"He attack me señor. Rape me. He attack other girls before. He hurt me."

Catebegian dipped his head and directed Moore to continue taking the woman's statement. He motioned for Cahill and Magliore to join him outside.

Again they isolated themselves from Kate Maxwell still seated in the area.

"What do you think?" Catebegian said eyeballing each man in turn.

Magliore did not hesitate. "Well! We now have the motive for Randy's murder and who did it. We need to arrest this Rudolpho character and the Finch brothers. They may not have participated in the actual murder but they know who did. And kept quiet. I'm sure the FBI and ICE (Immigration and Customs Enforcement) would like to talk to all these people."

Catebegian rubbed his baldpate and fortunately had no chaw handy to expectorate. "That still leaves O'Shea. Do we believe the woman?"

"She's not reliable on that," Magliore said. "These guys went to Fort Revere to scare O'Shea off. Maybe something went wrong. Johnny got testy. A struggle ensued. One of them pops him from behind. No way to know. The cigarettes prove they were there."

"Carlos wouldn't admit to his girlfriend he killed a priest," Cahill said.

"Well, let's find Rudolpho. He can clear this up if he's willing to talk," Catebegian directed.

"I'll take Kate home," Magliore said.

"After Moore gets her statement," Cahill said, glaring. "She's a big-wig in the Finch Company. She might not be an innocent in all this."

He crossed his arms and set his feet apart as if challenging them to contest his assertion.

Stunned, Magliore moved toward the Quincy detective with his fists balled until Catebegian stopped him with a massive arm thrust across his chest. He stood between the two men. "Knock it off, both of you," he said, his voice reflecting controlled anger. "This is not helpful."

Magliore backed away and Cahill relaxed his posture.

"OK," Catebegian said, seeing both men had regained their composure "We're all on the same team here. And like I said, let's locate Rudolpho."

Chapter 96

Rudolpho, "Little Hammer," Gonzales sat alone in a booth at Darcy's Village Pub in Quincy. He finished off a slice of pepperoni pizza, licked his fingers and guzzled the remains of an Adams beer.

He smiled as he thought about his business arrangement with the Finch brothers. Adrian was a *puta*, Roger stronger, but someone who could be manipulated by fear, Rudolpho's primary negotiating tactic.

So far he had been able to launder thousands of dollars through the company and provide work for the many desperate immigrants fleeing poverty and crime in their Latin American countries. He then exploited those workers by keeping them in debt. He knew Adrian abused some of the females. Such was the cost of business. Rudolpho liked to break in some of the women himself.

He signaled his two associates at the bar and one departed to bring their car around to the front of the building.

Rudolpho threw two twenty's on the table to cover his bill; he possessed no credit card. He slid out of the booth and hurried toward the exit behind his bulky "associate" who pushed open the front door, scanned the area to ensure it was safe and escorted his boss outside.

Their black Chrysler sedan rolled to a stop on the street. Other vehicles at the curb prevented it from getting closer. The bodyguard/associate stepped between two of those cars and opened the back door for Rudolpho, who ducked in and moved to the opposite window to allow his companion room to sit beside him. Neither of Rudolpho's protectors noticed a man who at that moment exited a vehicle parked ahead on the same side of the road.

The man strode up to the sedan and shouted "Hi" catching the associate on the sidewalk by surprise. Before he could respond or react, the approaching man drew a silenced pistol from a holster strapped to his side and shot the bodyguard through the left eye. Stepping over the fallen man, the assailant blasted both the wheelman and Rudolpho with well-placed rounds to the head finishing up his work by putting two more slugs into Rudolpho's heart and the driver's skull.

The assault took seconds and the silenced weapon attracted no onlookers. The man with the gun put it back into his holster, returned to his car with several long strides, slipped behind the wheel and drove away.

The three bodies left behind would not be the last.

Chapter 97

Roger Finch lived in a three story white Colonial on Main Street in Hingham, one of the homes Magliore had admired on his way to the Rockland Trust to search Hundley's safe deposit box. Roger was returning from his brother's bedside at the South Shore Hospital. The younger Finch, sedated and unconscious, did not have to explain to his wife and two daughters, hovering by his bedside, how he managed to get himself stabbed.

Roger had ignored and covered up Adrian's sexual proclivities and heavy drinking. But this recent incident threatened to expose everything—their company's secret alliance with a Mexican cartel, their reliance on illegal workers to cut costs and avoid taxes and their money laundering scam. He and Adrian faced federal prison for such rampant fraud and human trafficking. Murder charges might be tacked on as well. Roger considered fleeing but could not abide leaving his family.

At 9:35 p.m., Main Street was dark, the scattered streetlights providing little illumination. Roger was irritated when the automatically triggered exterior garage lights and the one above his front door failed to activate. He made a mental note to check them in the morning, his mind elsewhere. He grappled with how to tell his wife her comfortable life might end soon, their reputation destroyed, their kids future in jeopardy.

Roger pulled close to the garage. Its door didn't open when he pressed his remote. Another glitch. He cursed, opened the car door and stepped out onto the asphalt driveway, startled when someone called out his name. He turned toward the voice straining to see who it was. He never did. A silenced round from a revolver pierced his forehead blowing the back of his head apart. Two more rounds perforated his heart as the gunman stood over his body, surveyed the area to ensure he had not been seen, and walked away.

Chapter 98

It was 3:40 a.m. when the man found an isolated spot away from the handful of cars scattered throughout the South Shore Hospital parking lot. He exited his vehicle and walked toward a side entrance where he knew the door was often propped open by staff sneaking a smoke. He smiled when he spotted a piece of cardboard wedged between the door and door jam. Relieved, he climbed the stairwell to the third floor where Adrian Finch had been assigned a private room.

The man opened the fire door and faced a long corridor, sparkling white floor with a blue and red dot design in the middle, metal railings along each wall, paintings of seascapes and flowers above; no one in the hallway at this hour, the lone sound the low, audible buzz of the health equipment in the rooms.

The man strode down the corridor as if he belonged, his rubber soled shoes making little sound. He found the room he sought, pulled open the sliding concertina partition serving as the door and slipped in.

A quick scan showed Adrian Finch asleep, some type of device strapped to his right arm, an I.V. drip in his left. A flat screen T.V. high on the wall had the sound muted. The man took a quick peek through the window to ensure privacy and approached the bed. He snatched one of two pillows under Finch's head and pressed it over his face and mouth. Adrian's eyes snapped open, his legs flayed, as he thrashed around pulling his I.V. out in a vain attempt to breathe. Adrian, not strong despite his bulk, soon succumbed to the relentless pressure, his body limp. A bell sounded when the device attached to his arm disconnected during the struggle.

The assailant whispered into Adrian's ear as he removed the pillow from his face and placed it back under his head. He withdrew from the room, walked back down the hall and retreated the same way he entered. He reached his car unnoticed and drove off under control.

The nurses and doctors responding to the alarm in Adrian Finch's room found him unresponsive; efforts to revive him unsuccessful. His disheveled bed showed signs of a struggle. The doctor in charge notified the Weymouth police.

Chapter 99

A couple leaving Darcy's Pub stumbled onto the bodies of Rudolpho Gonzales and his two henchmen. The man called 911 and patrol officers arrived in minutes. Detective Brian Moore, working late, drove up moments later. He directed the officers to cordon off the area and then examined the bodies, all Hispanic males. None had any identification; the car was registered to a Boston investment firm.

On a hunch, he called Quincy Police Headquarters and requested the Finch cleaning woman, Yolanda Carrera, still in custody, be brought to the scene. Once there, she identified the man in the backseat of the Chrysler sedan as Rudolpho Gonzales, the other two as his bodyguards.

"Bad men," Yolanda said, dropping her eyes to the sidewalk. "They rape me, other girls too. We no can say anything."

These murders now linked to the state case, Moore called Ed Catebegian, who was having dinner with his wife and three kids for the first time in days. He saw Moore's name pop up on in his cell phone caller ID. "This better be important, Moore. I'm eating a nice pot roast cooked by my amazing wife."

She rolled her eyes and the children, two boys and a girl, roared until silenced by a "you could be in trouble stare" by their intimidating dad.

"We got three murder vics in front of a pub in Quincy, 93 Willard Street. The Finch cleaning woman ID'd them as Rudolpho Gonzales and two pals, all carrying, all dead. Looks like a hit."

"On my way," Catebegian responded. His wife shrugged, the kids studied their food.

Big Cat decided not to call Magliore, who would be bent out of shape, but someone deserved a quiet evening. Cat hoped Magliore was enjoying a meal with Kate Maxwell and perhaps more intimate interaction. He did contact the state CSI.

Catebegian lived on Gilbert Road in Weymouth, about a twenty-five minute drive to Darcy's Pub via Routes 3 and 93. Heavy traffic tacked on another twenty minutes, Big Cat grumbling all the way. He parked his unmarked car on the street and approached detective Brian Moore who was ensconced outside the crime scene tape, the state CSI team combing the car and corpses for evidence. They took prints and photos, bagged fibers and the guns carried by the dead men. They would analyze everything at the Boston crime lab.

One of the techs slipped under the tape and walked up to Moore and Catebegian. "Recovered a spent round on the floor of the backseat. Might be from a Glock 19."

193

"Thanks," Catebegian said. "Let me know what else you find."

The Investigator gave him a thumbs up and went back to work with his colleagues.

"OK!" Catebegian said to Moore. "If these guys supplied illegals to Finch, and other companies, who whacked them?"

"Cartel tidying up a mess or an illegal fed up with their crap?"

"Your first idea seems more plausible. But how did they know we were on to them. You've held the cleaning woman since earlier today, right?"

"Yeah. Doubt she would alert them though. Hell she hates them. Said these scumbags raped her and others. No way she tells them. But there were other women and maintenance workers at the Finch office when we apprehended her. Any one of them could have alerted the cartel."

"Don't buy that," Catebegian said. "These people are virtual slaves. No love for Gonzales."

"Right. But they have family members in Mexico, Nicaragua, wherever. Their lives might be endangered if the big bosses blamed someone here for blowing up their scheme."

Catebegian didn't argue with that reasoning.

Chapter 100

Vince Magliore and Kate Maxwell dined at Bridgeman's in Hull unaware of the murder of Rudolpho Gonzales and his henchmen. Kate dressed in a pink blouse, grey skirt; her long red hair knotted by a "scrunchie" and pulled over her left shoulder. Magliore wore a white polo shirt with black horizontal stripes, black slacks, Ferragamo loafers, no socks, his version of semi-formal attire.

Bridgeman's, located on Nantasket Avenue across from the beach, was one of the few upscale eateries in Hull that had survived over the years. A site with a better view situated on the beach opposite Bridgeman's opened and closed many times and was once again undergoing its ritual "renovation." The short life of such restaurants represented the difficulty of attracting businesses to town, something the latest redevelopment plan was designed to overcome; also something farthest from the minds of Vince Magliore and Kate Maxwell as they enjoyed each other's company.

Bridgeman's was billed as an Italian restaurant so Kate ordered shrimp scampi, house salad and a glass of Merlot. Magliore opted for chicken Parmesan, a salad and a California Cabernet. Only one other couple occupied the restaurant at this early hour. Vince and Kate sat a table on the first floor by the front window near an enclosed fire-pit of sorts surrounded by high-backed wicker chairs.

"I swear I didn't know, Vince. I swear," Kate leaned across the table and whispered, referring to the illegal workforce laboring at Finch & Sons.

Her protest reminded Magliore, an amateur historian, of the refrain many German's reiterated after World War II disclaiming any knowledge of the systematic extermination of the Jews and other's deemed inferior by Hitler's Third Reich. "We didn't know" absolved them of the guilt Kate struggled with now. Magliore didn't condemn Kate though; he believed her. And the German analogy was over the top, even for him.

"I wouldn't go back to work, yet," he cautioned. "ICE may be swarming over the company as we speak as will the state and Quincy police. I don't want you swept up in this."

"Will I be arrested?" she asked, body shaking, tears forming at the corners of her eyes.

Magliore reached across the table and took both of her hands in his. "No. I'll speak with Big Cat. He's fair. He'll have to interview you and ICE agents will also. We'll get you an attorney and I'll be with you anytime anyone talks with you if you like."

Kate squeezed his hands. "I'd like that very much," she said.

The waiter, a young man in white shirt and black pants brought their food and they ate in silence. Dark now, they could see the distant lights of ships, possibly freighters, plowing across the Atlantic.

They finished the meal, sipped wine and dipped their forks into a shared Tiramisu.

Magliore broke the silence. "You know what's puzzling. The cleaning woman we interviewed, Yolanda Carrera, confirmed the two men who worked for Finch killed Randy at the order of their boss, this "Little Hammer" thug. She swears they didn't kill Johnny O'Shea. Her boyfriend said they just intended to scare him off, threatened him. If that's true, we're back to square one on Johnny's murder."

Kate tasted a small bite of the dessert, licked her upper lip. "Do you believe her? Does Catebegian?"

"Can't speak for the big man. I'd like to believe they did it, wrap things up. Provide closure to everyone, especially Johnny's parents."

The waiter presented the bill and Magliore paid for the meal. They left the restaurant, walked across the street and beach parking lot and stopped at the metal railing on the concrete walkway. The moon was low in the sky, an oval shape, encased in its distinct aura, the tide high, ocean rough, slamming against the rocks below Green Hill.

"The ocean is always invigorating" Magliore said as he encircled Kate's shoulders with a bulky arm.

She put her head on his shoulder and, for the moment, they forgot about murder, human trafficking and the chaos surrounding them.

They would soon be jolted back to reality.

Chapter 101

"Christ on a crutch," Ed Catebegian fumed. The Hingham police had sent out an alert concerning a citizen found murdered in front of his home. The body hadn't been discovered until morning when the man's wife, walking her children to the school bus stop, saw him lying in the driveway beside their car. He hadn't come home the night before but the woman didn't worry. He sometimes stayed at work late and rather than drive home, stopped at a hotel, although he usually called to inform her. She didn't tell the police she suspected these overnight sojourns were a cover for some extra-marital dalliances.

"Roger Finch. Killed. We better send someone to the hospital to protect his brother Adrian," Catebegian said into the phone to detective Brian Moore who called to notify him of the latest twist in the Randy Hundley, Johnny O'Shea, Rudolpho Gonzales saga.

"Too late," Moore responded. "Adrian's body was discovered by doctor's and nurses responding to an alarm activated in his hospital room, suffocated."

Catebegian stifled a string of profanities. "Someone's tying up loose ends. Killing anyone with knowledge of the Hundley and O'Shea murders and the human trafficking scheme we uncovered."

"That's what Cahill and I are thinking."

"Your absentee partner showed up."

Moore ignored the jab. "We need to talk. Where are you?"

"I'm back in Hull, in Hundley's office. Get your butts down here pronto. I'll contact Magliore. He's got some good ideas, much as I hate to admit it."

"Why don't you come to Quincy, sir," Moore suggested buttering up the state officer. "We can re-interview the Finch cleaning woman we have in custody and question Kate Maxwell, who lives in Quincy."

Catebegian thought that over. "Makes sense. Mags and I will be there."

He had no idea Magliore and Maxwell had spent the night together in Hull.

***

The wine, the dinner, the stroll to the beach in the moonlight stirred passion in both Kate Maxwell and Vince Magliore, a craving that could not be expressed in public. Magliore, still staying at the Hundley's, couldn't take Kate there, not prudent. So they checked into the Nantasket Resort a short drive from Bridgeman's.

Their second floor corner room commanded a magnificent ocean view, which did not interest them now on this clear New England morning. The drapes were closed to maintain the fiction of night and the romantic mood; the king size bed ample room for sexual expression.

Kate lay on her back naked, while Magliore hovered over her anticipating the warmth of her embrace when his cell phone rang, shattering the mood.

He leaned over to examine his caller ID. Seeing Catebegian's name, he answered curtly. "What?"

"Am I interrupting something, I hope," Big Cat asked, releasing a characteristic guffaw.

"What?" Magliore repeated.

"New developments. I'll explain when you get here."

"Where's here?"

"The station."

Magliore sighed and gazed at Kate's enticing body; her head on the pillow, red hair disheveled, porcelain skin flushed with anticipation.

"Give me thirty-minutes," he said and broke the connection.

Kate's smile stirred Magliore. He longed to hold her tight, to never let go, and to protect her from all the ugliness in the world. The intensity of this emotion overwhelmed him. Not a romantic, he nevertheless remembered the lyrics from an old Leonard Cohen song: "I loved you in the morning, our kisses deep and warm, your hair upon the pillow like a sleepy golden storm..."

Kate saw the look in his eyes. "What?"

He smiled, bent over and kissed every nook and cranny of her face before pulling away and leaving Maxwell frustrated.

"Gotta go."

"I'm going to kill whoever that was," she said, throwing a pillow at him which he deflected by raising his hands in self-defense.

He drove to the Hull Police Station with the rest of the Cohen lyrics on his mind: "But let's not talk of love or chains and things we can't untie/ your eyes are soft with sorrow/ hey, that's no way to say goodbye."

Chapter 102

Catebegian regaled Magliore with the recent chain of events as they traveled along Route 3A to Quincy.

"It appears Randy's murder was triggered by his probe into the Finch Company," Big Cat explained as he drove and spit tobacco juice into his paper cup. Magliore focused his attention outside rather than watch the disgusting practice.

"Randy was looking into their background and fraud on the Big Dig as you learned from the newspaper clippings he kept in that safe deposit box. He wasn't aware of the company's alliance with the CJNG Cartel and human trafficking."

"That's just it," Magliore responded. "How did they find out? He didn't even tell his wife."

"Fitzgerald or Father O'Shea?"

"Nope. Fitzgerald uncovered irregularities in the books, financial stuff according to Kate. He confessed that concern to Johnny O'Shea. Neither one of them was aware of the trafficking angle. Johnny couldn't break the seal of the confessional and counseled Fitzgerald to go to the police. Fitzgerald's out of the picture, maybe dead, because he posed a threat to the whole scheme if he reported the fraud. Someone took him out."

Catebegian spit another stream of tobacco into his cup and Magliore flinched.

"So it comes back to Randy's investigation and how they discovered it," Big Cat concluded.

"Yeah! But who was in a position to find out?" he said surveying the passing scenery—the Hingham Shipyard, the 99 Restaurant, the condos in the distance. His mind was elsewhere, on the newspaper clippings he had found and the notes Randy had scribbled on them.

The notes. Shit. He turned back toward Catebegian.

"Cat, Randy jotted comments on a couple of the news articles he saved. He intended to call Fitzgerald, the state police and the state attorney general."

"So."

"What if he did? We can't ask Fitzgerald about it, of course, since he's missing and you have no record of a call from Randy into the state police."

"I don't. I can check further though."

"Do that. But what if he called the attorney general and someone in that office alerted Finch to a possible inquiry. The Finch's offered bribes to anyone and everyone who could help them."

FRANK J. INFUSINO JR.

Catebegian raised his eyebrows in disbelief. "You're accusing an employee in the attorney general's office of taking a bribe and, by association, acting as an accomplice to murder."

"That's all I've got. Fitzgerald never informed anyone outside of Kate Maxwell and Father O'Shea. O'Shea's dead. Kate told Roger and Adrian Finch about Fitzgerald's concerns unaware of Randy Hundley's research. No one knew unless he made a call either to the state police or attorney general."

The ramifications of those possibilities struck both men at the same time. Catebegian worked his mouth around his chaw; Magliore fell back on his seat, closed his eyes. "Gotta be it Cat," he said, "somebody at the Plymouth County D.A.'s office or the attorney general's office is on the Finch payroll. Son of a bitch."

"Shit," Catebegian responded directing his next stream of tobacco juice out the window... forgetting he hadn't opened it.

The brown stain inched its way down the glass capturing their mood. If someone in law enforcement tipped off the Finch brothers they were under scrutiny, heads would roll. And a stain, like that on the car window, would soil everyone, complicit or not.

Chapter 103

Phillip Cannon suffered a crisis of conscience. He lied about his whereabouts on the night of Father O'Shea's murder. His wife covered for him.

O'Shea's demise did not trouble him; he hated the priest and all those like him, deserved what he got. Randy Hundley was different, a good guy who did an excellent job as police chief. His death hurt the town.

Cannon, sitting at a picnic bench in the shadows, was at Fort Revere the night the priest died. He observed a car drive up, two men get out, joined later by O'Shea. He didn't know the men and didn't stick around to see what transpired.

Afraid of being seen, he left his perch and wended his way down the hill on one of the many trails through the woods kids and others trampled over the years. He was forced to jump back on the path when he reached the road; a car almost hit him as it sped by, lights out. He recognized the driver, one of his daughter's teachers, Susan Wilson. He kept his mouth shut unwilling to implicate her in O'Shea's murder. But Hundley's killing changed his thinking. He considered coming forward with his information.

He suspected the men he had seen at the fort killed the priest. Their car, a Dodge Charger, was the same make as the one the media reported ran down the chief. In the moonlight, the color appeared either blue or black.

He faced a dilemma. If he confessed what he saw, Mrs. Wilson, a probable innocent, would be dragged into the mess. Her reputation would suffer; she might be fired. If she did conspire with the two men to kill O'Shea and Hundley, on the other hand, she earned her fate.

His wife convinced him he was morally obligated to report what he had seen, even if it got him into legal difficulty.

He called the Hull Police station and asked for Lieutenant Catebegian. Told he wasn't available, he requested a call back, left no message.

His information would later prove crucial in identifying Father John O'Shea's killer and shock the town to its core.

Chapter 104

State police detectives combed through the phone records for the last two months at the offices of the Plymouth County D.A. and the state attorney general searching for any calls made by Chief Randy Hundley to either office and/or any calls from those offices to Finch and Sons.

"We struck pay dirt, lieutenant," detective Sidney Carpenter said in a call to Ed Catebegian.

"What have you got?"

"Chief Hundley called the fraud section in the attorney general's office last month. The call was forwarded to a records clerk who then contacted Finch. Under questioning, the clerk admitted the brothers paid him to warn them of any investigations or inquiries involving the company. He alerted them to Hundley's background inquiry. We can assume they notified their hoodlum buddies who put a hit out on the chief fearful their trafficking and money laundering schemes would be uncovered. We arrested the rat bastard clerk as an accessory to murder."

"Did he say anything about the priest's killing in Hull?"

"Swears he knows nothing about that and we can't find any connection to it from this end."

"OK, thanks Sid. That gives us the reason Hundley was wacked. Still leaves the killing of the priest, the Finch brothers, and their gangster pals open."

"Good luck with that," Carpenter said and broke the connection.

Catebegian punched off his cellphone and turned to Magliore who was with him at the Hull Police Station. "Pretty clear cartel operatives took out Randy afraid his unofficial inquiry would blow their sweet deal with Finch. When we ID'd the pair who did the deed and traced it back to Finch, the cartel higher ups decided to clean house. Hell, they've left bodies strewn all over Mexico as a warning to their enemies. No big deal to them. They'll regroup and find some other companies to do business with."

"What about Johnny?" Magliore asked.

Catebegian sat back in his chair and took a sip of coke from a paper cup. He hadn't resumed his chaw ritual since the incident in the car in deference to Magliore's pleading. "O'Shea didn't pose any danger to them. He couldn't reveal anything Carter Fitzgerald told him in the confessional. I believe the cleaning woman. Her boyfriend warned him off; nothing more."

"So now what?"

"We continue investigating O'Shea's murder. The FBI and Homeland Security will take over the Finch and cartel killings, beyond our reach and resources."

But the gunman who preyed on the cartel thugs and the Finch brothers was not finished. His continued rampage drew both men back into the hunt.

Chapter 105

A few minutes after nine in the evening, the gunman sat in his car in the parking lot of the Seaport Marina Bay Condominiums. He waited for Kate Maxwell, the one member of the Finch organization who hadn't yet been dealt with. Everyone in the company's leadership had to be eliminated to send a message.

He checked his weapon and opened the door to exit his vehicle, when he saw Maxwell coming out of the building. This promised to be easier than anticipated, no need to figure a way to enter and leave the housing complex unseen.

He parked close to Maxwell's car when he drove in, familiar with her Toyota Prius having shadowed her for the last two days; still two rows back though, he hustled to intercept her.

He wore a hoodie pulled down over his face to evade being identified. He cut her off, blocked her way and raised his gun. She stood transfixed, petrified, eyes wide with fear, unable to cry out.

He hesitated before firing, a mistake. A loud voice diverted his attention. "Hey! What are you doing man?" a male bystander shouted from a group of laughing young people emerging from the main entrance of the condominiums. The guy who yelled appeared stoned or drunk, oblivious to the danger in confronting an armed assailant.

Distracted, yet not deterred, the killer focused back toward his prey who, moved to action by the commotion, turned to run. Unsettled by the crowd of revelers now advancing toward him, he snapped off two shots without proper aim. He heard Maxwell scream as he sprinted to his car, dove in and sped off, sideswiping a Direct TV van entering the lot.

Several people surrounded the fallen Maxwell as she lay bleeding on the asphalt. A woman dialed 911 while two men knelt by the crumpled body straining to staunch the blood loss from head and neck wounds.

The assailant slapped the wheel of his car and uttered expletives as he slowed to the speed limit to avoid attracting police traffic enforcement officers. He wouldn't know until later if he had botched the attempt to gun down Maxwell.

No worry, though. He'd try again if necessary.

Chapter 106

Magliore and Catebegian stormed off the elevator on the second floor of the South Shore Hospital where Kate Maxwell rested in a private room after six hours of surgery. Two police officers, guarding the room, stood outside chatting with detectives Brian Moore and Corey Cahill. Two other men huddled with them looked like federal agents.

"How is she," Magliore asked to no one in particular.

Cahill stepped forward. "She's in a coma, lost a considerable amount of blood from head and neck wounds. Doctor says the next few hours are critical.

"What happened?" Catebegian asked, the concern in his voice evident.

"Lone assailant in her condo parking lot. Interrupted by a bunch of kids heading to a party, too dumb or drunk to see the danger."

One of the men not known to Magliore or Catebegian introduced himself. "FBI Special Agent Dante Culpepper, Boston Office. This is agent Johnson of Homeland Security. We believe the cartel dispatched someone to finish the job of eliminating everyone who worked at Finch. Feared the woman knew something that could hurt them."

"She has a name, man," Magliore said; moving toward Culpepper, his fists balled, jaw out.

Big Cat grabbed him. "Easy Mags."

Culpepper raised both hands in a surrender gesture. The fire in Magliore's eyes told him to back off. "Sorry. Didn't mean to be disrespectful."

"Let's get some java," Cahill suggested, wrapping his arm around Magliore and guiding him toward the elevator.

"Good idea," Catebegian chimed in.

Cahill and Moore escorted Big Cat and Magliore to a waiting room on the first floor of the hospital where they got coffee and took seats to await news of Maxwell's status.

"This is personal now," Magliore threatened. "I swear I'll rip the heart out of whoever did this."

"No way Mags," Catebegian cautioned. "Let the Feds handle it, their case now. Kate needs your support. Stay by her side."

"I don't even know who to notify, Magliore said, cradling his head in his hands, elbows on his knees."

"Taken care of," Moore interjected. "Her parents are on the way from Cohasset."

Everyone settled in for a long wait.

Chapter 107

Vince Magliore spent five days by Kate Maxwell's side, holding her hand, whispering words of encouragement, pacing the room, staring at the TV, keeping in contact with Catebegian by phone.

Kate's parents maintained a daily vigil. They were in their late sixties, dad, tall and lean, full head of white hair, chiseled features, strong nose, high cheekbones, leathery skin from much time outdoors; mother, petite like Kate, yet frail, thinning red hair neatly coiffed, porcelain complexion now sallow. They sat together in Kate's room holding hands, solicitous of Magliore once assured he cared for their daughter. They shared stories of her childhood, college years and struggle to make it in the male dominated construction industry. They stayed in a Weymouth hotel and visited each day to sit in her room praying though neither was very religious.

Magliore prowled the hospital corridors, snatching sleep in chairs, eating in the cafeteria when he remembered, pestering nurses and doctors for updates to the point they tried to avoid him as much as possible.

Detective Cahill came by twice a day to share news of the federal investigation and to visit Kate, exhibiting genuine concern for her recovery.

His report, though, was not encouraging. ICE agents, the FBI and Quincy police raided the two houses shielding the illegal workers who were interrogated, cleared of participating in the murders and the attempt on Kate Maxwell's life and relocated to a Homeland Security detention center for deportation. The hit man, or men, the Feds suspected, escaped to a safe haven across the border, any arrest doubtful.

Cahill and Magliore bonded during this time, Cahill grateful Magliore had not "outed" him to Karen Hundley or revealed his tryst with her husband; Magliore heartened by Cahill's interest in Kate's health.

The Quincy detective, though upbeat, hinted in their conversations Kate's assailant might not be apprehended. Magliore resisted that assumption though his resolve weakened as the days passed.

"How's Randy's wife doing," Cahill asked as they sipped coffee in an employee break room made available to them by the staff.

"Hanging in there. I've been staying there since it happened, helping her over the hump."

"Sure you're not doing some "humping" yourself," Cahill kidded, regretting his words when he saw the hardened expression on his new friend's face. "Sorry man, that was thoughtless."

"Karen's good people, known her since high school. Under different circumstances...." His voice trailed off as he stared into space.

"Understood. Sorry again," Cahill said and changed the subject. "Does she know we got Randy's killers?"

Magliore shook his head. "Not unless Big Cat notified her. I want to tell her in person."

"Makes sense. By the way, you need rest, get cleaned up, the nurses and doctors move to the other side of the corridor when they pass you. You stink man."

Magliore sniffed an armpit, made a face. "You're right buddy. Promise to keep me updated if anything changes with the investigation."

"Will do."

They dropped their coffee cups into a trashcan, stood, clasped hands, bumped shoulders in the manly way to hug and left the room.

A twist of fate would draw them together in a different and dangerous way.

Chapter 108

Magliore returned to Hull reassured by Kate's parents and hospital staff he would be notified of any change in her condition. He was irritable, needed a shower, a decent night's sleep and a distraction. He hoped working with Catebegian on the still unsolved murder of Father John O'Shea would provide that diversion.

He got to Hundley's house at 5:00 p.m. and rang the doorbell even though he had a key. He didn't like barging in unannounced, frightening Karen Hundley who hadn't recovered her equilibrium since Randy's death.

Karen answered the door, gave Magliore a hug and pulled him through the doorway. "Ewe," she said, holding her nose. "You need a shower, a change of clothes and a big glass of wine."

Magliore didn't protest. He showered in the bathroom across from the guest room, shampooed his hair, scrubbed every inch of his body and let the hot water pummel him, drawing out the tension and pent up emotion, tears mingling with the cascading water.

Later, he pulled a pair of jeans from his travel bag, tugged a turtleneck sweater over his head, slipped on his running shoes and joined Karen in the living room. She sat on a multi-colored couch, wine in hand. A glass for Magliore and a can of mixed nuts rested on a low coffee table between the couch and two overstuffed matching chairs. Magliore fell into one of the chairs, grabbed his wine and lifted the glass. "Here's to justice for Randy."

Karen raised her glass, a tear escaping from her right eye.

They finished one bottle and opened another, taking time out for Magliore to cook steaks on the patio grill and Karen to fix a salad they devoured with gusto.

As the night wore on, their conversation covered topics from high school escapades to Johnny O'Shea's death. By the end of the second bottle of vino, both slurred their words, giggling and telling nonsensical jokes they found hilarious.

"Do you remember the Great Pumpkin Caper in our senior year?" Magliore asked, glassy eyed.

Karen giggled, which Magliore took as a yes.

"We stole most of the pumpkins in town from house porches, front steps and lawns, even the police station, piled them up on the roof of the high school. Pissed off half the town. We made all the newspapers at the time. Never got caught. Never told anyone."

Karen burped: "That was you?"

"Yup. Randy, Johnny and me, the three Musketeers."

Both became quiet at Magliore's reference to Hundley and O'Shea, remembering better times.

At some point, Magliore sat next to Karen though he couldn't recall when or how. She laid her head on his shoulder, crying. He stroked her hair and pulled her close. She rubbed his arm, patted his chest, let her hand fall to his lap, where she felt him stir.

"Your little guy wants to come out and play," she said, snickering while struggling to unzip his fly, her fingers unable to accomplish the task.

Though aroused, Magliore hesitated. Even in his drunken stupor he sensed Karen's behavior was fueled by more than the wine or any sexual feelings she might have for him. Randy's death devastated her. She sought, needed, love and protection and reached out to him in her loneliness and despair.

Magliore struggled to clear his mind, no easy feat after the night's consumption of alcohol. He respected Karen and the memory of her husband too much to take advantage of her vulnerability. He gently took her hand, moved it to his shoulder and wrapped his beefy arms around her as her body convulsed and her tears soaked his sweater.

They remained locked in that desperate embrace until Magliore stood, scooped her in his arms, took one step and plopped back on the couch, Karen falling on him. Laughing, he tried again, succeeded, stumbled around the coffee table, navigated between the two chairs and carried her down the hall to the bedroom plunking her on the bed. He hovered over her, swaying back and forth, a vacant expression on his face, unsure of his next move.

Karen had landed with her arms and legs spread, as if making a snow angel. She gazed up at Magliore with a goofy grin. His attempt to return the smile failed as his eyes rolled back in his head and he fell face forward landing by Karen's feet.

He awoke later still dressed under a blanket at the foot of the bed. Karen lay under the covers smiling down at him. She patted the bed beside her.

He crawled up next to her, wrapped his arm around her and they fell asleep in that position; she beneath the sheets, he above, their faces wet with tears.

***

They awoke an hour later.

"Let's shower, go get something to eat," Karen said as Magliore rubbed the sleep from his eyes. Forty-five minutes later they sat at a window seat in the Saltwater Diner, ordered coffee first, oatmeal and wheat toast for Karen, bacon, scrambled eggs and wheat toast for Magliore.

When the waitress left, Karen said: "Nothing happened last night, you know."

"Close."

"But no cigar."

"Definitely no cigar."

That evoked another spasm of laughter attracting disapproving glances from a couple at the counter and a smile of approval from an older gal in an adjoining booth who probably thought they were lovers.

"So what's next?" Karen asked.

"I should find another place to live, for one thing."

"No way. We were drunk, emotional, let down our guard. One glass of wine at dinner will be our new limit."

Magliore raised his eyebrows, sipped his coffee and changed the subject. "We need to find out who killed Johnny now that it's clear his death wasn't connected to Randy's."

Karen nodded and reached for his hand.

Magliore hesitated, reluctant to pursue an issue he knew he must. "Did you and Johnny, ever, uh, have sex?"

Karen pulled her hand away, dropped her eyes and frowned. "One time. We got drunk while Randy was at one of his so called conferences, no doubt chasing his own piece of ass."

Her face flushed, she stopped and took a sip of coffee when the waitress brought their food, then resumed. "I was ashamed. Johnny offered many Mea Culpas, worried how Randy would react if he found out; we never went there again, I swear."

Before Magliore could respond his cell phone rang, Big Cat calling.

"One moment," he said and stepped outside to avoid additional scathing disapproval from the couple at the counter. He moved to the edge of the sidewalk. "OK. Go ahead."

"Where are you?" Big Cat asked.

"Having breakfast."

"We got a tip on O'Shea. Meet me at the station in an hour if you want in."

"I'll be there."

Chapter 109

At noon Magliore joined Ed Catebegian at the Hull PD. Big Cat, ensconced behind the Chief's desk, had resumed his tobacco chewing.

Magliore stared at him in disbelief. "Didn't the incident in the car tell you something about that nasty habit of yours?"

"Yeah. Never try to spit out an unopened window."

"Brilliant. I can see why you're a respected state police lieutenant; a mind like a steel trap, closed."

"Are you going to break my balls or are you interested in the lead on the O'Shea case?"

"I'm all ears, no pun intended," Magliore retorted, a jab at Big Cat's protruding lobes.

"You never quit do you, asshole."

Magliore shrugged, an impish grin on his face.

Catebegian leaned forward, struck a professional tone and recounted Phillip Cannon's story about being at Fort Revere the night O'Shea was killed and having seen Susan Wilson along with the CJNG thugs.

"Could be covering his own ass."

"Yeah. But why come forward now? We had written the guy off as a suspect."

"Afraid if we dug further we'd discover the truth."

"What truth? That he was there. So what. We've got nothing to tie him to the killing."

Magliore kept silent for a few minutes before speaking. "Sue Wilson mugged Johnny at the reunion, nearly raped him on the dance floor. She was infatuated with the guy and not reluctant to show it even though he was a priest. What's her motive?"

"How about jealousy, for starters. We know O'Shea wasn't exclusive. He was banging a lot of women, their denials aside. Could be Susan wanted him all to herself. Hell hath no fury like a woman scorned, as the old saying goes."

"Actually it's a quote from the Book of Proverbs."

"Whatever. The meaning is: piss off your woman and suffer the consequences."

"Wisdom from he who spits tobacco for pleasure."

"Are you going to continue to annoy me or are we going to talk with this lady? She might open up if you're there, being a former classmate and all."

211

"Point taken. Let's wait till school is out. I don't want to confront her with kids and colleagues around. I'll call the school, get a message to her, to meet me at her house around four, should give her enough time.

"I want to check in with Kate's parents, find out how she's doing and with Cahill. He's in touch with the Feds regarding the attempt on Kate's life. I'll meet you back here a few minutes to four. Wilson lives on Rockland House Road, a short drive from here."

Catebegian nodded, spit into his cup and opened a folder on his desk. He didn't anticipate the near tragedy that awaited him.

What could happen confronting a female schoolteacher?

Chapter 110

Magliore and Catebegian pulled up in front of Susan Wilson's house at 4:05 p.m. It was a two-story grey clapboard structure with blue shutters flanking each window and a blue door at the top of steep stairs leading to the first floor; the cement foundation enclosed a cellar common to many New England homes.

The house was across the street from and four lots down from the Seawatch Condominiums, a huge building not suited to the residential area, which blocked the once great ocean view of many residents. It long ago replaced the dwelling of a man named Simmons who owned the Fun House, once a popular attraction in Paragon Park with its giant slides, rotating walk-through barrel and crazy mirrors transforming humans into those resembling alien beings. It burned down before Magliore's time but his parents had shown him pictures of them riding a gunnysack down a huge, wide slide.

Magliore, disheartened, stared at the condos. They represented another sign of so-called progress stamping out the town's unique history. He doubted any redevelopment plan could revive it. Shrugging his shoulders, he led the way up the stairs to Wilson's and rang the bell. The door opened on the third ring. Susan Wilson stood there dressed in a color-coordinated outfit more conservative than the one she had worn at the class reunion. She donned a green knee-length skirt, a white blouse buttoned at the top with a green and white scarf around her neck and green wedge heels.

She gave Magliore a hug and stepped aside to let the men enter. They stood in an expansive living room, with two couches perpendicular to a brick fireplace, a low rectangular coffee table between. A reclining lounge chair sat at the opposite end of the room with an adjacent table and lamp. A book rested on the table. A staircase on the far wall with a mahogany railing led to the upstairs bedrooms.

Magliore introduced Catebegian. Susan nodded, didn't smile. "Can I get you some coffee? I just made a fresh pot. Need a caffeine fix this time of day."

Both men said yes and reclined on opposite couches as Susan walked to the kitchen. They waited without speaking until she returned with a tray holding steaming mugs and a plate of Italian style cookies. She placed everything on the coffee table and sat next to Magliore. Everyone selected a mug while Big Cat snatched two of the cookies.

Susan broke the silence: "How can I help you." Her eyes shifted from one man to the other, expectant, concerned.

Catebegian deferred to Mags who took the cue: "Uh, Sue, uh, someone claims to have seen you at Fort Revere the night Johnny was killed."

She straightened as if slapped. "He or she is mistaken Mags, wasn't me. I was here with my daughter."

"The person is pretty certain it was you. His child is in your class and he's met you at parent/teacher conferences, can identify your car."

Her eyes darted from one man to the other, reflecting fear. Her hands trembled and she clasped them in front of her in an attempt to regain composure. "He's wrong, Mags. Let me show you something."

She got up and walked to the table beside the recliner, opened the drawer and took something out before turning to face them, holding a 38 special revolver to her head.

"I didn't mean it Mags. The son of a bitch molested my daughter. I went to the rectory to confront him, saw him drive to the fort and followed. He met two men; they talked for a while then left. I hid nearby, couldn't hear their conversation. When they left, that fucking pervert called some woman, girl, and whispered things to her, the same words he said to me. I got pissed, grabbed the first thing I could find, a rock and smashed his head. I ran when I understood what I had done. Didn't know anybody had seen me. I won't go to jail, disgrace my daughter, I won't."

She pressed the pistol tighter against her right temple.

Both men stood, Magliore inched toward her in an attempt to calm her. "Sue, if what you say is true, you didn't plan it, acted in the heat of passion; a good lawyer can help you. You might not serve much time."

"I don't believe you."

"He's right Mrs. Wilson," Catebegian said, in an effort to distract her. "We can recommend leniency, explain you were defending your daughter. A jury will be sympathetic. The district attorney will be open to a plea, may not even go to trial. It's a no win case for him."

Catebegian moved to his right, Wilson's left. He released the holster snap on the weapon he carried on his belt. Sometimes suicide victims turned on those attempting to help. He worked the gun out of his holster, held it close to his leg, ready.

"Trust me, Sue. I'm telling the truth," Magliore pleaded, catching Big Cat's movements out of the corner of his eye. "You can't do this to Victoria. You know how cruel kids can be. Even friends will torment her; remind her every day of what happened. You don't want her walking in on this."

Wilson's hand trembled; tears clouded her vision, confused and desperate—dangerous.

Magliore kept talking, painting a grisly picture if she made good on her threat. "Head wounds are messy, Sue, Victoria will have that image in her mind forever. Can't be erased or explained. She may hate you. Better a flawed mother than a dead one."

Wilson's eyes flicked from one man to the other, she waved her weapon without apparent purpose, her knuckles white. She didn't sense how close Magliore had crept, in a position to grab the gun, a risky move considering her fragile state. A sudden lunge might force her to pull the trigger, a reflex.

"Sue please," Magliore tried again. "I promise we'll do everything we can to help you, protect your daughter, the other children who may have been assaulted. Johnny and all the other predators win if you do this; kids might see this as their only way out, some have done that. Don't send the message this is okay, the way to end their pain."

Magliore now stood about a foot from Wilson. Her eyes locked on his and in that moment he knew she'd do it. His arm lashed out a split second before she fired. The bullet, its trajectory deflected by Magliore's swift move, grazed Wilson's skull and lodged high on a wall above a front window. She cried out as Magliore wrapped her in a bear hug, his vise-like grip forcing her to drop the gun.

Sobbing, her body convulsing, she buried her face in his massive chest while Catebegian darted over and scooped up the weapon. He moved to handcuff Wilson. Magliore waived him off. He lifted her off the floor and put her down on one of the couches holding her tight. The blood from her head wound saturated his shirt though it was not deep or dangerous. Catebegian put the gun in his pocket and went to the bathroom in search of a first-aid kit.

"I'm so sorry, so ashamed," Wilson said.

Chapter 111

Paramedics transported Susan Wilson to South Shore Hospital in Weymouth to be treated for her head wound. Catebegian arranged a private room under state police protection. Assured by doctors her head trauma was superficial, Catebegian recited her Miranda rights and suggested she have an attorney present. She declined.

"Susan," Catebegian asked for the record. "Did you kill Father John O'Shea?"

"Yes," she answered, tears forming at the corners of her eyes.

"Tell us what happened."

She frowned and told them the story:

"I found some photos and emails from Johnny to my daughter. She had posed for him and he told her how nice she looked and felt. I lost my mind."

She asked for a couple of Kleenex, dabbed her eyes and blew her nose before continuing.

"I drove to the rectory that night determined to confront the bastard, missed him by minutes. I followed him to Fort Revere, maneuvered up Farina Road with my lights out and didn't see anyone else around.

"I stopped next to the old water tower when I saw cars parked at the top of the hill. Johnny stood talking with two men then they disappeared from view descending toward the concrete gun emplacements and ammunition bunkers.

"I played at the fort as a kid, like you Mags, so I knew a trail that would get me close to where I anticipated they would stop, at least I hoped so."

She patted her eyes again and asked for some water.

Magliore poured her a glass and handed it to her.

"I was right," she said, with a half-smile. "They were outside a large darkened room next to steps leading up to where the big guns used to be."

She paused, sipped the water, gazed out a window and sighed.

"I slipped into a small room near the men with Johnny. It was dark and smelly and my skin crawled worrying about spiders or other bugs."

She shivered. "These rooms and tunnels always freaked me out even in the daytime. Didn't believe the ghost stories, still...." Her voice trailed off and her eyes drifted toward the window, again distracted.

"Susan," Magliore prompted.

Her head snapped back. "Sorry. Where was I?"

"You were hiding near Johnny and the two men."

""Oh! Oh. Right. Didn't hear much of what they said, though. The wind was blowing. Made it difficult. I do remember snippets like 'Fitzgerald,' 'audit,' 'confession,' and 'police.' The man speaking had an accent, maybe Spanish, which confused me. He sounded threatening until Johnny said something about 'the seal of the confessional.' The man said, 'bueno padre.'

"After that, the men climbed the wooden steps nearby and left. Johnny remained behind, which I thought strange."

She rested again, drank more water and stared at the ceiling as if considering her next words. Magliore and Catebegian kept silent until she regained focus.

"I was pissed and ready to confront him but I stayed hidden, not sure why. Not sure about anything I did that night."

Her eyes misted and she swiped at them, sniffed, and blew her nose.

"I peeked through a small hole in the wall, watched him take out his cellphone and punch in a number. He faced the inside of the darkened room saying things like 'honey,' 'sweetheart,' 'your body,' 'want you.'

"I went crazy, imagined him flirting with my daughter; picked up a rock lying by my foot, snuck up behind him and smashed his head before he could turn around. He fell to the floor, dropped his phone and didn't move. I stood over him screaming; don't know what I said. Didn't know if he was dead or not. Didn't care."

Her body shuddered and her hand trembled as she reached for the water, put it back when she couldn't raise it to her lips.

"I was so angry. I wanted to expose the rat bastard as a pervert. I didn't want to touch him, but I undid his belt and yanked his pants and underwear down. 'I hope everyone sees your naked ass,' I yelled and kicked him as hard as I could."

She stopped again, put both hands in her lap and stared outside, her eyes and nose red. After a few moments, she dipped her head as if acknowledging she should finish her story and began again.

"I'm not sure how I got back home. I almost ran off the road a couple of times going down the hill from the fort. I sat in the car in front of my house for a long time, crying as much for my daughter as for me. I embarrassed myself with Johnny. Let him do whatever he wanted. Believed he cared for me, loved me. What a dope.

"He shouldn't have messed with my little girl, he shouldn't. He had to be stopped, didn't he?"

Her gaze flicked from one man to the other seeking confirmation. Neither gave it to her although Magliore reached out and squeezed her hand.

"Susan," Catebegian said. "You're under arrest for the murder of Father John O'Shea. You should get an attorney and say nothing else until then. Do you understand?"

Wilson nodded, let her head fall back on the pillow and stared through the window at the darkening skies.

Chapter 112

Special Agent Dante Culpepper summoned Ed Catebegian to the new FBI headquarters located in Chelsea. The facility, eight stories high, was hailed for its heightened security, state-of-the art technology and expanded capacity to house additional task forces like the one Culpepper now led to investigate the CJNG and its participation, if any, in the murders of the Finch brothers and its own henchmen operating in Quincy.

Culpepper dissuaded Catebegian from bringing Magliore to the meeting. He was testy on the phone perhaps embarrassed because the former FBI Assistant Special Agent in charge of the Boston Office (ASAC) recently pleaded guilty to perjury and obstruction of justice in connection with his testimony at the trial of James "Whitey" Bulger, an informant who committed at least eight murders while being supervised by the ASAC.

Catebegian did not want to exacerbate any ill will the FBI might harbor against the state police, or Magliore, so he did not mention the Bulger fiasco but he did bring Magliore with him. Culpepper, not happy, nevertheless escorted both men into a conference room adjacent to his office. A huge oak rectangular table and ten chairs dominated the room and the one person who was there, Homeland Security Agent Johnson who had been present at the hospital after the Kate Maxwell shooting. He halfway stood, smiled, and shook hands with the detectives as they entered.

Magliore and Catebegian grabbed seats opposite Johnson while Culpepper sat next to his counterpart in Homeland. Culpepper had a blue folder in front of him. "I cannot over-emphasize the confidentiality of the information I'm about to share with you," he said, staring at Magliore. "I swear I'll bring you both up on federal charges if any of this leaks."

Magliore shrugged. Catebegian did not flinch. Even sitting, he could be intimidating. He placed his elbows on the table and leaned in to Culpepper. "We're both sworn officers of the law, agent. We know the consequences for leaking information. Don't disrespect us. I don't appreciate it and won't accept it."

Magliore stifled a grin, put his head down and shielded his face with an open hand, palm down, as if blocking the sun.

"Just so everyone is clear," Culpepper responded, his face flushed. He did not like the dressing down.

Culpepper opened the folder and glanced at it for a minute before closing it. "We have information proving the Mexican Cartel, CJNG, did not orchestrate the murders of the Finch brothers or take out their own operatives in Quincy who had killed Chief Hundley. We're dropping our investigation. It's your baby again."

Magliore and Catebegian sat back as if punched.

***

"Are you sure about this?" Catebegian asked.

"Yeah," Culpepper said. "We've got an informant at the highest levels of the CJNG. He's a friend and confidant of the group's leader, a crazy named Nemesio "El Mencho" Oseguera Cervantes."

Big Cat and Magliore exchanged glances. "Never heard of him," Catebegian said.

"Few people have. CJNG is the new kid on the block, more dangerous than the Zetas or Sinaloa's under Guzman. They're trying to dominate the drug trade in the Northeastern United States and also dabble in human trafficking. That's how they wound up laundering money through Finch and Sons Construction and placing workers there."

"What does this have to do with our murders?" Magliore interjected.

"When we identified the guys in Quincy as CJNG soldiers, we asked our mole to find out what he could. He told "El Mencho" the FBI and Homeland were irate the cartel would kill U.S. citizens on American soil. He let him know the heat would be turned up and could undermine their whole operation in New England."

Culpepper took a breath, got up and poured some coffee from a pot on a long counter bordering one wall of the conference room. He held up the pot, a gesture inviting others to join him. Magliore did.

Culpepper returned to the table with coffee and a donut. Magliore got up and grabbed two donuts and some napkins, slipped back into his chair and put the treats down in front of Catebegian whose face lit up.

Culpepper continued his narrative. "El Mencho assured our man CJNG did not kill the Finch brothers. He admitted Little Hammer went rogue in taking out Chief Hundley and tried to cover his tracks by eliminating his own hit men. But, 'Bodies are bad for business,' our guy quoted El Mencho as saying."

"And you believe this?" Catebegian asked devouring a donut in one mouthful.

Culpepper winced at the sight of Catebegian's dreadful manners but answered. "We do. Our informant's information is reliable. He's helped us dismantle extensive crime networks in Boston, Maine and New Hampshire. We'll assist you in any way we can but we can't divert scarce resources to a local matter."

Catebegian licked his lips, eyed Magliore and said: "OK. We'll work with the Quincy police on the latest killings and the attack on Kate Maxwell."

Culpepper and Johnson stood signaling the end of the meeting.

Chapter 113

On their way back from FBI headquarters, Catebegian and Magliore stopped at the Quincy Police Station to inform detectives Brian Moore and Corey Cahill of the FBI's withdrawal from the case, omitting details. They found Moore in, Cahill pursuing another matter.

Moore had been included in the FBI investigation so he gave Big Cat and Magliore an update. "Everyone in the Marina parking lot that night was interviewed. Conflicting eyewitness testimony, of course. The shooter described as over six-feet, under six-feet, wearing a black hoodie, grey hoodie, blue hoodie, gloves, no gloves. They agreed no one heard shots, so we assume he used a silencer. He escaped in a Toyota or Honda SUV, the model with the tire on the back door, dark color.

"The driver of the TV van sideswiped didn't see the man behind the wheel; everyone at least agrees it was a man. State lab techs took samples from the side of the van and should be able to determine if the paint was from a Honda or Toyota. The driver side rear view mirror may also have been damaged. We're checking local body shops. So far, nothing."

"The state will take the lead on this since it's linked to Chief Hundley's murder," Catebegian said. "We'll expect and need your help. My friend here has a personal stake in this, as you know, and because of that should be excluded."

Moore avoided eye contact with Magliore.

"But," Big Cat said, "against my better judgment, he's in. We'll consider him an unpaid, very unpaid, consultant."

Moore understood. He liked Magliore and assumed his partner did too. Cahill likewise was solicitous of Kate Maxwell's health and checked on her daily. In fact, Moore suspected that's where he was at the moment.

Catebegian interrupted his thoughts. "If the cartel guys did not kill the Finch brothers, it might be someone who had a beef with them, personally or professionally, perhaps a business rival jealous of their success. My detectives will examine their files and determine if anyone stands out. You and Cahill follow up the personal angle. Maybe one or both diddled someone else's wife, stiffed a friend on a loan, anything."

"Will do," Moore responded.

Magliore spoke up. "If it was a personal thing Cat why include Kate?"

Before Catebegian could respond, an awful, unthinkable thought jolted Magliore. He dismissed it as soon as it surfaced but his gut told him otherwise. Love knows no bounds; jealousy or revenge often stokes murders, witness Sue Wilson's reaction toward Father John O'Shea.

"Hey," Catebegian said, noticing Magliore's far away stare. "You check out to planet Magliore again?"

Moore laughed.

"Sorry Cat. Just had a thought although I know that challenges your belief in my intellectual capacity."

"Got that right pal. Don't make me regret involving you in this case."

"I won't."

They shook hands with detective Moore and headed back to Hull, Magliore dreading his instinct might be correct.

Chapter 114

They faced another dilemma when they returned to Hull, ambushed outside of Police Department Headquarters. Not shot at! Rather assaulted by a member of the Fourth Estate, one Gwen Garner, a reporter for the Quincy Patriot Ledger who contributed to the paper's Cops & Courts section that chronicled criminal activities throughout the South Shore.

Garner blocked the entrance to the station. She was a petite brunette, hazel eyes, pale complexion, marvelous figure. She wore a beige skirt cut an inch or two shy of her knees and a white, long sleeved blouse, top two buttons open. A silver pendant hung around her neck and nestled in her cleavage. Magliore and Big Cat were wary despite her seductive appearance; perhaps because of it; reporters could be treacherous and mean spirited, part of their DNA.

"Lieutenant Catebegian," she asked, "what can you tell me about the investigation of Father O'Shea's murder? I understand you have a suspect in custody."

"Gwen," Big Cat responded. "We can't comment on an ongoing case. The press will be notified as soon as we have something to report."

"Noted," she said and smiled, revealing a perfect set of teeth. She turned to Magliore. "I've heard you grew up with him. I'm seeking some background. To make him more real to our readers."

"He was a great guy, super athlete, fine priest. We all liked him."

"Was he true to his vows?"

Magliore expected the zinger. He gave her a twisted grin and shrugged. "You're looking to trash the guy's reputation to sell papers. I'm not going to comment."

"So you're implying some truth to the rumor?"

"I'm not suggesting anything," Magliore insisted. "I'm a consultant here. Anything official will come from Lieutenant Catebegian."

Sharp lady, Magliore thought. Smart and pretty, a winning combination for a reporter. He suspected she pried information from more than one guy as he drooled over her rack. Not immune to her looks, he knew better than to say anything that could be misconstrued or twisted to fit the story she planned to tell especially if one misstep would get him kicked off the case.

"Like the lieutenant said, the press will know something as soon as we do."

Catebegian cut off the dialogue as he pushed by her. "Nice talking with you Gwen." Magliore followed.

Once inside they faced another challenge posed by Gwen Garner. "She's going to pick up on Sue Wilson's arrest sooner than later," Magliore cautioned. "We should go see O'Shea's parents before the shit storm hits."

Catebegian concurred. "We'll go together, but they'll take it better coming from you."

Chapter 115

Before they left the station, Magliore changed his mind. He stuck his head into Big Cat's temporary office, formerly Chief Hundley's. "Cat, I'll talk to Johnny's parents alone. Not sure how it will go down but they'll be more comfortable with me. They're in denial but the dad knows, I'm sure of it. He's trying to shield his wife from all this."

"What are you going to tell them?"

"Not sure. I may take a ride to think about it before I go."

"OK. Get it done and let me know when. We have to put out an announcement soon."

For his drive, Magliore chose one of the more scenic routes in the area along Jerusalem Road to Cohasset Harbor. He took Atlantic Avenue past the former St. Mary's of the Assumption Church, now condominiums, then through Gunrock and a flat rock-strewn area sandwiched between the ocean and Straits Pond, an area devastated several times from monster storms, water cascading over the seawall and flooding many homes, some of which have now been placed on tall concrete foundations with a hole in the middle so future flood water may pass through; that's the idea anyway.

Magliore executed a left turn at Rocky Beach onto Jerusalem Road and climbed a small hill with stately homes on either side, some new, some dating back over eighty years, all with panoramic ocean views. He marveled at the opulence of the mansions, as he thought of them, and continued to Sandy Beach where he stopped rather than continue on to Cohasset Harbor. He ignored a residence only warning sign and parked facing the water. He took girls here often during his high school days, sometimes doubling with Randy Hundley and his date.

He got out of his car and sat on one of the large rocks bordering the beach. Clouds blanketed the sky, blocking the sun, portending a storm. Winter approached. Rough seas had washed some lobster pots ashore and they lay entangled in a heap close to the water's edge.

Magliore shivered in his short sleeve polo shirt braced by the cold offshore breeze. Despite the discomfort, he enjoyed the solitude and time to reflect, something he did a lot of lately. He raised his face to the wind and wrestled with how to tell Johnny O'Shea's parents their precious son, a priest, violated his sacred vows and had been murdered as a result.

No easy way to do that.

Chapter 116

Rain forced Magliore back into his car raindrops playing a steady drumbeat on the roof and hood as he leaned back in his seat, eyes closed, waiting out the storm.

He dozed for ten or fifteen minutes and awoke to find clear skies, a typical New England cloudburst. He dug into his pants pocket, pulled out the container with his pain pills and popped two into his mouth. By now, he couldn't tell if the aching in his leg was real or imagined; didn't matter. The painkillers made him feel good, needed or not. His resolve to end his dependence on them a distant memory.

He drove out of the beach parking lot, retraced his route and wound up in front of the O'Shea house in less than twenty minutes. The moment he opened the car door, another cloudburst swept through the area. He slammed the door shut, vaulted the stairs to the O'Shea's, slipped on the wooden porch floor and fell on his butt, sliding into a wall as if stealing a base on a ball field. Before he could get up, the front door of the house opened and Mr. O'Shea peered out. "Nice slide but an unusual entrance."

"Sorry. Didn't plan on making such a noisy entry."

"Well. Come in and dry off."

Magliore grinned, stood up and walked into the living room. A fire raged in the stone fireplace, wood crackling as flames consumed bark and continued their onslaught on the logs stacked on a metal grate. Mrs. O'Shea sat on the same couch near the fireplace she had on Magliore's last visit, a cup in hand which he presumed to be tea. Both parents gawked at him, fear and hope reflected in their eyes, anticipating news of their son. Neither asked him to sit.

Magliore plunged in: "The state police have arrested a suspect in Johnny's murder. She has confessed."

"She?" Mr. O'Shea blurted as he stood by an arm of the couch next to his wife hand on her shoulder.

Magliore still wrestled with how to tell them the reason for their son's murder but he thought the truth best—perhaps not the whole truth.

"Johnny was killed by Susan Wilson, a teacher at Hull High School."

"Susan," Mrs. O'Shea gasped. "We know her. Johnny dated her in high school. She's been to our house. We liked her."

Tears cascaded down her cheeks; the teacup wobbled in her hand. Mr. O'Shea grabbed it before it dropped into her lap and placed it on a nearby small table.

"Why! Why! Why did she do it?" Mrs. O'Shea whined.

This was the hard part for Magliore. He stood statue-like until Mr. O'Shea prodded him with a piercing glare.

"Jealousy. I'm afraid she and Johnny were intimate. She believed he was cheating on her."

Mrs. O'Shea, stunned, cried out and buried her head in her husband's lap. He patted her shoulders and held her tight, his expression a confirmation of his worst fears; his son hadn't been true to his vows. He stood rigid for a moment, swiped his sleeve across his eyes to wipe away moisture forming there and then caught Magliore off guard with a seemingly unrelated question. "Mags. Did you know this house once belonged to Ralph Crossen, the guy they named the street after?"

"No I didn't sir," Magliore answered, unsure where the man was going with his query, afraid he was becoming unhinged.

"He was a decorated World War II soldier, a hero," Mr. O'Shea declared. "A hero."

"Yes sir," Magliore said, shifting his weight from one leg to the other, still confused until Mr. O'Shea connected the dots.

"Johnny was our hero, Mags. Our hero. He was a warrior for God." He then bent over, wrapped his arms around his wife and rested his head on hers, the conversation over.

Magliore couldn't wait to extricate himself from the tragic scene but he offered some reassurance. "Not everything you hear or read about Johnny will be true. He lost his way is all," he said as he opened the door to leave. "Call me at the police station if you have any questions. I'll be in town for a few more days."

He stepped onto the porch, shut the door behind him and stood motionless. For some reason thoughts of Kate Maxwell flooded his consciousness. She was still in the hospital, still not awake. His feelings for her remained unchanged yet he questioned his commitment to her or to any other woman.

Hell, a little wine and he and Karen Hundley almost played hide the salami.

He'd never had a long-term relationship no matter how intense the initial passion. Truth be known, he enjoyed the single life, freedom to come and go as he pleased, not beholden to anyone. He could go to the gym when he wanted, eat and sleep when he chose. A relationship was difficult, stressful; he doubted he had the self-discipline to make one work.

Now, still standing on the O'Shea porch, he dismissed thoughts of his own inability to bond, long-term, with a woman and again grappled with the feeling that had unnerved him when he had discussed the Finch murders with detectives Moore and Catebegian.

If cartel gangsters didn't take out Roger and Adrian Finch and attack Kate, someone with a personal vendetta did, someone who blamed Kate along with the brothers for Randy Hundley's death: someone who sought revenge.

Chapter 117

Revenge is often listed among the top three reasons for murder along with sex and money. Susan Wilson killed Father John O'Shea because of jealousy and fear he abused her daughter. Cartel thugs murdered Chief Randy Hundley to protect their money-laundering scheme from being exposed.

And Magliore now believed payback was the motive for the slaying of those same goons, the Finch brothers and the attack on Kate Maxwell. Someone overwhelmed with grief by the loss of a loved one and willing to punish those deemed responsible despite the cost both personally and professionally.

Magliore, disheartened by this knowledge, knew from personal experience the strong pull to exact revenge, a pull to which he himself succumbed. He returned to Hull to recover from his wounds and to deal with the anguish resulting from an act that threatened his mental health as well as his physical wellbeing

The circumstance that led to his crisis of conscience began when a fired Los Angeles police officer declared war on his brethren and their families by killing a young woman and her fiancé in the city of Irvine. The twenty-eight year old was the daughter of a police captain who the cop blamed for inadequately representing him during a dismissal hearing. In a *Manifesto* posted online the rogue officer proclaimed he would continue his vengeance until the LA Police Department exonerated him.

From February 3rd through February 12th the man blazed a trail across the counties of Los Angeles, Orange, Riverside and San Bernardino wounding two officers and killing another. The attacks so unnerved LA police they fired upon three civilians driving pick-up trucks matching the description of one driven by the suspect. Two of the civilians included an elderly woman and her daughter delivering newspapers. Their truck was riddled with over one hundred rounds discharged by rattled officers.

The other civilian was a young man heading to the beach to catch some morning waves. He was not hit by gunfire but suffered injuries when police rammed his vehicle. These misadventures proved embarrassing and costly to the agencies involved and displayed the level of tension existing in the manhunt for the murderous cop.

Finally, on February 12th, the report of a hijacked vehicle and the description of the hijacker in the San Bernardino Mountains west of Los Angeles gave police hope they had found their man. Their suspicions proved correct when two San Bernardino Sheriff's Deputies responding to the sighting were attacked; one killed the other wounded.

Other pursuing officers cornered the suspect in a remote cabin but did not launch an assault because of a report the assailant held hostages. Efforts to talk him out proved futile.

While commanders considered their options as darkness descended on the mountains, a lone figure crept away from the police line, approached the cabin undetected and slipped inside through an unlocked door. The renegade cop, distracted by flares fired by the encircling lawmen, did not hear or see the man sneak up behind him and was knocked unconscious by a blow to the back of his head. But instead of notifying the fearful cops outside that their prey had been disarmed and rendered defenseless, the man retrieved the rogue cop's gun from the floor where it had fallen, wrapped the guy's hand around it, placed it to his forehead and pulled the trigger.

Vince Magliore slipped away and was crawling back to the perimeter line when a fusillade of pyrotechnic tear gas canisters, burners, was launched into the cabin causing a fire and igniting ammunition from within. The intense heat and exploding rounds prevented officials from putting out the conflagration and two rounds hit Magliore as he crawled away.

A charred body later found in the remnants of the cabin was identified as the rogue cop. An autopsy stated he died from a single self-inflicted gunshot wound to the head.

Magliore, along with hundreds of police officers in southern California, attended funerals held for the men slain by the rebellious cop, one of whom had been Vince Magliore's partner. As he stood by the man's grieving wife and children, he experienced no remorse for his actions.

But now, in Hull, a quote from the Chinese philosopher, Confucius haunted him: "Before you embark on revenge, dig two graves."

No doubt the man who exacted revenge for his friend and lover felt no regret, but his grave had already been dug.

Chapter 118

Magliore returned to the Hull Police Station and found Catebegian behind the Chief's desk leaning back in the swivel chair and spitting tobacco juice into his cup. He shook his head and sat down. "How does your wife tolerate that?"

"She doesn't," Big Cat said, dropping his legs to the floor and facing Magliore. "I brush at least three times a day and use mouthwash before I go home. Chew gum as well."

"Why don't you stick with the gum? Cheaper and less offensive."

"Not the same high."

"You have seen pictures of those old baseball players who chewed, faces eaten away by that poison?"

"I'm touched by your concern but drop it. Heard all the arguments before."

He spit into the cup again. "What did you tell O'Shea's parents?"

"The truth. He had an affair and his jealous lover killed him. I didn't detail how many affairs or include his abuse of kids. Can we keep that out of the news?"

"Doubt it and I don't plan to lie. The son-of-a-bitch got what he deserved. We're not sweeping anything under the table like the Church did. I need to sleep at night."

"Understood. I'm sure Miss Gwen from the Patriot Ledger will find and reveal all anyway."

"That's fine by me. This shit pisses me off. I've got kids."

Magliore tried to understand the emotions of a parent as he struggled to empathize with O'Shea's mother and father. No winners there so he changed the subject. "I've had a bug up my ass ever since the FBI removed the cartel from the Finch slayings."

"Good for the bug."

Magliore twisted his mouth into an awkward attempt at a smile. "I'm serious, Cat. I believe I know who killed Adrian and Roger and attacked Kate and I'm afraid he may try to finish the job on Kate."

"We've got a guard on her door twenty-four seven."

"Won't help if I'm right!"

Catebegian repeated his spitting ritual and scowled. "What are you saying? Who is it?"

"I need to check this out myself first. Trust me on this."

"Don't jerk me around, pal. If you're wrong or go "rogue" on me, a bug up your ass will be the least of your worries."

Magliore grinned and stood up. "I won't do anything stupid."

"Fat chance," Catebegian retorted, moving a chaw from one cheek to the other.

Chapter 119

Magliore drove to South Shore Hospital in Weymouth to visit Kate Maxwell. He pulled into a parking space next to a Toyota, Rav4, white. He inspected the car for damage, found none but near the left rear tire the white paint had flaked off and revealed a darker color beneath, perhaps blue. He stood up, took out his cell phone and punched in detective Brian Moore's number.

Moore answered on the third ring.

"Brian. Mags."

"Yeah, I can read."

Magliore ignored the jab. "Brian. What kind of car does Corey drive?"

"Why?"

Magliore hesitated, then improvised. "I'm at South Shore Hospital, pulled in too close to a vehicle and scratched the driver's side door. A Quincy police vest is on the back seat."

"He drives a Rav4, dark blue. He's going to be pissed. Some jack-off backed into him in the department lot. He's had the car at my brother-in-law's for the last three or four days. He's a mechanic and does some bodywork on the side. He'll give you a good deal if you ever need it."

"Thanks but I'm driving a rental. In examining it closer, I didn't put much of a scrape in Cahill's car. I'll pay for the damage."

He broke the connection and jolted upright as Cahill eyed him from three cars away. "You figured it out, didn't you," he screamed, pulling out his service revolver.

"Yeah."

"Those slime bags deserved it. Walk away man."

"I might have, if you hadn't hurt Kate."

"She's as guilty as the Finch's."

"She wasn't in on it, Corey, I promise you."

The Quincy detective turned back toward the hospital. "Too late anyway. Too late."

Magliore understood. He darted between some cars and sprinted in the direction of the hospital entrance. Cahill made no attempt to stop him.

Taking the stairs two at a time, Magliore reached the second floor, burst through the fire doors in time to see a doctor and two nurses rushing into Kate's room pushing a crash cart.

Magliore froze when he got to the room and watched in horror as the physician pounded Kate's chest. The monitor above the bed displayed a flat line, no heart activity.

"IV/IO push, 40 units of Vasopressin," the doctor shouted to the nurses.

Within seconds a nurse injected a syringe containing the drug into Kate. And after what seemed like an eternity to Magliore, the video screen again displayed the peaks and valleys of brain activity and the frenetic commotion in the room ceased.

The doctor, whose nametag read, Stephanopoulos, approached Magliore still standing transfixed outside the room.

"She's stabilized for now," he said. "Can't rule out further brain injury though. We won't know until, or if, she recovers."

"If she recovers?"

The doctor reached out and put his hand on Magliore's shoulder. "Not a certainty. I'm sorry."

Magliore inched into the room, stood by the bed and grasped Kate's hand. It was cold. He bent over, kissed her forehead and stroked her cheek remembering her smile, their instant connection at the high school reunion and their frenzied lovemaking in her condo. It seemed so long ago.

As he stood there, his cell phone rang. Prepared to ignore it, he glanced at the screen, knew he had to answer. He pushed the accept call image on the phone.

"I'm not done," Cahill said, his maniacal laugh echoing in Magliore's ear.

Chapter 120

The call unnerved Magliore. The Quincy detective sounded deranged and planned to continue his revenge spree.

Who could his next victim be?

Two possibilities came to mind—the man who spied on Chief Randy Hundley at the behest of Attorney Francis Prescott, PI "Billy" Brown, and the attorney himself. Cahill would see them as part of the conspiracy that killed his lover.

Magliore called Catebegian, "It's Cahill."

"Nope. My phone says Magliore."

Not amused, Magliore retorted. "Cahill's our guy. He gunned down Gonzales and his bodyguards as well as the Finch brothers and attacked Kate. Tried to kill Kate again at the hospital moments ago."

Catebegian responded after a brief pause: "Are you outa your mind? A Quincy detective, a cop, one of the investigators on the case, is the killer? You gotta lay off those pills you pop every five minutes. Your mind is fried."

Catebegian would be even more pissed once he discovered the reason for Cahill's rampage and that Magliore withheld that info from him. "They were lovers," Magliore announced, his voice low, restrained.

"What?" Catebegian stammered. "Who?"

"Cahill and Randy Hundley."

The sound of Catebegian spitting into his cup reverberated through the phone connection; the big man no doubt apoplectic over this new information. "I should throw your ass in jail Magliore for impeding a murder investigation. I had to schmooze my boss to let you work with us. This is a fucking nightmare."

"We can debate this later, Cat. He's gonna go after two more people as we speak."

"Who?"

"Attorney Prescott and PI 'Billy' Brown."

"You know this how?"

"For Christ sake, Cat. I'm guessing. They are the two people left connected to the murder of Randy. Cahill called to tell me he's not through. He's gone over the edge."

"Ya think?"

"I do. And if we don't act fast we'll have two more victims on our hands."

"On your hands, asshole."

Magliore took a deep breath, regretted not telling Catebegian about the relationship between Hundley and detective Cahill. His effort to protect Randy's reputation and spare Karen Hundley additional grief backfired; a mistake but no time to rehash that now. "Can you get some state police officers over to Brown's and Prescott's? We don't have much time."

"On it," Catebegian said aware that to continue with recriminations wasn't helping.

"Good. If I'm right, he'll take out the attorney first, bigger fish than Brown. I'm going to head there."

"I'll alert Quincy PD as well," Big Cat said. "It'll be awkward but they'll do their job."

"They will, I'm sure. I'll contact Cahill's partner, Brian Moore. Fill him in. Ask him to meet me at Prescott's office."

Catebegian ended the call without comment.

But Cahill was one step ahead of them.

***

Quincy detective Corey Cahill disconnected his call to Magliore by punching his cell phone off with the index finger of his right hand and stuffed the phone in the pocket of his Member's Only Jacket. He wore civilian clothes so as not to sully the uniform he once donned proudly, a ludicrous decision in light of the murderous acts he had recently committed. Thinking about it, he threw his head back and cackled like a witch in the midst of stirring her dangerous brew.

He suffered no guilt for his past actions or for what he now planned, no longer restrained by the boundaries of the law he once swore to uphold. American justice was slanted towards protecting the rights of criminals instead of those of the innocent. The cartel scum and the Finch brothers would have cut deals with the Feds and no doubt walked after serving time, or in the case of the Finch's, paying a fine.

Corey Cahill made sure that didn't happen and now he intended to make the greatest culprit, in his mind, pay the ultimate price as well. Lawyer Francis Prescott twisted the law to suit his purposes and those of his clients and amassed a great deal of money in the process. Cahill deemed him the worst offender because his defense of criminals freed them to repeat their crimes. He regretted that he wouldn't get to exact revenge on Kate Maxwell and PI Billy Brown, who he believed, also contributed to Randy Hundley's murder. But he doubted he would walk away from his next act.

He checked his weapon and exited his car, which was parked in front of the offices of Francis G. Prescott. He glanced to his left and right, no cops in sight. Magliore hadn't alerted the Quincy police in time. He darted inside the building taking the stairs two at a time.

He couldn't wait to confront that bastard Prescott.

Chapter 121

It took thirty minutes for Magliore to drive from South Shore Hospital to the office of Francis G. Prescott on Hancock Street in Quincy, which the police now had barricaded. Patrol officers guarded the perimeter, their cruiser lights flashing.

Magliore parked parallel to the barrier and approached two uniforms who regarded him with concern. One signaled him to stop. "Sorry sir. You can't come any farther."

Magliore held up his Anaheim, California badge. "I'm working with the state police."

The skeptical officer motioned him to step closer so that he could inspect his badge. His partner unlatched his holster and placed his hand on the handle of his gun, alert, prepared.

Magliore stopped. He didn't want a confrontation. He saw detective Brian Moore standing beside a SWAT captain near the entrance to the building housing the Law Offices of Francis G. Prescott. They were behind an armored vehicle shielding them from the high windows of Prescott's office, which opened onto Hancock Street.

"Officer," Magliore asked. "Do you know detective Moore?"

"Yes sir."

"Good. I see him. Would you tell him that Lieutenant Magliore is here and would like to speak to him? Please."

The officer hesitated, then ducked under a sawhorse type barrier and strode up to Brian Moore. Their conversation lasted seconds after which Moore spied Magliore and waved him forward.

Magliore thanked the officer as he walked passed him and stopped next to Moore who introduced SWAT commander, Captain Leo Block, who offered his hand. Block was dressed in standard SWAT gear, camouflage clothes, helmet, combat boots, black vest with a flash-bang grenade attached, Sig Sauer P220 semi-automatic pistol strapped low on his right thigh.

Block spoke first. "We're too late. Prescott, his office staff and two clients are hostages. Cahill's threatening to kill everyone unless we let him leave with Prescott, which ain't gonna happen."

"Can I talk to him?" Magliore requested.

Block shook his head. "As I understand it, you're a civilian with no police authority in Massachusetts. We'd be crucified if you participate in a hostage standoff and things go south."

Magliore stared at Moore, eyes pleading, intense. "Detective Moore knows I've been working on this case with the state police, been "snapped in" to the investigation since before Chief Hundley's death. I have a relationship with Cahill and I'm the one who discovered he killed those cartel guys and the Finch brothers. I know why he did it. I can talk him down. At least let me try."

At that moment, State Police Lieutenant Ed Catebegian, all six foot six, two hundred sixty-five pounds of him sauntered up to the group, his tie askew, his jacket wrinkled, his face red. He appeared poised to take someone's head off. Even SWAT commander Block stepped back as Catebegian thrust his chin forward and inserted his bulk into the center of the group. He eyed each man in turn before asking without preamble, "What have we got?"

Block was superior in rank to Catebegian but not prepared to tangle with the state police. His response was calm, deferential. "Our man has five or six hostages."

By calling Cahill "our man" instead of using his title, Block relegated the detective to the status of any criminal; that point not lost on the other law officers present.

Catebegian then surprised everyone. "This is your operation, Captain. What you're trained to do. You call the shots."

Block nodded, relieved, as two SWAT team members joined them, one carrying a U.S. Marine M403A sniper rifle, the other an MP5/10 submachine gun. Both appeared eager to employ their extensive training; too eager to Magliore. "Please let me at least talk to him, Captain."

Block shrugged. "He's refused to speak to our negotiator, called it bullshit. Promised to execute a hostage if we tried again."

"He won't do that, Captain. He's after those he blames for Chief Hundley's murder. He's off the rails, yet still a cop. He won't kill innocents."

Block grimaced, unconvinced.

"I don't like it any more than you do Captain, and I've got a few issues with this meathead," Catebegian said, shifting his focus toward Magliore. "But we don't have a lot of options right now. Cahill's a cop. He's familiar with our tactics. He might not want to kill innocents as Mags says, but if cornered—."

Block held his hands up as a sign of surrender.

Magliore didn't hesitate. He pulled out his cell phone and tapped in Cahill's number. "Let's talk, man," he said when Cahill, to the surprise of everyone answered.

Chapter 122

Ten pairs of eyes riveted on Magliore as he held the cell phone to his ear and chatted with Cahill as if arranging a casual meeting at a local pub. The onlookers heard his side of the dialogue, enough to discern the meaning.

"Look man," Magliore said. "You don't want to do this. Randy would not want you to do this."

Magliore nodded at something Cahill said. "I know. Lawyers are scum. But let the court's determine his punishment. If he knew his client engaged in illegal acts, he had a duty to report those actions. He'll be held accountable, I promise."

Catebegian, Block, Moore and the two SWAT team members watched as Magliore listened to Cahill, at times nodding his head, at other times twisting his mouth into an awkward grin."

"I'm coming up man," Magliore announced and cut off the conversation.

"No way," Block said. "We're not going to provide him another bargaining chip."

"He talked to me Captain; a good sign, right? Something hostage negotiators strive for?"

Once again Catebegian lent his support, not sure why. "Your call Captain. But as much as I hate to admit it, Magliore has a point. He's got him talking."

"My partner's not a murderer," Brian Moore chimed in, then stopped, embarrassed, realizing the foolishness of his statement. His partner having killed at least five people.

The SWAT leader rubbed his chin, dropped his eyes to the ground. When he raised them, he had made his decision. "OK. Your number one goal is the release of those hostages. Failing that, maneuver him in front of the big windows fronting this street. We'll take him out."

He turned to the SWAT team member with the sniper rifle. "Get in position on the roof of the building behind us. Take the shot on my command.

Thinking it over he said. "Wait! Belay that. Take the shot if you've got it."

The rifleman gave him a thumbs up and sprinted away.

"Put on a vest Magliore," Block ordered. "And you're wearing an ear-piece mic. Talk to me every step of the way."

Chapter 123

Magliore limped toward the entrance to the building housing the Law Offices of Francis Prescott and nodded to the SWAT team aligned single file by the doors. SWAT tactics called for troopers to enter buildings or approach dangerous situations in single file cutting down the opportunity for gunman to take out more than one officer at once with one volley. The point man, of course, was most vulnerable reminding Magliore he was fortunate never to have been in that position.

He entered the building, and contrary to any police tactic in such a situation, rode the elevator up to the office reception area certain Cahill was not lying in wait to ambush him. He was relieved when the door opened and he stepped into an empty room. Unbeknownst to Magliore, the SWAT team by the front door had been ordered inside. They used the stairs and waited on the stairwell poised to strike.

As Magliore stood alone, he thought of Kate Maxwell in a coma in a hospital bed put there by Corey Cahill. His face reddened and he clenched and unclenched his fists, every nerve tingling as he fought the hostility within him. He had a weapon concealed under his shirt at the base of his spine protection against a possible attack by Cahill or the means to take him out if given no other choice. He kept the frightened captives in mind as he inched toward the open door of Prescott's office not sure if he would be attacked or would be the attacker. He might have only seconds to decide his fate and those relying on him to help.

"Heading toward Prescott's office," he said via his earpiece microphone.

He stopped at the door and swept the room with his eyes. Four of the hostages sat with backs against the wall to his left. An elderly couple, no doubt clients and two young women, staff. One was the receptionist who greeted him and Catebegian on their initial visit. The older women, possibly in her seventies clung to her husband's arm, head on his shoulder. The two younger females, twenty or thirty something, sat with their legs outstretched, clasping their short skirts to their thighs, eyes wide, lips pressed together, faces pale.

Francis G. Prescott sat behind his desk, a red gash on his forehead, blood dripping in his eyes, his usual smug demeanor replaced by fear. He stared at Magliore, pleading.

"Let these folks go," Magliore said, speaking first and gesturing to the hostages. "They don't deserve to be caught up in this."

"Insurance," Cahill said. "Keep the hounds at bay."

"You've got me now and Prescott. No one's going to charge in here and risk our lives."

Cahill shrugged. "Hell, I'm going to kill this bastard and you too."

Chapter 124

"In position," the SWAT sniper reported as he stationed himself on the roof of the building across the street from the Prescott law offices.

Mike Pawlinski, a former Marine "Hunter of Gunmen" (HOG) with over twenty confirmed kills in Afghanistan, had a direct line of sight through the windows of the attorney's office. At twenty-nine years old, Pawlinski was a solid six-footer with a build honed by years of training and grueling combat. His long fingers belied his thick body; they were almost delicate enabling him to exert just enough pressure on the trigger to be surprised by the rifle's "report" when he fired. Something all marksmen strived for.

Cahill's failure to close the blinds in Prescott's office was an egregious error by a cop aware of police tactics, but perhaps one too blinded by rage and revenge to care. Pawlinski welcomed the mistake; made his job easier; a job not as challenging or dangerous as his military experience. In his two years with the Quincy PD, he had yet to fire his rifle in anger. Now, the possibility of doing what he trained for put his mind and body on alert.

Pawlinski did not worry that his target was a brother officer. In Afghanistan, he adopted the mantra: "Take a life to save a life," a phrase popularized by Prince Harry of England to justify his killing of insurgents while deployed in a war zone.

Pawlinski repeated those words as he set up his weapon on its tripod. The Marine Corps M40A3 he carried was a modified Remington 700 with a Schmidt and Bender High Power digital scope with laser range finder. He determined the distance to target as ninety-five meters about fifteen meters longer than the shot fired by Lee Harvey Oswald when he assassinated JFK. And Oswald had used an old bolt-action Italian Carcano rifle no match for Pawlinski's modern equipment.

Pawlinski had checked Oswald's perch in the Texas Book Depository Building when he toured the site while on a trip to Dallas to see a Cowboys-Patriots game. He was struck by the closeness of Oswald to his victim although conspiracy theorists at the time dismissed Oswald's ability to make the shot.

Piece of cake, Pawlinski thought at the time, as he did now. If he got the opportunity, he'd take a head shot, aim for the base of the skull to contact the part of the brain that controls involuntary movement, to ensure immediate death. In Afghanistan, like most military snipers, he aimed for the chest, which over distances of 600 to 800 meters offered a larger target and greater chance of success.

Unlike Afghanistan, the rooftop occupied by Pawlinski did not permit him to lie down. His rifle and tripod rested on the edge of the building about thigh high, forcing him to hunch over, rigid, eye focused on the windows, waiting.

No guilt. *Take a life to save a life.*

Chapter 125

The SWAT team leader on the staircase outside the Prescott Law Offices, like his colleague, sniper Mike Pawlinski, also related he and his men were set. Magliore, hearing the exchange through his earpiece, whispered, "back off."

"I don't like flying blind Magliore," Captain Block responded. "I need more info."

"I'm working here, captain. I don't want to spook him."

All eyes in the office of Francis Prescott pivoted toward Magliore when they became aware he was talking to someone unseen. Cahill's jaw tightened and he pointed his weapon, a .45 caliber Px4 Storm pistol, at his friend. The Storm was designed for combat and very accurate, as Magliore knew. He took a deep breath, exhaled and held up his hands.

"It's Big Cat, Corey. They're no doubt antsy having not heard from me since I came up here," he lied.

"Tell him everything's under control but I'll start shooting if they try to come in."

Magliore conveyed the message and added one of his own. "Corey's gonna let the office staff and two clients go as a gesture of goodwill. He'll still have Prescott and me."

Cahill grinned and leaned against the wall to Magliore's right, near, but short of the two large windows opening onto Hancock Street. "Risky move, pal. What if I'm not inclined to do that? No reason to. Hell, you're expendable and Prescott's a dead man anyway. They know that. You two don't help me."

"Not so, Corey," Magliore argued. "Releasing these people gives them the idea you're a reasonable man. That they, or me, can talk you down. They'll hold back. Why risk lives in an assault. They're always messy, unpredictable. They get much more favorable press if things end without shots fired and lives are saved."

Cahill crossed his arms, weapon pointing down churning that argument over in his mind. "Tell Catebegian four people are coming out; a win for the good guys. But I swear if they bust in here, I'll take old Francis here first and you next. I'm not walking out of here alive either way."

Magliore didn't respond, relayed the message.

As the hostages squeezed past him, Magliore made eye contact with each and sucked in his breath and expelled the air as you do in a doctor's office during an examination. Four people spared. He didn't care about Prescott but the man didn't deserve to die. He still had work to do.

"Nice move Corey," he said, "now let's figure out how to end this."

Cahill aimed the Px4 at Prescott. "Already have."

Chapter 126

Magliore considered reaching for the gun concealed in the small of his back, rejected the thought. Pissed at Cahill for his attack on Kate Maxwell, he called him on it.

"You shouldn't have attacked Kate, Corey. She wasn't aware of what the Finch's were up to and when she found out her first call was to me."

"Bullshit. She was their second in command, had to know."

"I'm telling you she didn't."

"Bullshit. Too late anyway."

Cahill's face reddened, his eyes twitched, he stared at Francis Prescott cringing in his chair. All that he had done, all that he had lost overwhelmed the detective, shook him to his core, pushed him to act. He rubbed beads of sweat from his forehead and brandished his weapon at the cowering attorney.

"You son-of-a bitch," he screamed. "You scumbag. You're going to die like the sniveling coward you are. I'm going to watch the life ooze out of you. I'll dance on your grave while you rot in hell."

In his rage, Cahill stepped toward the object of his hatred oblivious of the windows behind him. Before Magliore could shout a warning, glass shattered and Cahill's head exploded spewing blood and brains everywhere, some splattering on a screaming Francis G. Prescott.

The SWAT team poised outside the office rushed in at the sound of crashing glass. They found detective Corey Cahill lying face down on the carpet in a pool of his own blood, Magliore on the floor, his back to a wall, elbows on his raised knees, head in his hands. Prescott lay on his back behind his desk, no visible wounds.

The SWAT team leader, Sergeant Leo Urbansky, a six-foot two imposing former Army ranger, called Commander Block using the tactical radio built into his helmet. "Target down. Hostage Prescott unconscious, doesn't appear to have been hit though, possible heart attack, request paramedics ASAP. Lieutenant Magliore unharmed."

"Copy that," Block responded. "Secure the area. No one in or out except medical personnel. Ask Magliore to report to me now."

"Yes sir," came the reply.

Chapter 127

Vince Magliore had slipped to the floor, exhausted by the mental effort to resolve the standoff. He struggled to his feet, looking down at Cahill and Prescott, grief mixed with anger at Cahill, contempt for Prescott. A foul odor engulfed him; the attorney had soiled himself. Shaking his head, Magliore limped toward the elevator.

Once outside the office building, Magliore hobbled to Catebegian, his limp more distinct as a result of his mental exhaustion or his pain pills having worn off, he didn't know or care. Moore and Block stood where he left them. He gave them a thumbnail overview of how events unfolded in Prescott's office.

"Nasty business," Block responded. "You did good work getting those people out. We can be thankful for that."

The SWAT commander turned to Catebegian. "Your show now, Lieutenant. I'll submit my action report to you by tomorrow. You get to handle the press, meet with next of kin. All the fun stuff."

Catebegian grunted as Block walked away. He pivoted toward detective Moore. "I'll order a state forensics team to process the scene. Have Quincy PD secure the perimeter until that's finished."

Moore acknowledged that with a dip of his head, his face a mirror of shock and sadness for the loss of his partner and friend.

Still holding Moore's gaze, Catebegian asked: "Can you handle the notification of Cahill's next of kin." Might be better coming from you. No doubt the press will delight in reporting all the sordid details."

"Will do," Moore said. "Corey's never been married. He has a sister who lives out of state; father's dead, mother resides in one of those senior living complexes in Brockton. May not be very lucid; she's suffering from dementia."

"Can we leave out his relationship with Chief Hundley?" Magliore asked.

"What relationship," Moore asked; clear by his response that he did not know

"Tell him," Catebegian said, in a voice that sounded like an order.

Moore was no dummy and by the expressions and body language of the two men he had worked with for the past few weeks, he understood his former partner and the Hull Police Chief were more than colleagues. He raised his hands, turned around and shuffled away.

As they watched him go, Catebegian and Magliore became aware of the throng of newspaper and television reporters being held at bay by the Quincy police barricade and uniformed officers. They noticed Patriot

Ledger newswoman Gwen Garner in the front row, eager to pursue the story. Vans, with satellite dishes on top, from the three major TV channels along with a CNN affiliate flanked the noisy group who shouted unanswered questions to detective Moore as he pushed through the horde.

Observing the chaos, Catebegian had a change of heart. "I can stonewall for a day, maybe two, about Cahill's motivation for the killings and the scene today. I'll say we're still investigating the cause of his actions. Give you time to talk with Hundley's wife, prepare her."

Magliore offered a weak smile. "Thanks Cat. I'll do it ASAP."

"One day, two at most, pal. My superiors will cut me a new asshole if they find out I'm withholding information. The cover up is worse than the crime, *Capiche*."

Magliore smiled. *He's definitely Italian at heart.*

"Understood big man," he said and ambled toward the crowd concealing his limp as best he could. Gwen Garner of the Ledger knew him but would be forced to interview Catebegian, the official in charge not him.

In other circumstances he'd be amused by Catebegian's discomfort at having to face the press onslaught, yet sadness overwhelmed him and he didn't know when he would feel anything else.

He did not look forward to telling Karen Hundley about Randy's gay tryst.

And he was blindsided by her response.

Chapter 128

The traffic was bumper to bumper on the drive from Quincy to Hull. Magliore parked in front of the Hundley house a little after 5:00 p.m. He exited the car and waved as Karen Hundley nudged her Toyota Corolla in behind him.

"Mags, great to see you," she said as she left her car and gave him a hug. "I coach field hockey at the high school; practice today. Join me in a glass of wine. You look like you need to unwind and I sure do."

They clinked glasses as they sat on the couch in the living room, Karen charged up from coaching, Magliore dreading the conversation to come.

Karen noticed his demeanor. "What's wrong Mags, bad day?"

"Karen. We found out who killed Randy and why."

"Oh my god," she exclaimed and spilled some wine as she placed it on the coffee table in front of them. "Oh my god."

Magliore also put his drink on the coffee table and took her hands in his as he told her the story.

"That stupid investigation," Karen responded shaking her head, tears running down her cheeks. "Wasn't any of his goddamn business; stupid."

Magliore got up, went into the bathroom and brought back a box of Kleenex. He handed it to Karen and sat down again.

Karen dabbed her eyes, waited. "There's more isn't there?

Magliore turned away and leaned forward with his elbows on his knees. "You've heard about the murders of the Finch brothers right?"

"Yes. Their company was supposed to do the redevelopment project."

"Well. A Quincy police detective killed them as payback for Randy's death."

Karen, confused, stared at him. "Why on earth would he do that? Did they work together on a case or something?"

"Karen," Magliore answered, his throat dry; "they had a personal relationship, a very personal one."

"What are you saying?"

"They were intimate."

Karen Hundley fell back on the couch eyes closed and remained like that for a long time.

When she spoke, she kept her eyes shut. "He was Randy's lover?"

Magliore reached for her hand but she recoiled from his touch.

"Get out," she yelled, "and take your fucking stuff with you. Don't ever come back here again. You lied to me."

"Karen!"

"Get out."

Magliore hung his head, got up and trudged down to his room to collect his belongings. He was half way there when Karen shouted his name. He swiveled on his toes and caught her as she fell into his arms.

"I'm sorry Mags. I'm so sorry," she said as she wrapped her arms around him and squeezed. He fought to catch his breath.

"I didn't mean it," she said. "I know you were trying to protect me."

Her tears soaked his shirt as she buried her face against him.

He held her as her body quivered and lost the battle to contain his own emotions as his tears mingled with hers. The loss of his friend and the tension of the hostage situation hit him hard.

He would leave soon. Not because Karen ordered him to but because it was time. Very little had gone as planned. The peace and quiet he envisioned on that first day in town was shattered almost before he settled in.

That damn call from Randy Hundley.

If anything, he was in worse emotional shape than before he arrived. As he patted Karen's back and stroked her hair, he mentally packed his bag.

Chapter 129

In the aftermath of the slaying of Corey Cahill, a missing piece of the puzzle in the murder of Father John O'Shea turned up.

The Hyannis Inn is located on Maine Street in downtown Hyannis on Cape Cod. It's comprised of two elongated two-story buildings with parking on site. Those with a first floor room can pull up almost to their door. The motel's amenities include an indoor pool, banquet rooms and flat screen TV's. The Bluebirds Restaurant on the property has a full bar.

The JFK Museum, with a bronze statue of the former president in front is a short walk away. The Museum, which also houses the Cape Cod Baseball Hall of Fame, chronicles the Kennedy family exploits on the Cape.

Carter Fitzgerald, Hull selectman did not care about the motel's conveniences or the tourist sites available in town. He had been held captive since his abduction from the parking lot of a restaurant in Plymouth weeks before. His abductors, two Hispanic males, spoke little English and made no attempt to converse with him. They did not harm him although he suffered minor bruises in the scuffle during his kidnapping, bruises long since healed.

The guests in room 115 puzzled Marta Weintraub, one of the cleaning women on the staff at the Inn. Since their arrival, they had not requested cleaning service and left the "Do Not Disturb" sign dangling from their doorknob day and night. She notified the manager lest she be accused of shirking her duties. The manager, having called the room and spoken to the inhabitants, though with difficulty understanding them, told her they wanted privacy and would leave the room in good order when they left. This was curious but during the off-season the motel coveted occupancy and the men paid their bill on time. They even offered to pay a higher rate for this convenience.

With all of this as backdrop, Marta Weintraub was surprised on the day she made her morning rounds and discovered the "Do Not Disturb" sign no longer displayed on room 115. She was more shocked when she opened the door to find Carter Fitzgerald trussed and gaged on one of the queen beds. Her screams brought other staff rushing to her side. The manager alerted the Hyannis police who, with a substation across from the motel, arrived in minutes. Their interrogation of Fitzgerald led to a call to the Hull police and interim chief, Lieutenant Dan Porter, who dispatched a cruiser to pick up Fitzgerald.

Chapter 130

Carter Fitzgerald was dumbfounded when he learned of the firestorm resulting from his audit of the Finch Company; relieved to hear he was not responsible for the death of Johnny O'Shea but disheartened by the news Susan Wilson killed him. He regretted not going to the police in the beginning as O'Shea recommended.

He also fretted that the redevelopment plan, for which he toiled for years, was again delayed for the foreseeable future. Undaunted though, he sat in the conference room at Hull Police Headquarters plotting ways to revive it. His thoughts were interrupted when State Police Lieutenant Ed Catebegian and acting Hull Chief Porter entered the room and took chairs opposite him. Porter asked him to recount the story of his kidnapping and subsequent detention by the cartel henchmen.

Carter related the details and asked a question of his own. "Why didn't they kill me?"

Catebegian offered an explanation. "You were their point man in Hull. They needed you to push the redevelopment project ahead. If you turned up dead, the plan might have been shelved. The kidnappers meant to intimidate you into backing off the fraud issue and force you to remain committed to the Finch Company."

Catebegian paused before continuing. "Do you have any relatives in the area?"

"One, a sister in Duxbury. My mother lives in Florida."

"I suspect they intended to threaten to hurt them to keep you in line," Big Cat said.

"Jesus."

"Once their leader, this Rudolpho Gonzales character, was taken out along with the Finch brothers and the two hit men, the guys holding you panicked, thinking they might be next, and disappeared."

Fitzgerald put his elbows on the table and held his head in his hands. "My god. What a nightmare. I'm lucky to be alive."

"The chief wasn't so fortunate," Lieutenant Porter said. He pushed his chair back, stood and left the room.

Fitzgerald kept his head down shocked by the anger in Porter's voice. *He blames me for Hundley's death.*

Catebegian followed Porter out of the room leaving Fitzgerald behind, and symbolically, the case that unsettled him like no other. He'd never lost a colleague in his years in law enforcement and, though they served in different departments, he considered Chief Hundley a brother. He looked forward to going home to his family and, perhaps, some well-earned time off. A grin creased his face. And he no longer would have to deal with that whack-job Magliore.

Epilogue

Vince Magliore stood on Telegraph Hill amid the ruins of Fort Revere shaking his head in disbelief. His hopes of finding solace in Hull from the ravages of his wounds and the secret he harbored had crumbled like the walls and stairs of the old fort. Two high school friends were dead---murdered---another was a murderer. His new love interest lay in a coma, her recovery uncertain. Once again, a redevelopment plan for the town stalled, disrupted by the collapse of the construction firm chosen to implement the project; a result of his investigation and the maniacal behavior of the deranged lover of the town's police chief.

Magliore shivered in the cold breeze as clouds swept towards him. Lightening gashed the sky above Hull Bay followed by an artillery volley of thunder. His gloom matched that of the impending squall. A quote from some unknown author stuck in his mind: "The tragedy of life is not death, but what we let die inside of us while we live."

The once fond memories of Randy Hundley, Johnny O'Shea and even Susan Wilson tugged at his heart while the knowledge of their fate troubled his soul. Rain pelted Magliore's face mingling with the tears he now shed for his past and unclear future. He took shelter in his car as the downpour, whipped by strong winds, lashed at the windows. He waited a bit before turning on the ignition and guiding his vehicle down the narrow road leaving behind the ghosts of the long dead French sailors and marines and perhaps those of the newly deceased.

He doubted he would ever return.

But as he drove away, the rainsquall abruptly ended, as often happens in New England; the sun poked through the dark clouds promising a brighter day. The effect on Magliore was instantaneous, a transformation. He realized he was wallowing in self-pity as if his life was over. He pulled into the Hull Yacht Club parking lot, stopped and turned off the car's engine. He sat up straight in his seat with his hands on the wheel and grinned. The past needn't define him. Depressing memories could be erased and new, uplifting ones, made.

He stepped out of the car and raised his face to the sun. The warmth restored his courage and determination. He extracted a pill bottle from his pocket, emptied the contents on the ground and crushed them under his shoe. He vowed not to rely on meds any longer to relieve his physical and emotional pain. It wouldn't be easy and he'd need help and a plan.

He smiled as a plan took shape.

His first step would be to make an appointment with Mavis Fisher, the psychologist recommended by Randy Hundley. She could help ease the burden of keeping his secret; perhaps guide him toward a resolution. It was worth a shot.

In the meantime, he'd go to South Shore Hospital and look in on Kate Maxwell, stick around until she recovered, work on establishing the long-term relationship that had eluded him for so long.

Finally, he'd surprise Ed Catebegian at his home, meet the man's wife and children...and maybe apply for a job. He thought he'd make a great state police detective and couldn't wait to see the "joy" on Big Cat's face at the prospect of having him as a colleague.

His laughter echoed across the bay.

Acknowledgments

A good resource for the early history of Hull is the book, <u>Old Nantasket</u> by Dr. William M. Bergen, a former Hull selectman. As Bergen points out, the town was first called Nantascot by the Wampanoag Indians until it was incorporated as Hull in 1644. Nantascot was later Anglicized to Nantasket, which is now a small section of the larger coastal community despite the tendency of many non-residents to use Hull and Nantasket interchangeably.

I spent my childhood and early adult years in Hull so I am familiar with the landscape and some of the later history involving redevelopment plans. I worked in Paragon Park as many of my classmates did and also served as an altar boy until the age of twenty-one. I served with priests who were pious and excellent role models and also assisted at mass, one time, with a priest later accused of molesting a young boy. This wasn't revealed until many years later when the Boston Globe exposed massive abuse in the Catholic Church. I have no personal knowledge of this abuse. This story is not intended as an indictment of the Catholic clergy but only as an interesting plot device pulled from my imagination.

Some of the incidents in the book, like the Great Pumpkin Caper, were extrapolated from incidents remembered by former classmates. Those offering mostly fond remembrances of Hull were: Jim Doyle, Susan Berman Davis, June Sumner Hiracki, Anna Bonnano Lucia, Don Benjamin, Bobby Neal, Pat Laramee, Joyce Olsen, Ed Anderson, Ed Burke, Marcia Savage and Alan Tubman. One classmate whose real name is used in the book is Heleana Brickman Drossin, the high school assistant principal character.

Special thanks to those intrepid souls who read the draft manuscripts and offered invaluable ideas and suggestions: Debbie Pavich, Jeanie and Duke Conway, Jessica Miller, Jack and Carol Curtiss, Phyllis McKown, Chris Haraden and, of course, my "helper" and wife, Carol whose encouragement and support I have always relied upon.

Frank Infusino

CPSIA information can be obtained
at www.ICGtesting.com
Printed in the USA
FFOW02n1027290618
47213852-50027FF